The Madonna Files

The Madonna Files

by Stephen Ryan

Printed in the United States of America

Published by
WHISKEY CREEK PRESS LLC
Whiskeycreekpress.com

Jesus declared:

"I thank you, Father, Lord of heaven and earth, that you have hidden these things from the wise and understanding and revealed them to little children" Matthew 11.25

Pope John Paul II:

"If victory comes it will be brought by Mary. Christ will conquer through her, because He wants the Church's victories now and in the future to be linked to her."

Dedication

I would like to dedicate this book to my wife Tania. She gave me the freedom to pursue this project while running the trains on time at home (not to mention working full time). My kids, Andrew and Meredith, are probably more grateful than I am, for her support. Tania's editorial ear was also enormously helpful.

I would also like to thank Daniel Klimek. I think, without Daniel finding me through my website, I am not sure this book would have gotten out of the starting gate. Daniel has done magnificent academic work on Catholic mysticism and the scientific investigations into Medjugorje and I rely on his work often, in this book.

The term "Miracle Detective" comes from the incredibly generous Randall Sullivan who wrote the great book *Miracle Detectives*. The book explores how the Catholic Church goes about investigating miracles, supernatural phenomenon, and apparitions of the Virgin Mary. Randall's short emails, over the years, have been very motivating to me.

I would also like to thank Brooks Savage for taking the time to read this book, in its earliest most hopeless form. His encouraging words, that he did not hate the book, were more helpful than he even knows. Also thanks to his law partner Salah Abed, who took time to read early segments as well. The idea for this book hatched itself over many beers, over many weeks, with Brooks and Salah at an undisclosed watering hole in Washington, D.C.

Lastly I would like to thank my mother and father for being book lovers and loving parents. God Bless you, Mom and Dad.

Chapter 1:

April 1994 - Rwanda

While in Rwanda, the priest never met the small arms dealer, but he had heard the Russian was tough as a hammer. As luck or irony would have it, maybe the Russian had saved Father Dan's life that day after all.

He had certainly left a mess that was for sure. Hard to believe that was twenty years ago.

The gun dealer didn't like much of anything except his walkabout safari shirt and maybe the whistle he wore around his neck. He never blew it much, most of the time it just hung there stupidly against his chest; odd for a man so finely pressed—the whistle—seemed out of place. The whistle was nothing more than a shiny, decorative, piece of bling for a man who shot people for a living. Perhaps in a pinch it scared off hyenas or maybe a stray wildebeest now and then. No one knew for sure, no one asked. The whistle belonged to Nicholas Alexi, who was already having a bad day before things took a turn for the worse…

It was early afternoon and the skies were cloudy and gray over Gitesi, Rwanda, when Nicholas Alexi pulled his van into the church parking lot and stopped hard. With the van still rocking, the panel door slid open and four Hutu men spilled out. Two men, holding machetes, trotted to the church to fetch the nuns; the other two, Idi Kambana and his side-kick, headed to the rectory to find the priest. Not far from the church, in a small plaza, at the center of town, a different matter – but a similar disturbance, was beginning to take form. Fear was the common link and it was beginning to grip Gitesi.

With the men out of the van, Alexi lit a cigarette, fiddled with the radio knob, and looked back towards the entrance to the small wood church and scanned the grounds. It was like breathing to Alexi, instinctive—the doorways were always first - nothing unusual. He scanned the church structure and out buildings—a need for fresh paint, a cracked window pane, doves on the roof top; his eyes shifted to the perimeter: dirt, weeds and dead grass, then from the corner of his eye he noticed, to the right of the church doors, something white and gleaming.

From inside a small courtyard, a white concrete statue seemed to be looking his way—the statue's effect was of a deliberate stare. A ray of light poked through the clouds and the lone sunbeam bathed the peaceful womanly figure in an incandescent light. Then something else—Alexi squinted—he worked his eyes into focus; the glowing stone visage looked to be bleeding or maybe crying. The gun dealer took a long draw from his cigarette, and after a moment, he exhaled forcefully, snapped open the van door and made his way to the courtyard. Coming face to face with the statue, Alexi studied the glistening stone figure. He looked up to the clouds searching for the source of radiant light then returned his eyes back to the statue; the dark streaks he had seen from the van were running down the sculpture's face. As he leaned forward to get a closer look, the ray of light retreated into thickening clouds; a gunshot in the distance startled him, and the song birds in the shade trees drew silent—the peaceful nature of the courtyard vanished. A foreboding darkness descended around him.

The dark streaks on the statue, he noticed, were actually murky red. The red streaks on the face started from the eyes and from there they worked their way down the stone cheeks. He pulled out a handkerchief from his pocket and wiped the streaks clean. He felt the dampness on his bandanna and rubbed the dark red substance between his fingers. As he looked back at the statue he saw the fluid run down from the eyes – heavier this time. He stepped back a few feet and looked hard at the bloody red streaks dripping from both eyes. The sky darkened further and it seemed to close in on him, he felt a slight tingle behind his head and the hair on his arms began to stand. Alexi felt danger—sensing danger was a well-developed sixth sense that the Russian had learned to trust over the years.

He looked back up to the cloudy sky, then towards the church, looking for a source, anything, to explain the mystery, and in the darkening sky he saw smoke. He traced the smoke back to a large cross at the top of the church steeple. He could not really tell, but the cross looked to be pulsating with a flicker of light or burning. Were there flames? Was the cross on fire? Had Idi and his men set the church on fire? He looked at the church roof, and the windows and doors and saw no sign of fire. The smoke and fire came only from the cross on the steeple.

He went back to the statue. The red substance continued to flow and it began to dot the statue's gown. Alexi had no doubt that the red liquid was blood, he could tell from the consistency, the way it flowed, and the way it dripped off the face. He had seen blood on still faces so many times before.

Alexi looked back up at the steeple, at the burning cross; he was surrounded by unknown forces. He felt threatened; a station he was not unfamiliar with, and so he reacted in a way that was ordinary to his character. Alexi pulled his pistol out of his shoulder holster, stepped over the iron fence, and took aim right between the statue's eyes. As he was ready to pull the trigger, the stone eyes opened and turned blue, then blinked, and the red streaks transformed into tears. Horror shot through him.

"*Good God,*" he thought. He momentarily lowered his gun, but the good soldier stood firm. He quickly covered his face with his left arm and took aim, and as he was ready to pull the trigger, he saw the statue's mouth open—and then he heard a sound, a voice, a word. What he heard was unmistakable. The stone figure cried softly and said, "I am the peace."

Alexi shook his head sternly and steadied his feet again; the Russian's work was not finished. This time he took the gun in both hands, looked down the barrel of his pistol with resolve and shot the head off the statue of the Blessed Virgin Mary with two quick rounds from his 9mm pistol.

After the fragments settled, he bent over, put his hands to his knees and spit to the ground. Still hunched over and with the cigarette in his mouth, he cocked his head towards the church almost looking upside down to inspect the roof top. The smoke was gone; the fire and glow had left as well.

Straightening his posture, Alexi tossed his cigarette to the ground, and walked back to the van, stepped in, turned up the radio and waited for Idi Kambana to come out of the church.

Chapter 2:

On the restaurant terrace overlooking the lake, the short shadows of the early afternoon sun made room for light and color. Pink stucco walls, white stone walkways, and red terracotta pots nurturing blue and yellow blossoms presented their splendor in the midday light along the banks of Lake Como in Bellagio, Italy.

As the headwaiter arrived with a bottle of champagne, Carl Beckett nudged the iPad towards the center of the table. He could not believe the Arctic Mariner was missing—his cargo ship had vanished into thin air.

"Ottima scelta, Signore, la nostra migliore!"

Sitting alone at a table overlooking Lake Como, on the veranda of the Grand Hotel Villa Serbelloni, Beckett acknowledged the waiter's zeal with a slight nod of his head. Beckett looked across the table at the empty seat, then back at the waiter, thinking of his Russian freighter and the deepening crisis. Beckett needed something to hit, someone to blame; he thought of piñatas. None, of course, were to be had, so instead, he spoke—rhetorically. As much as the question was intended for the waiter, he, nevertheless, flung the words up to the cloudless sky, a small foolish gesture, hoping the world would understand their weight. He bit down hard on each word as he shot them out.

"Young man, do you know that Vladimir Putin wears a crucifix around his neck?"

The waiter darted his eyes towards Beckett, pinched his lips and shrugged his shoulders and continued to work the champagne bottle.

Beckett got the answer he expected. He glanced at his watch then turned towards the white peaks of the Italian Alps across the lake; Father Indellicotta was late.

With his eyes set on the mountain tops, Carl Beckett, owner of MediaCom, a sports cable TV network, motioned to the waiter with a tap of his finger to have his glass filled, then went back to thinking about the wire reports coming in from shipping news bulletins.

"A cargo ship has vanished in the Strait of Hormuz eighty miles from Iranian waters. Two weeks before the voyage, The Arctic Mariner, was in Kaliningrad, a Russian port known as a hub for Russian smugglers, and there its bulkhead was disassembled so something large could be loaded."

In another report:

"The Arctic Mariner was carrying a mysterious cargo and being tracked by unknown agents. The payload was not timber, as reported, and not from Finland. To put it simply, the Arctic Mariner is carrying some sort of state of the art surface—to—air missile system, most likely the SS-300, or a nuclear apparatus bound for Syria or Iran."

"Tracked by unknown agents? What do they know? Hell with it!" Beckett thought. Right now there was nothing more he could do about it anyway, so he decided not to worry about his tramp freighter; he would be in Washington, D.C. tomorrow, and by then he would have more information. He would have his answers; the piñata would open. Besides, he had other important business to attend to with Father Roberto Indellicotta. He and Roberto were now so close. The Pope was not well; it was now just a matter of time, perhaps days, and by morning the 'Codex de Rio Grande' would finally be his. Beckett picked up his glass and took a long drink. A gentle breeze blew across the terrace and his thinning gray hair rustled in the wind. He put the glass back down, pulled out his phone, and punched in a number. As the phone rang, he looked back out across the glittering lake and smiled, thinking about the dying Pope.

Chapter 3:

Landini Brothers' awning flapped in the wind and the tree tops along King Street shook towards the banks of the Potomac River like pom-poms; remnants of tropical storm Amy spit and lingered over the Mid-Atlantic.

Standing on the brick sidewalk outside the restaurant, Father Dan Baronowski, pushed back his sandy blonde hair, then took a hold of Rene's pretty warm hands, hands he once knew so well. But before saying good-bye, the priest peered over Rene's shoulders and caught the small bulging eyes of a fat, pudgy-faced man, in a disheveled raincoat, smoking a cigarette by the entrance to a busy Irish pub across the street. The man in the coat was staring right back at him. After making eye contact, the pudgy faced man cocked his finger in the direction of Dan and smiled as he playfully pretended to shoot the priest. He dropped his cigarette to the ground, squashed it like a bug and glanced back at Dan with a hard, menacing look before he slid into the restaurant. As Dan watched the fat man disappear, Rene surveyed the priest's eyes. His blue eyes were alert, but his attentive eyes were not for her, adding vagueness to his fidgety state. Dan sorted through his options, which were getting fewer each hour, then turned his attention back to Rene.

"I know I said this earlier, Rene, but you really do look beautiful tonight, and I am sorry about dinner; I know I wasn't great company; I was a total bore."

Rene agreed, but she would bear the burden without a fuss; dinner was good, and she did not get out much these days.

"Don't worry about it Dan; you have a lot of irons in the fire. I know how it goes sometimes."

The priest let go of her hands and with the tree tops stirring in the wind, Rene Estabrook moved her black bangs away from her eyes, and off her glasses, and kissed Dan good-bye on his cheek.

Parting ways, Dan walked down the street towards the river to an outdoor parking lot; Rene headed home on foot in the opposite direction. She lived six blocks from the restaurant in Alexandria, Virginia—an historic seaport town located across the Potomac River from Washington, DC.

Making her way home, Rene felt the warm, humid breeze rush across the back of her neck. A stout puff blew her hair around her eyes and the unsettled weather and damp air put her mind on boats. Wind on the face—it's how she drove boats at night—that's all she needed; she could feel wind shifts on her cheeks and neck before thirty thousand dollars worth of boat electronics could calculate new target boat speeds. The guys on the boat watched the digital displays on the mast like floor traders in a market crash—not her.

"Head out of the boat boys" she would say to herself, "T-bone at night was just a matter of time, if the guys didn't get off the junk and scan the horizon from time to time."

As Rene turned left onto Royal Street, Father Dan sat in his car in the quiet parking lot by the river, and pulled out a note from his jacket lapel pocket. Before reading the note, he had a flashback - the suicide in Rome—the stranger who looked him in the eye as he stepped backwards into a speeding bus.

Dan winced at the memory. He never should have followed the stranger.

He shook his head. Looking back would solve nothing. He went back to the note. He had memorized the words, but when he reached dead ends he liked to see the words on paper, hoping something would shake loose, hoping somehow the answer would come to him.

They protest and dismiss me, yet my son they adore
He loves me like no other but they choose to ignore
With blood and tears, a trail has been made
I cry with the memory of the last one they laid

Find the canyon where my child is buried
And there you will find a painted young virgin named Mary

The Blessed Mother, the Virgin Mary, that was the answer to the riddle, he knew that much, but which "painted" Virgin? The earliest artistic images of the Madonna are found in the Catacombs of Rome. After the Council of Ephesus in 431, artistic representations of Mary exploded. She was everywhere. Renderings of the Virgin Mary were so pervasive in art that it gave rise to the phrase "iconic image". For over a thousand years, from the countless Madonna and Child icons of the Byzantine era, through the Medieval and Early Renaissance periods, the Virgin Mary was far and away the most celebrated artistic subject in history.

The most famous painters and sculptors—Duccio, Leonardo da Vinci, Michelangelo, Giovanni Bellini, Caravaggio, Rubens, Salvador Dali, and Henry Moore—dedicated their enormous talents to capturing the transcendent beauty and eternal grace of the Mother of Christ. Mary, as an artistic subject, reached its zenith with Michelangelo's breathtaking sculpture the "Pieta", the most exquisite work of art in history. For centuries, Jesus Christ himself would have to take a back seat to his mother as an honored object of art.

Dan knew what the finish line looked like—it was a painted image of the Virgin Mary—he also knew he would find her at the Basilica of the National Shrine of the Immaculate Conception in the District of Columbia. One big problem: there were hundreds, maybe thousands, of images of the Virgin Mary in the National Shrine—the magnificent shrine is colossal; it is the largest cathedral in the United States and the eighth largest church in the world. The answer to the riddle did not come to Dan that night, and he was beginning to wonder if it ever would.

Dan slipped the note back into his pocket, turned the car on, then reached under the seat and felt the smooth cold steel of the gun barrel. The pistol was there; it was right where he had left it, but, right now, the gun was the only sure thing he could put his hands on. Before putting the car into drive, he thought of Rene, and what he had to do.

Chapter 4:

Rene turned the corner onto a dark, tree lined street, a few blocks from her house. She popped the collar of her red Musto's, and zipped the jacket up tightly. A Pavlovian move, to be sure; the rain had basically stopped, but she had learned in a hurry that being wet offshore on racing boats, as the veterans liked to say, 'sucked big time.'

Rene noticed a car roll by slowly without its lights on; another Old Town barhopping reveler who forgot to turn their lights on, she thought. After the car passed she looked up at the night sky, at the fast moving clouds and thought about the boat race. Winds were twenty, maybe twenty two knots out of the north, gusts higher. It was going to be a crazy spinnaker run down the bay tonight for sure; port pole, dead down, and most likely a nasty 3 am jibe at Point Lookout in big following seas—shrimping was a distinct possibility. The Annapolis to Newport race was underway, and her brother was charging down the Chesapeake Bay on Wharf Rat, a forty-two foot sloop, dodging tugs, freighters, and other race boats—race boats littered with barking alpha males—all gunning for Castle Rock Light—the entrance to Newport Harbor, in Rhode Island, four hundred miles away. The prize? Bragging rights and fish chowder. Not just any fish chowder—but Black Pearl's, the best fish chowder in the world.

Rene watched the clouds race past the moon. "When am I going to get a life? I should have been on that boat."

She let it go; she had made her decision months ago. Rene then got to thinking about her strange dinner with Dan.

The evening got off to a good start. Dan looked great; he clearly had time to work out in Rome, and when he talked about a town called Medjugorje—a place steeped in mystery and sacred drama, he seemed himself. He called the town of Medjugorje the spiritual lung of the world and a miraculous place of peace. He said that God is speaking to the world through the Virgin Mary from Medjugorje and that Medjugorje is proof that God exists. But after a while the topic turned gloomy and unsettling. He said that, although Medjugorje offers special graces, it also has a dark side. Stitched into the fabric of its divine messages are secrets—ten secrets in fact—and warnings of upheaval, even punishments against mankind. Dan said Russia, of all places, was the linchpin—the regulator—he called it, of some timetable. He said in 1981 the Virgin Mary made a shocking prediction about communist Russia's future. He said a religious revival in Russia would be a sign.

"End times", heavenly warnings, secrets and chastisements, Dan never talked that way before, and then, out of nowhere, he had to know where the last American Indian was killed by the U.S. Government—the last Indian killed in action. Dan needed to know his name; he needed to find the location of the last battlefield. It was in some "canyon" he had said. It was as if somebody's life depended on it.

"The last Indian killed," he asked in a clenched whisper, "where did he die?"

Then, almost as if he was talking to himself, "It wasn't at Wounded Knee, South Dakota. Many historians think Wounded Knee marks the final battle in the American Indian wars, but it wasn't."

She told him she didn't know for sure, it wasn't her area of expertise. Finally, she texted a colleague, but that wasn't good enough for him.

"You're an American History Professor, for Pete's sake."

It was twilight zone at Landini Brothers. Dan seemed distant, detached, except when he talked about the Virgin Mary. But she wanted the conversation to be more about them—not his work. She had hoped to feel closer to Dan. She wanted to talk about family, his life away from work, old times—normal stuff. She wanted to laugh. She had looked forward to the evening, but dinner seemed rushed, and by the time the check arrived the night seemed to have no point. As they stood up from the table to leave, he picked up Rene's purse and slipped a book into her Coco Blanco shoulder bag—a book about the Virgin Mary. He urged her to read it right away.

Almost home, she looked back up to the clouds—she missed her brother and the open waters—but what she missed most was feeling close to someone, it was something she had hoped for, before dinner, and now that was gone. Rene's heart felt empty as she reached for the door.

Chapter 5:

June 12, 1:00 pm - Boston, Ma.
On the Campus of MIT—The Professor's Office

A pretty graduate student stepped into Professor Bob Baronowski's office and right away went searching for the thermostat.

"How about a little A/C, Bob? It's an inferno in here."

On a hot June day in Boston, MIT Statistics Professor, Robert "Bob" Baronowski, ignored the fact that it was eighty-two degrees inside his office. It was summer school after all. The former standout left tackle had suffered through August two-a-days for years and he couldn't stand it when people complained about the heat just days after moaning about the long cold spring.

"Bring it on Darcy, gimme ninety degrees for a month."

It was one o'clock in the afternoon, and two of Bob's best students, Darcy—tall, skinny, pretty, Goth—and her friend, Tim—a Pillsbury dough boy with perfect math boards and Nantucket reds, dropped in to watch a low budget film about an odd religious event that was taking place in an obscure village in Bosnia/Herzegovina. The village, with the difficult name, was called - Medjugorje. Tim and Darcy were told the video was part of some kind of math problem Bob was working on.

Bob stood up and cranked opened a window then pointed at two chairs set behind his desk.

"Have a seat, guys."

After opening the window, Bob moved across the room to get a cup of coffee. To Bob, coffee in the afternoon was like having a smoke—liquid Chesterfields. He was completely addicted.

Teasing Darcy, who was flapping her arms like wings trying to cool off, Bob offered up his white Styrofoam cup.

"What'll it be, Darcy? Cream, sugar, or just black? It's fresh, hour old, max."

Darcy rolled her eyes, and maneuvered her way around Bob's desk, still flapping her arms with some kind of black lace streaming behind her.

"*That's it.*" Bob thought to himself. "*Adam's Family—Wednesday—all grown up.*"

Bob looked at Tim and wondered if he saw a little Pugsly in the preppy dough boy.

As Darcy and Tim took their seats behind Bob Baronowski's desk, the professor took a sip of coffee and thought about the documentary that was taking over his life. Bob had lost count of how many times he had seen the video about the Virgin Mary; he now watched it almost every day, and with each viewing it seemed like the religious paradox was taking him somewhere further down a path—a dim trail without markings. Bob kept walking down the path; when at some point he stopped looking back, he decided not to turn around. He was going to find his way out to the other side. There had to be an answer—science and religion were in a tug of war and for the first time in his life, like a fish on a hook, he felt a tug from the other end.

Bob's interest in religious supernatural phenomenon began after his brother, Father Dan Baronowski, sent him a package of information from Rome about the strange events taking place in Medjugorje. The priest had asked his brother for a favor. Dan asked him to crunch some numbers. Dan thought it would help with a secret project that he was working on in Rome.

In Rome, Father Dan worked as a Consultor for the Prefect of the Congregation for the Doctrine of Faith, the oldest of the nine congregations of the Roman Curia. Back in the day, before a public relations maneuver in 1904, Dan's employer was better known as the "Holy Office of the Inquisition." Today, the duty of the office is to safeguard the Catholic faith.

Dan investigated reported cases of supernatural phenomena for the Catholic Church. He was a detective of sorts—miracles, beatifications were his specialty, but on rare occasions he investigated ghosts. Father Dan was the Vatican's chief "Miracle Detective" in charge of investigating alleged appearances of the Blessed Virgin Mary—the appearances are better known as apparitions.

Dan—the miracle detective—on this occasion, asked Bob to help with the Vatican's secret investigation into the astonishing claims that the Virgin Mary is appearing to six children at Medjugorje.

"Can you calculate the probability," Bob's brother had asked, "the probability that six children from Medjugorje—unsophisticated—a hodgepodge of normalcy, unrelated to each other, could sustain a hoax for thirty years, a narrative lie with no end in sight; a fraud so audacious and sublime that the conspiracy would, over time, grow into the most sensational religious event since Jesus Christ walked on earth?"

"The Pope is involved," he said "and the Vatican, behind closed doors, is splitting in two, because six children say they see a ghost; they say they see and talk to the Virgin Mary." Dan added, "The spiritual phenomenon of Medjugorje is based on the belief that Mary, the Mother of Jesus Christ, is quite literally revealing herself to the world and proclaiming the existence of God in a way that is unique in the history of the world. The Virgin Mary says now is a special moment in history, and we are now in 'A Time of Grace' granted to mankind from God".

Most amazing, to Bob, was that fifty million people, perhaps many more, take the children's words as Gospel.

It was all nonsense to Bob at first.

But Dan had done his homework. The package Bob got from Rome included extensive interviews with the six children, Communist party police reports, documented threats against the visionaries of incarceration into mental institutions, scientific examinations, and private letters from Pope John Paul II to his friends. The package from Rome about Medjugorje even had a letter from Mother Teresa supporting the claims of the apparitions. At first, Bob didn't touch any of Dan's data dump—including the DVD; it all just sat in a yellow envelope in his desk drawer collecting dust.

Then Dan called from Rome on Thanksgiving Day. "Bob, I really need your analysis; you have to give me something."

A month later, two hours before picking up Dan at Logan Airport for the Christmas holidays, Bob shoved the DVD into his laptop and watched one of the Medjugorje visionaries, an attractive woman with stylish blonde hair, stare into space, and move her lips—talking to no one, just smiling, and chatting away. Maybe she was talking to Jimmy Stewart's imaginary pink bunny—who knows—but then he saw the woman's tears roll down her face and it changed everything. The tears were followed by a haunting sorrow. Then came an aching, wrenching sadness—a sadness that seemed immeasurable; it was unlike anything he had ever seen before. He hit replay and watched it again—then again. The woman's face—mournful, penetrating, and authentic—grabbed him like an ocean's riptide. He reached into his desk drawer and took out Dan's notes—five other young adults were experiencing the same thing—the sadness.

Twenty minutes late to the airport, he asked Dan as soon as he stepped into the car, "What the hell is going on with that woman in the video, and what is she looking at in the empty space that makes her seem so abandoned and sad?"

Dan had heard the question so many times before. As was often the case, Dan was never sure how to explain Medjugorje. From the first days it had been that way. He never felt he had the right words; there were really no "right" words to describe what was taking place at Medjugorje. So Dan simply decided to start with Bob's specific question; he decided to first talk about the tears—the sadness.

Dan stared out of the passenger side car window as he spoke.

"She sees the end."

Bob turned off the radio and powered up the small crack of the car window and looked over at his brother.

"What's that?"

Dan took his eyes away from the highway guard rails and the dirty snow rushing by and slowly turned his head towards his brother.

"She sees the end, Bob; she sees the end of the world."

Bob looked away from his brother and stared straight ahead—eyes back on the road.

Rather than unload his entire sack of MIT, PhD, king of the world,

God is dead weaponry, Bob held his fire. He thought of the young lady's tears—the sadness in the visionary's eyes. He thought of Dan's data dump—he had no answers. Bob loved to kid Dan about his career; the truth is he trusted Dan. Dan was also smart—UVA, Harvard Law. With Dan, Bob had learned to ask questions first, then shoot.

"Come on Dan, for real, the end of the world?"

"I don't know Bob. It's part of it. I guess it's part of the whole thing."

Later that night, on Christmas Eve, they talked until two in the morning and by sunrise, the six strangers, the so called "seers" in Dan's video from a small village called Medjugorje, a village previously known only for tobacco, brambles, and violent thunderstorms, had become Professor Bob Baronowski's obsession.

At first, Bob thought solving Dan's religious mystery would be as complex as finding a toy in a box of Cracker Jacks, but the more he dug, the more he was beginning to believe his brother's fantastic assertions that the phenomena at Medjugorje may be the most extraordinary event of modern times. Dan said Medjugorje could change the world. He said it was already changing the Catholic Church in unknown ways – perhaps dangerous ways. A schism was starting. According to Dan, Medjugorje was a ticking time bomb inside the Vatican…

"Hey professor!" Darcy spoke up, "Are you going to join us or are you planning on staring at your navel for the rest of the afternoon?"

Bob topped off his coffee and quickly sat down at his desk and with the foam cup in his teeth he slipped the DVD into his laptop.

But before hitting play, Bob's thoughts, once more, returned to his brother. He saw his brother in the car. He saw his brother's head again turn towards him. He thought about what he had said.

"She sees the end, Bob; she sees the end of the world."

Chapter 6:

June 12, 7:54 pm- Alexandria, Va.
Rene's Home

As Rene opened the door to a small row house, located on a quiet cobble-stoned street, tucked in among grand townhomes, Luke, her yellow lab, greeted her like a long lost war veteran. Her home was furnished with family antiques - Persian rugs, porcelain lamps, and a sofa covered with yellow fabric decorated with polite monkeys wearing tailored red culottes. Almost all the items came from the house she grew up in. After Rene's mother died, her father came by regularly delivering furniture and looking for companionship.

His visits made her happy most of the time, but on occasions, she would go to bed in tears after he left. The family photo albums were how the trouble would start. Pictures of her mother gently holding her hand, or photos of her mom just looking happy and messy in a kitchen full of life, were at times devastating. She asked her father not to come by with the photo albums; she would sit with them when she was ready.

Rene tossed her keys on the kitchen table and looked at the clutter. The coffee mug sat on the Washington Post, and a stained spoon rested on baseball box scores. She picked up the newspaper; a headline beneath the front page fold mildly caught her attention—"Russian freighter missing in Strait of Hormuz." She dropped the paper back onto the table—she would read it later. She looked around the kitchen—the place was a mess; she hadn't picked up a thing since last night. She was doing that more often she thought, not picking up; it was easy when you are thirty-eight years old and lived alone.

Rene Estabrook's home was not the only victim of her untidy ways; her office at Georgetown University, where she taught American History, was a cluttered mess as well. Rene was a popular professor at Georgetown University. Her class was a favorite at the University, but for some, the reasons went far beyond her thoughtful lectures. The young Romeo's queued up early to register. Her dress—elegant simplicity—blue sweaters over a white collarless blouse and jeans. Her mouth was full and wide—a mouth one noticed in a line of dancers. In college, Rene, was tagged with the nickname, "Espy," for her intramural heroics. Tall, slender and athletic, Rene still smiles when she daydreams about flag football—such silliness—running down a field with little white flags bouncing off blue denim jeans. "Come and get it boys," she would say to herself, as she raced towards the end zone.

The name was fine; her brother even started calling her Espy. It sure beat Ester—her nickname during the reign of terror known as middle school, a time when she towered over mean skinny boys who despised her for her oversized glasses and her undersized bra.

Rene lived quietly and alone and it had been that way since graduating college. She was in love once, but now that was long ago. She even experienced the thrill of being engaged, but that fairy tale lasted for eight months before the cart spilled, leaving behind, at the scene, the words "I do." Her mother had seen to all the details of the wedding. Her wedding day had been set, invitations mailed, and reservations for the rehearsal dinner and wedding reception made. The boy she loved was named Dan. The love of her life broke up with her the night before her wedding day, one hour before the rehearsal dinner, to become a priest. Dan loved her with all he had inside of him, but something else kept calling, chasing him, and on the night of the rehearsal dinner he stopped running. That night, Rene's heart was shattered; her heart was lost in an ocean full of emptiness. Some pieces were still missing—pieces of her heart were flotsam, drifting alone, under endless gray skies.

Of course they had talked about Dan's interest in becoming a priest; she wasn't totally blindsided, but in the end it still split her in two.

Rene made her way upstairs to get ready for bed. Undressing in her small walk-in closet, she felt weary from the long day, most of it spent at the Smithsonian, working on a Civil War exhibit. She had started the day at 5 a.m. and it was now 8 o'clock in the evening.

Taking her blouse off, Rene looked into the full length mirror and stared vacantly, thinking of the night, thinking of Dan. As she reached for the fourth button, she stopped. Her gaze caught the souls of her eyes and in the soft dim light something startled her. She saw herself standing alone in the mirror, not by herself, but alone. The figure in the mirror seemed unmistakably, lonely.

"*Good Lord,*" she thought, "*I really don't need that tonight.*"

But there was no other word to describe the mirror's message. Loneliness seemed to be seeping into the edges of her eyes. Her stomach sank briefly, but it wasn't her nature to brood. At times she had considered its pursuit - brooding; she had seen the condition work wonders for some of her friends, but, for her, she never seemed to have the time to commit fully to its calling.

To meet the truth, she stepped towards the mirror.

"*Was I really lonely?*" The word resonated with a heaviness that surprised her. Could she really be that person? Loneliness was a sad feature she sometimes recognized in others; she would spot them most often at the grocery store, holding fruit usually, like mateless silverbacks you see in a zoo. But, she never dreamed that she would succumb to its affliction. Lonely? Her? Probably. Why not? She got what was coming to her; she got what she deserved. Hell, all she did was work these days. All she ever did was work. What was she to expect—the only man she ever loved was a priest.

"*Good Grief*" she said out loud. She wondered how she had pulled into that port in the middle of the night without running aground. She had not seen it coming. She had missed the rocks she figured, she wasn't unhappy, but she had to accept the fact that she had lost her way and run into muddy waters in a lonely creek. But rather than mope, she decided to take a trip, maybe a long trip; put the work down—get a life—like Dan had recommended, time and again. Take some chances.

She walked out of the closet and from her bedroom window: a faint flash of lighting—strobe like—came into her room. She looked at her watch and thought about her brother's boat race. She figured the boats were probably near the LNG plant north of Cove Point.

Rene looked down at her phone, for a moment, picked it up and called Monique, her best friend. No answer. She was about to hang up, but instead, she spoke to the answering machine: "Monique, I need to get out of here; take a plane ride—anywhere. Sooner the better, I am done with classes 'till fall. Call me, bye."

If she was to take a trip, she wanted her best friend with her. Dan had introduced Monique to Rene a number of years ago when she arrived in DC from Rwanda to go to law school. Monique was a walking talking travel guide. "Anytime, anywhere" was Monique's promise to Rene, when she was ready to get on an airplane.

They would talk in the morning. Monique would start planning adventures before breakfast, but first, as it always seemed, Rene would start a new book. Tonight, it was the book Dan had slipped into her purse at the restaurant, the book about the mysterious events taking place in Medjugorje. With Luke at the foot of her bed waiting for her to get in, Rene pulled the book out of her purse, which was sitting on top of her bureau, and opened the book to a random page.

"From 1985 to today, I received the apparition from the Blessed Virgin Mary once, every year, on June 25. But at that last daily apparition I was given the greatest gift, not just for myself, but for the entire world. And because every single human being is asking is there a life after this life on earth, I am standing before you here today, I am standing before the entire world and I can easily answer that question. Yes, there is a life after this life, because by God and Our Lady I was given this great grace, that I was able to see my late mother during that apparition time and my mom told me: 'My dear child, I'm proud of you.'

For twenty eight years, Our Lady has been telling us which road we need to take in our life. She is showing us the way and we have to decide which road we are going to take in our life." Visionary Ivanka

Rene closed the book and looked at the cover. Medjugorje—Proof of Heaven. She thought about Dan's words, "The phenomenon of Medjugorje may be the most extraordinary event of modern times."

She opened the book up again to another random page.

"*You go to Heaven in full conscience: that which you have now. At the moment of death, you are conscious of the separation of the body and soul. It is false to teach people that you are reborn many times and that you pass to different bodies. One is born only once. The body, drawn from the earth, decomposes after death. It never comes back to life again. Man receives a transfigured body.*"
Visionary Vicka

She gently closed the book, and then her eyes, and thought about her mother. The passages, strangely, made her think about where her mother might be, right now—physically—if she could actually be in a place. She had never really thought about her mother in that way—that she could be somewhere. Rene had not thought of heaven since she was a child—or maybe for a moment, at her mother's funeral. Her eyes welled up and a few tears made their way down her cheeks. It had been a while since she cried over her mother. God, she missed her. She shook her head a couple of times.

"*Not tonight,*" she said to herself, "*Not tonight.*"

Rene closed the book and softly rubbed the cover. She decided she was going to be patient with the book about Medjugorje.

As she turned and looked at Luke, who was staring her down, waiting for her to get in bed, Rene heard a loud "smack," then a pounding on the front door.

Chapter 7:

June 12, 9:30 pm Annapolis, Md.
"D" Dock - Annapolis Yacht Club

After the rain, the wind came around from the north and the steady June breeze worked its way along the waterfront. Light clangs ringing off boat masts mixed peacefully with sounds of small boats puttering under the Spa Creek Bridge; now and then gulls and terns argued over dinner. Tucker Finn never tired of the maritime musical arrangements. His boat, "Pilar," a custom, ninety-two foot ketch, docked at the Annapolis Yacht Club, had been Tucker's home for better part of a year. Pilar had eased into her slip early in the morning after leaving Bermuda four days ago.

It was 9:30 in the evening when Tucker Finn hit send on his smart phone, launching an e-mail to his old friend, Manny Menendez. "*Almost done. made landfall U.S. this morning, Mexico in a month—see ya.*"

Tucker reached into a cooler, opened a beer, put his feet up on the wheel, and thought about the beautiful stormy sail up the Chesapeake Bay the previous night. After a few minutes of blissful contemplation, the handsome, deeply tanned, and slightly graying forty-two year old, Tucker Finn, got up and shouted down the companionway.

"Hey, Sanjay, I think I am in love with this damn boat. Last night was crazy. Blew like hell! Close reach in twenty-five knots, gusts to forty, surrounded by lightning and you and I are trimming two thousand square feet of A-Sym like it's the Volvo Cup. We have Bono and Pavarotti cranked up singing "Miserere"; we draw twelve feet, we're in fourteen feet of water off of Sharp's Island Light and we are screaming up the Chesapeake Bay at sixteen knots."

Tucker waited a moment for a response, and hollered again into the boat's luxurious interior.

"Yo, Sanjay, are you down there?!"

Tucker's ninety two foot boat, his home for almost two years, was a custom made, two masted, sailboat and she was magnificent. The boat's name was "Pilar"; a name inspired by the great Ernest Hemingway. Tucker Finn thought Hemingway was one cool cat. The ending was pretty messy—for sure—but the big guy lived a hell of a large life. Sadly, as Tucker now saw it, Hemingway's trail blazing invention of the modern male, has been strip mined, and dumbed down by American men, who have replaced real adventure with the innocuous art of completing something called a "bucket list,"- jumping out of airplanes, or ball camps with ex-pros. Perhaps, that's why Hemingway left early—didn't want to stick around to watch men spend their evenings counting friends on Facebook.

Tucker was convinced a perfect correlation existed between the number of collected Facebook friends and utter banality. The larger the group, the more the group resembled a pond of farmed cat fish. Tucker Finn finally weaned Sanjay off the Facebook Kool-Aid, somewhere in the middle of the Indian Ocean.

Tucker took to the name "Pilar," after he discovered that Hemingway chose the name for his beloved fishing boat in Cuba, in part, to honor the Virgin Mary.

Hemingway, after collecting his Nobel Prize for Literature in 1954, made a bee-line straight to the "Patroness of Cuba" to a shrine called Caridad del Cobre—the shrine commemorated a small set of sublime miracles of the Madonna. Hemingway offered his Nobel medallion to the Virgin Mary as a gift, and laid it at her feet to keep a secret promise. Santiago, Hemingway's hero of <u>The Old Man and the Sea,</u> had made a similar promise to the Blessed Mother, "if he should catch this fish."

The Virgin from Cuba was not Hemingway's first encounter with the Mother of Christ. Years earlier, Hemingway had gone to bullfights in Zaragoza, Spain, and there, he encountered another shrine of the Virgin Mary—the shrine of "Our Lady of Pilar"—the first recorded apparition of the Virgin Mary, which would inspire his boat's name.

Today, Hemingway's famous boat, Pilar, is a popular tourist attraction in Cuba.

Tucker poked his head further down into the companionway looking for Sanjay.

"Hey, Sanjay, are you down there? I thought you were coming up."

Sanjay clicked the TV remote off, stood up, and turned towards the companion way.

"Huh? What did you say, my man?"

Tucker rolled his eyes at Sanjay.

"I said, will you be my best man if I marry this damn boat, you pin wheel."

Sanjay made his way up to the cockpit smiling.

"Come on, Tucker. I heard you dude."

Sanjay, standing by the wheel, looked around for the beer cooler and continued to talk.

"Look, my man, the way I see it, nobody deserves this boat more than you. You are living the American dream. You give hope to all the slackers around the world. Check it out, my man—a day in the life of Professor Tucker Finn."

"Sanjay, I've heard that one before—like a hundred times."

"No, no, Tucker, you are going to hear it again—listen up."

Sanjay Singh, twenty-eight years old and ex-Google programming wunderkind, reached into the ice chest and grabbed a cold beer. He held it up to Tucker, then turned towards the harbor to give his speech to the animal life on the bay.

"Check this out—take a good look around at this splendor and listen up, you lazy varmints, you might learn something."

Sanjay popped open the beer bottle, took a big gulp, moved up towards the portside toe rail and leaned against the lifelines.

"My man, The Finn man, built his empire from an oceanside cot on a Mexican beach, pounding Coronas for breakfast. After eating lunchtime bowls of sugar frosted flakes, my man Tucker tended bar until midnight before spending the rest of the night playing cards with tourists he had just over served, hustling money from the very same people who tipped him too much in the first place."

Sanjay then made a grand swooping gesture, acknowledging the splendor of Tucker's home and his surroundings, and looking right at Tucker, he raised his beer bottle.

"And now this; you earned it my man. Don't ever forget your keys to success. You worked you're tail off, my man. I salute you."

Sanjay hopped back into the cockpit giggling.

With Sanjay mentioning Mexico, Tucker, for a moment, thought about the true price he had paid. But he didn't want to go there, tonight. Last night was fantastic—perfect—and he was going to keep it light with Sanjay. Keeping it light, enjoying the moment—after three ocean passages it was something he was finally getting better at.

Sanjay nudged Finn on the shoulder and motioned to clink bottles.

"Hey, Tucker, you earned it, buddy. And yeah, sure, I'll be your best man—go ahead, marry the damn boat."

Looking at Sanjay, a smile quickly returned to Tucker's face. He tapped Sanjay's bottle.

"Yeah, I guess you're right. I guess I should just enjoy the fruits of my labor."

Tucker looked back up at the moon that was starting to poke through the clouds, and stood up.

"Hey Sanjay, are you hungry? Let's go to the Boatyard Bar and Grill and get a burger."

Chapter 8:

June 12, 11:30 am - Near Bellagio, Italy
Father Roberto Indellicotta

Roberto's car hummed along Highway A1 heading north to the Italian Lake district. Off to the west, the sun rested easily on the Tuscan hills of Italy. Father Roberto Indellicotta, Chief Exorcist to the Diocese of Rome, was on his way to have lunch with Carl Beckett at the Villa Serbelloni, in Bellagio, Italy.

Roberto, sitting alone in the back seat of his chauffeured Mercedes Benz, finally felt a sense of peace now that he was set to ask his old friend for help. His stomach and chest pains had eased as well. The mysterious pains had been with him for months.

With the fleeting sense of peace, out of habit—a tiny ritual—Roberto patted a small leather bag of relics that he kept in his trousers' pocket. Like a set of worry beads, he took the leather sack with him whenever he traveled.

He should have accepted Beckett's offer to help from the start. He had to find the letter known as the "Third Secret of Fatima". The letter contained the most closely guarded secret in Catholic Church history. The letter had been stolen from the Pope's apartment. Roberto now had his opportunity, but it would also be his last chance. Roberto needed the Codex De Rio Grande; the Codex —a pictorial Aztec calendar with coded messages—would lead him to the secret letter. With the secret, the truth would be revealed, the Church would be restored—the crisis would end, the healing would begin.

There was now a cancer inside the Vatican, and rumors of a schism were taken seriously—a terrible unease was beginning to grip Rome. Roberto decided a heavy hand was called for—a man willing to kill—and Carl Beckett, his old friend from Yale, was the man for the job. Carl Beckett loved the Catholic Church with all his heart, but despised the sitting Pope—and any prelate that supported Vatican II with an unhinged fury.   Roberto needed Beckett—his ways of doing business. The incompetents, his zealous young acolytes, had failed him; they had not been able to persuade Father Dan Baronowski to hand over the Codex de Rio Grande.

Roberto gazed outside the car window and thought about the Virgin Mary and the three secrets of Fatima. It was impossible to overestimate Fatima's status inside the hearts of the men who run the Vatican. He also thought of the great miracle of the sun that took place at Fatima, Portugal in 1917. The miracle is the most extraordinary intervention of God since Jesus Christ raised Lazarus from the dead. The "Miracle of the Sun", to this day, is the most definitive example of a supernatural event in the history of the world. The sun appeared to rip away from the sky as seventy thousand people watched in horror. But, it was Fatima's three famous secrets that mattered most to the Church. The Church claims all three secrets have been disclosed, but that assertion is hotly disputed. The "Great Deceit," Roberto called it. The third secret of Fatima was still hidden and the Church was lying to the world about it.

The first two secrets, "The vision of Hell," and the prophecy that Russia would "error" by turning away from God in the form of atheist communism; an "error" that would lead to the greatest slaughter of humanity in the history of the world, had been revealed and accepted by the faithful. But the third secret is shrouded in controversy. The third secret of Fatima, the so called "hidden fragment", is said to be the authentic words of the Virgin Mary. The fragment was the key, the cure, the Church's savior. Roberto believed that the words of the Virgin Mary were prophetic and a succession of Popes, for political reasons, had kept the truth away from the world.

The Church's official version claims the prophecy of the third secret only pertained to the assassination attempt on Pope John Paul II. But Roberto believed the secret had to be about a crisis of faith, that would attack the Church. For decades the rumor, of that prophecy, had hardened into a truth for millions of Catholics—the most devout and militant were known as "Fatimists".

A collapse of faith, among Catholics, was *THE* prophecy of Fatima. It had been simmering for years, but, today, the crisis of faith had erupted into a full-fledged disaster after the discovery that thousands of priests, for decades, had sexually abused children on a massive scale. Catholics were leaving the Church in record numbers.

The Titanic had hit an iceberg. Seeking blame for the cause of the sex abuse epidemic, the Vatican was splitting in two. Roberto, and many others, blamed Vatican II. With the passage of Vatican II, the sacred traditions of the past, over time, had been cast aside and replaced with man-centered philosophies. The church was becoming an NGO—an institution serving the poor—a welfare office, and by abandoning sacred traditions, millions of souls were on the road to perdition. The Holy Spirit was flickering and nearly out. The very soul of the Church was transforming into the creature – into the "Beast". And now with the Pope ailing, a power struggle had emerged. Two hundred Cardinals were beginning to take sides—few words were spoken—hand gestures, code words, or subtle allusions were all that was needed to understand entrenched positions. A schism in Rome—it was now secretly cardinal against cardinal, bishop against bishop.

With the Church ailing, Roberto believed the final prophecy of Fatima was beginning to unfold and the future of the Church was at stake. If he had the letter he could prove it.

Roberto's jacket buzzed quietly and he reached into his coat pocket and answered his cell phone.

"The Pope has taken a turn for the worse, Father. He has made his decision to end treatment and there is concern that it is just a matter of time before he falls into a comatose state. There is talk that the College of Cardinals will be asked to return to Rome at any time. A Papal conclave is imminent, I am afraid to say, Sir."

"Has the New York Times agreed to delay publishing until Cardinal Lombardi's office has had time to properly respond?"

"Two days sir, they will give Cardinal Lombardi until Thursday and then they are going to run the piece as is."

He hung up the phone. The Pope had been ill for some time, and now Roberto's friend, and the savior of his faith, the man who must be the next Pope, Cardinal Lombardi, was in trouble. Roberto already had a contingency plan in place to assure the proper apostolic succession, but the timetable needed to be changed and changed quickly. The Pope was gravely ill and succession was now unclear. DC would have to be a go, even without the Codex in his hands.

Chapter 9:

June 12, 1:00 pm - Boston, Ma.
The Professor's Office

Darcy spoke up again.

"You're on pause, Bob; hit the play button."

"What? Yeah, yeah, okay. Here it comes, guys, just a second."

A voiceover from a BBC reporter started in: "Mirjana Soldo says she first saw the Virgin Mary when she was a child, when she was fifteen years old. The visionary claims she saw the Blessed Mother on a rocky hillside in Medjugorje, for the first time in June of 1981. Thirty years later, Mirjana still sees the Virgin Mary and today she stands patiently in prayer, at the foot of Cross Mountain, outdoors, surrounded by hundreds of witnesses waiting for the arrival. She is dressed comfortably—urbane, chic—and with her eyes closed, head down, and her hands clasped in prayer, holding rosary beads, she waits for the Blessed Virgin Mary to arrive—to arrive literally from heaven, at least as claimed by the Croatian "visionary" from Medjugorje."

Bob put his arm out like a railroad gate blocking the students from moving.

"Wait, wait, waaaaaaiiiiit...THERE! Right there! Did you see that? The blond woman is with Her, the Virgin, real time—right now. The visionary is peering into another dimension. She is actually talking with someone—a spirit, an apparition, a ghost—not sure what—but right now she is actually engaged in conversation with a "being" from another world."

BBC voice over: "And then, Mirjana opens her eyes and looks up to a point slightly above her head. Mirjana's eyes, mouth, her entire face, explode into ecstasy. The Virgin Mary, known as the Queen of Peace, has arrived with a crown of twelve stars, and is now with Mirjana in Her full bodily presence. For the next eight minutes, the crowd watches in complete silence as the visionary encounters the Virgin Mary—the Mother of Christ. The crowd studies every facial expression—happiness one minute, then tears, then sadness, then agonizing sadness. As the apparition comes to its end, Mirjana, holding back tears, covers her face with her hands, then, after a moment—after a return to the realities of being an earthbound mortal— she breaks down into a full heaving cry—the Blessed Mother has gone, and taken with her the tantalizing glimpse of eternity."

The scene fades and moves to an interview with the visionary sitting at a table at an outdoor café on a sunny day in the town of Medjugorje.

BBC: Emotionally speaking, if you had to use one word to describe how you feel when you are in the presence of the Mother of God, what word would you use?

Mirjana: That is heaven. They ask me did I see heaven and I say I did not see heaven, but to be with Our Lady is to be in heaven. You simply feel you don't want it ever to stop. The greatest love on earth beside love for God is love for your children. Imagine when you do not even think about your children. You forget that they exist. Only Our Lady, so she may look at you.

Bob clicked off the DVD.

"That woman you saw there on TV, the visionary, claims she just spent eight minutes peering into another dimension—a dimension she calls heaven—talking with a 'being' she insists comes from the afterlife, and after unprecedented testing—no medical or scientific explanation has been established; no answers at all—not yet—and there are five others that swear they see the same thing. They all believe what they see and feel is real and beyond space and time."

Darcy interrupted the professor.

"Come on, Bob, you don't really believe that stuff, do you?"

"I didn't at first, not at all. But now I'm not so sure."

Bob reached into his desk and pulled out two large yellow envelopes and tossed them to the two students.

"Check this data out, guys. Look at the DVD again on your own, but leave your 'snarky' hats at the door before you do, there is more to it than you think. The Roman Catholic Church is fit to be tied over this, and they are desperately looking for an answer—for the truth. I'm putting this all into my Bayesian models and it's just not adding up. The results from my analysis suggest that there is a staggering low probability that this religious phenomenon is a fraudulent human conspiracy or that it is a hoax of some kind. I mean these so called "visionaries" hide nothing—it's now all on TV—you can watch the apparitions, these episodes of ecstasy, in fact, on YouTube; it's completely transparent—nothing is hidden."

"YouTube? I am supposed to believe this because you saw it on YouTube? Come on, Bob."

"No, not entirely, but it's part of the mystery—the transparency—the willingness of the six people to stand before the world, unfiltered, so that each witness can judge for themselves. It's definitely part of it—all part of the equation, the math problem. Just read the stuff I gave you; we are talking six sigma standard deviation. There is astonishing evidence supporting the claims of the visionaries."

"Honestly, Bob, I think the heat's getting to you; this is a bunch of religious mumbo-jumbo."

Tim interrupted the debate.

"Hey, Darcy, knock it off. Bob, turn the DVD back on; I want to see more."

For the next twenty minutes, the three sat in silence, and watched Father Dan's documentary about the mysterious events taking place in a small Eastern European village.

Bob's mind drifted again and he thought about Medjugorje.

"The greatest mystery of modern times", that's what Dan had called Medjugorje, and on this hot afternoon in June, Bob was beginning to believe his brother, and he was not alone in his growing devotion. Some of the professor's students were beginning to believe. Some students had started going back to Mass, even confession. Medjugorje is no longer just a town; it is an ideal, and Medjugorje was changing his own views of faith.

Bob wondered if he was beginning to believe, to believe in God; he wondered if he was being pulled in all the way. One thing he knew for certain—he wanted answers.

As the documentary was coming to its end, the Chairman of the Mathematics Department, Jim Cromwell, stormed into Bob's office, waving sheets of papers in his hand like a matador and shouting like his pants were on fire.

"Bob, what the hell is this all about, for crying out loud? The Virgin Mary? Jesus Christ, Baronowski!"

Bob ignored the Department Chair and calmly turned around in his swivel chair, coffee in hand, and looked at his two students.

"Okay, guys, the nanny is here and he wants to change my diapers. I'll see you guys in class, tomorrow."

Chapter 10:

June 12, 8:10 pm - Alexandria, Va.
Rene's Home

The pounding on the door wouldn't stop.

Luke jumped out of the bed barking his head off and ran to the door.

"*What? Who could that be?*" Rene looked at her watch.

She then heard a voice. She buttoned her blouse and hurried to the front door.

"Espy, Espy, open up, it's me, Dan."

Rene quickly opened the door.

"Dan, what are you do…"

Dan charged into the foyer.

"We need to leave. We need to leave, now!"

Rene's mouth fell open; her eyes met his with a startled silence.

Dan's eyes quickly left Rene's and searched the room frantically.

While still scanning the room, Dan said, "Get your purse and I need the book."

Rene shook her head coming to her senses.

"What?" she snapped. "Get my purse? Leave? What do you mean leave?"

Dan went straight to the kitchen looking for the book and purse, and wildly swiped the newspapers off the kitchen table, sending the coffee mug crashing to the floor.

"Where's the book, Rene, the book I gave you at dinner? Rene! Is it still in your purse?"

The coffee cup, crashing to the floor, shook Rene out of her daze.

"Dan, stop, stop. You are freaking me out. If you don't calm down, I am going to call the police."

"Tell me where the book is and I'll explain everything."

"The book is in my bedroom, on the chest."

Dan exploded upstairs into the bedroom, found what he was looking for, and rushed back down into the hallway. Dan took Rene's wrist and started pulling her towards the door.

"We've got to go. I'll explain everything in the car."

Rene stiffened and dug her feet in.

"Let go of me! I want to know what is going on—now!"

She struggled harder, trying to pull her wrist away. Dan let go of her wrist and quickly grabbed Rene by both of her shoulders and faced her directly.

"Rene, I will explain everything, but right now there is no time. You are in danger in this house."

The word, 'danger,' had always seemed so abstract to Rene. And at first, the word had no real meaning or impact, but then she saw the anguish in Dan's eyes. Suddenly the word, 'danger,' became tangible; the word moved quickly though her body, past her heart, and settled low in her stomach. Her mind was churning as she looked for answers. She thought about dinner and suddenly, the strange night with Dan seemed to have no end. She looked at Dan pleading for it all to go away.

"Rene, if we don't leave right now, Russian hit men are coming over here with guns and two bullets—one for you and one for me. That's just a fact. I need you to trust me."

She felt sick and her mouth went dry. She looked at Dan's white collar and then back at his eyes. She searched for something that made sense. Then she remembered the night they broke up. That night, through lots of tears and even some laughter, they promised that they would always be there for each other, if the time ever came—till death do us part. If he needed her now, she would be there for him. She realized the torment that Dan must be in to be at her door; she knew he would give up his life to protect her, but assassins? It seemed impossible. What kind of trouble was he in? There had to be a reason he was putting her life in danger. A real good reason, she hoped.

Dan sensed he was getting through and let her go. She knelt down, hugged Luke then looked back up at Dan.

"Okay, but I am not leaving, not without Luke."

"Okay, bring him, but let's go."

As Rene went to get her purse and the dog's leash, Dan stepped out of the house and looked down the street. He saw headlights turn quickly onto Rene's street. They had arrived sooner than he had planned. Dan called out to Rene.

"Look, Rene, slight change of plans."

Dan put the book down on the stairs and took out a pistol from a shoulder holster.

"You need to go hide right now, and take the dog. Go back to the kitchen."

Rene turning around gasped when she saw the gun, then shouted, "Daniel!"

The bubble burst. She was done with Dan's cloak and dagger games. The gun was too much. She ran to the phone in the kitchen to call the police. Dan chased her into the kitchen and yanked the phone cord out of the wall.

"Look, Rene, right now the police can't help us—other people will be put in danger. It is never going to end; more people are going to die until they get what they want from me."

"What? What are you talking about? They want something from you? You came into my house to tell me THAT!?"

Rene stepped back away from Dan and threw the wireless handset at the priest.

"It's that book, isn't it?"

Rene lunged past Dan and went for the book. With the book in her hands, she shouted, "Just give them what they want. What you have gotten yourself into is none of my business. She began to cry softly. "Just get the hell out of my house and take your precious book with you."

She weakly tossed the book towards Dan.

"Dan, just go. Just leave me alone."

Dan had no choice now—in forty-five seconds the front door would be kicked in—and Rene would go down first. He pointed the gun at Rene.

"Take Luke back to the kitchen now, or we are both going to die."

Rene, staggered at the gun pointed at her, stiffened, and decided to give up. But rather than raise her hands in surrender, she saluted. She saluted Dan with her middle finger as she walked away, heading for the kitchen. Luke loyally followed Rene to the back of the house.

Dan looked through the hallway window. He saw there were only two in the car. One got out wearing a rain jacket and some kind of European beret. Dan, his heart pounding, looked upstairs, then at the small closet by the front door. He chose the closet to make his stand. He stepped in, leaving the door slightly ajar, and waited; his anger and adrenaline were raging. How dare this monster walk into Rene's house looking to kill her in cold blood. He did not have to wait long. The man outside the door turned the door knob of the unlocked door slowly, and walked in confidently with his gun drawn—clearly unafraid of a bumbling priest and his ex-girlfriend.

The priest didn't hesitate—as soon as the door closed, he put a shot of lead into the assassin's throat. The blast of the gun shot pounded into Rene's ears and shook her to her core—she put her hands over her ears and knelt down beside Luke under the kitchen table. The bullet sliced through the assassin's flesh, shattered his cervical before smashing into the front door.

Dan looked down at the dead man and started to say a prayer:

"God have mercy on your..." He stopped. Forget it he thought. Maybe now he would begin to awaken from his nightmare. It felt good to finally fight back. These men were enemies of the people he loved, enemies of his faith. He could barely live with himself any longer knowing that everybody he cared about was in danger. "It's game on, now."

He quickly took the rain jacket off the dead man, put on the man's beret and trotted out to the car with the hat pulled down over his eyes. Dan opened the car door, sat down, drew his gun and pointed the pistol at the drivers head—it was the pudgy faced man with the small bulging eyes.

"You move and you're a dead man, just like your friend in the house, simple as that." He cocked the gun, reached into the man's coat pocket, and took his gun and passport. "Sergei Yeltsin, Republic of Russia, nice to meet you. Now listen up; one silly, little, Russian macho-man act, and I am going to blow your head off. Step out of the car, nice and slow."

Dan walked the man back to the house. A few neighbors had gathered outside of Rene's home at the sound of gun fire.

"Been a suicide." Dan opened the rain jacket and revealed his collar. "We are going to take the body to the funeral home. It's all been taken care of, thank you. The police have been notified."

Dan whispered into the Russian's ear.

"You are going to take your dead friend out of the house and put him in your car. We are going to leave together. Now listen to me carefully; I have no problem painting this side-walk with your blood in front of all these people. I have things to do—you are just slowing me down. If you're not helpful, you are dead. You make this quick, you go home; you live another day."

With the dead body in the back seat of the car, Dan got in the car. "Drive."

The car approached the four way stop at the end of the street.

"Go ahead and make a full stop like the fine law abiding citizen that you are."

When the car came to rest, Dan shoved the transmission into park, put the gun on the drivers knee cap, and pulled the trigger. The Russian shrieked in pain. He needed to slow down the men who were after him, anyway he could. He pressed the pistol up against the driver's temple.

The priest believed the Catholic Church can play rough too, when it needed to protect the faith.

"Now listen to me. You tell whoever you are working for I am going to find him. I am going to track him down and I am going to punch his ticket to hell with a bullet to his brain. You understand that?"

Dan jammed the pistol harder against the Russian's skull and thought about Rene, and what these men had almost done. He had a huge urge to pull the trigger. His adrenaline was pulsating, and his anger now had no bounds, but he eased the gun off the Russian's temple.

Dan stepped out of the car with the gun still pointed at the Russian. He took a few steps back toward Rene's townhouse, but stopped and went back to the car—this time to the driver's side. The Russian was still tending to his wound. Dan tapped on the window, pulled out the Russian's passport, put it up against the glass and motioned to the driver to roll down the window. The Russian ignored the gesture and went back to his wound. Dan took a hold of his pistol by the gun barrel, and with the butt of the gun shattered the car window. He rammed the gun against the driver's head and worked the barrel into the Russian's mouth. He shoved the passport in the Russian's face. His days in Rwanda were fueling his anger. *Never again*, he thought.

"You see your passport right here? I know who you are, you son of a bitch. You understand that? You are Sergei Yeltsin. Anything happens to Rene and I am going to find you. I am going to hunt you down and hurt you. I will make it my life's work. Now, get the hell out of here and take your friend with you—and stay out of my life."

Dan hurried back to Rene's house and went inside.

He picked up the book and said, "Rene, there are going to be more of these men. The police cannot keep you safe. We have a death warrant on our heads. I need to hide you—take you somewhere where you will be safe."

Rene, totally defeated and in shock, took Luke's leash from the pedestal table by the door, and followed Dan out of the door to a car that was parked a block and a half away.

Nobody spoke for twenty minutes as they made their way down Route 50, heading east. Finally, Rene looked over at Dan, then down at the book that was resting between them.

"Dan, where are we going?"

"Annapolis"

Another five minutes went by without a word. Rene looked back at Dan.

"Dan, why's your hair wet?"

Dan patted the top of his head.

"Huh?"

Chapter 11:

June 12, 12:25 pm - Near Bellagio, Italy
Father Indelicatto and the Smoke of Satan

As the Vatican's Chief Exorcist, Father Roberto Indellicotta had spent years battling the stench of evil. The demonically possessed often spat out rusty nails or splinters of glass, even rose petals—the small relics he still kept in bags and leather pouches. Today, however, he faced something different. Roberto understood his time had come. His battle, this time, would not be against a possessed child, but rather, his fight would be for his own salvation. Satan had begun its possession of his body. It was just a matter of time—he knew the demon better than anybody. Roberto was sure the pains inside his chest were signs of the onset of his possession—the heavy blows were coming directly from the demon.

For Roberto, it had been the woman's flesh; it was how the demon found his way in, and his salvation was now gravely at risk.

Roberto's downfall began after writing a series of bestselling books about his work as an exorcist. After the publishing success, and a major motion picture, he became a popular speaker throughout the Catholic world. He was a celebrity in Rome and he enjoyed his success immensely.

Human pride—ego, a sin yes, but easily confessed away each month. But after Roberto took a young mistress, his life became darker and more secretive. He stopped going to his confessor; it had led to furious attacks, but he could not abandon the Holy Mass. When he neared the tabernacle, in his state of mortal sin, enduring internal pains, he had to force himself to take the Eucharist. For a moment, with the consecrated host on his tongue, the demon would retreat; the promise of Christ's peace would reign. But later, as Roberto's thoughts found their way back to the girl, the demon would return—angry, and armed; the demon would come at him hard, like an abusive, merciless father seeking vengeance with a belt tightly wrapped around his fist.

But he could not give up the girl. Instead, Indellicotta looked to blame others for his weakness. With the girl, he had fallen victim to the temptations of the flesh, and like many victims, he searched for something or someone to blame. His fall from grace, he concluded, was due to the great lost traditions of the Catholic Church. The Church was weak, the fear of God had diminished, the rite of exorcism was now ridiculed by his own colleagues—the rite embarrassed them. The devil was nothing but a comic strip for children. It was the wretched state of the Catholic faith that had made him weak and vulnerable.

The phone buzzed again—it was Carl Beckett.

Father Roberto Indellicotta had met Carl Beckett in Connecticut, at Yale; their friendship had been nurtured by cigars, scotch, and late night debates on the meaning of life, women, and the reality of God.

"Where the hell are you, Indellicotta? You're late. I've just opened a bottle of the best champagne in this town, and trust me; they have the best in the world. Right now I am staring at a Krug 1995 Clos d'Ambonnay."

"I'll be there in a few minutes, Carl. You're a bit early, nevertheless, my apologies."

"No worries pal. Time to celebrate, Roberto; the gates of hell are beginning to close and I am ready to dance on the devil's grave. Everything is in place. We will have the Codex tonight, and with it, we will have our proof that the Catholic Church is in a state of apostasy."

"Carl, we may have new complications."

Carl Beckett sensed in Roberto's voice a concern that caught him off guard, and Beckett was in no mood for surprises. He had enough on his plate already.

"Complications—I hate that word, Indellicotta. Christ sake, I don't want to hear your Debbi Downer whining all over again."

Beckett wanted good news from Roberto. Beckett had a major problem developing. His cargo ship, the Russian freighter was floating around somewhere in the Persian Gulf near Iran—missing. A three hundred and fifty foot freighter had vanished—a complete communication blackout. He had not heard a word, and Beckett had one hundred million dollars of his money tied up in the venture. Rumors were that Israeli

Mosaad had boarded the ship. There was nothing Beckett could do at the moment—he needed to hear from his point man on the ship. Beckett was not going to worry about it now. He didn't get to the top of his company by wringing his hands and worrying. Keep taking hills, keep fighting, and never give in. It was how Beckett got to the top.

Roberto groaned, but Beckett carried on.

"Look Roberto, we have waited years for this moment, so when you get here, keep your worry-wart bull crap to yourself. That phony Pope is dying, not soon enough, as far as I am concerned. Souls are at stake, Roberto, and we have our guy ready to go."

"Carl, the Pope has taken a turn for the worse—looks like life support is going to be removed shortly. A Papal Conclave may be called soon and Cardinal Warwinka is in DC—he may head straight back to Rome before his speech."

"So what, Indellicotta, sounds like good news to me; the Pope will be dead; it is what we have been waiting for, and for the life of me I don't know why Warwinka continues to matter to you so much; Cardinal Lombardi is going to be Pope. His time has come. He has promised to destroy Vatican II - to relegate that heresy into the dustbins of history. He has the votes; you've assured me."

"It's not that simple any longer, Carl, Lombardi has rivals—Cardinal Warwinka has a lot of support. The power center of the Church is moving south—Latin America, Brazil is the largest Catholic country in the world; Africa—that's where the Cardinals see the faith growing. Believe me on this. Now, are you sure you will have the Codex del Rio Grande tomorrow?"

"I'll have it tomorrow; I am heading to DC to pick it up. Don't worry about that, but what the hell are you talking about—a lot of support? Don't give me that—Warwinka! Impossible. He's a commie from Honduras, for crying out loud."

"I'll explain everything when I see you, Carl. Like I said, it's not that simple. Sit tight. But I need your man in DC, now. Get him on the first plane out."

"He's already in the States. He's in Boston."

"Good, but, he needs to be in DC, tomorrow. We will talk about it when I see you."

It all had happened so quickly. The Church was facing ruin—he was left with no choice; he had to take action and Beckett was his man. Cardinal Warwinka had to be stopped; he could not become Pope. It looked like Washington, DC would now have to be a go. Cardinal Warwinka was speaking in Washington, on the campus of Catholic University. He needed Cardinal Warwinka in a place where he could get to him. If Cardinal Warwinka made it back to Rome, it would be too late. Security inside the Sistine Chapel would be impenetrable during the Papal Conclave.

Nearing the outskirts of Lake Como, Roberto put his phone back in his jacket and thought about his upcoming lunch with Carl Beckett and what he was going to ask him to do. He reached into his pocket and felt the little bag of relics, hoping to put his mind at rest. He wanted to think of a simpler time—a time before his sins, when he loved God—a time when he made a difference in people's lives—before his first exorcism, before his early encounters with the demon.

He held the bag of relics in his hand, but the simpler times did not come. Instead, Sofia, his mistress, entered his daydreams. She often did. Again, he thought about her hands; how they had changed everything a few years ago on a Sunday drive through the Tuscan hills. That day, she took the bag of relics from his pocket and replaced it with her warm hands and friendly fingers. After that day, he made peace with the demon, and Roberto began to love the world.

"Sir, we're here—Grand Hotel Villa Serbelloni—Bellagio."

The chauffeur waited another moment, looked in the rear view mirror and saw Roberto blankly staring out of the car window.

"Is everything okay, Father? Shall I get the door?"

As Roberto reached for the door handle, the sense of peace had evaporated, replaced by a small pang of nausea. He was about to set in motion an act that would condemn his soul to hell.

Chapter 12:

"What about my hair?"

"It's wet. Your hair is wet."

"Oh, yeah, right—the Russians believe I'm in the shower...Or they did."

Rene looked at Dan, sharply.

"Is it a custom of yours to take a shower before you shoot people, Dan? Is that some kind of Catholic ritual that I missed hearing about at CCD?"

"No, no, no...Let me explain. I met the Russians at the hotel to finish a deal."

Rene cut Dan off in mid-sentence.

"A deal? You show up at my house with a gun because—what—some 'deal' went bad? What are you talking about?"

"Just a second, Rene, hear me out. The Russians are working for somebody in Rome. I don't know who, but they want a document I have. I gave it to them tonight at the hotel. I told them to review it while I took a shower. I had booked a room on the first floor of the hotel. I turned the water on, wet my hair, popped my head back out into the room and asked the men how things were going. They ignored me; they had some expert looking at the document. I closed the bathroom door, jumped out of the window and into this rented car. I had the gun stowed in the car. I don't think the Russians considered, even remotely, I'd have a gun, and would be ready to use it. And the document I gave them, by the way, is a doctored fake. They are not happy."

Rene could barely take it all in—jumping out of windows, guns, shooting people—in her house—it was overwhelming, but she gathered her thoughts. A transaction? What was he talking about, and why her. She looked at the book as she spoke.

"Okay, let's forget about your hair; what is this about a transaction, and documents?"

"What matters, Rene, is that they made you part of the contract. It was made clear to me that you would be kidnapped or killed if I did not cooperate. At first, I agreed to work with them, but things changed. Bottom line is I didn't trust them and that's why you are with me, right now."

"Damn right things changed, and you certainly didn't hold up your end of the bargain."

"Huh? What do you mean?"

"Cooperate—you didn't cooperate. Shooting people is not cooperative—at all—and it looks like I've been kidnapped—at gun point, you may recall. Is that what this is all about, Dan; are you the bad guy?"

"Rene, this whole thing has just gotten out of hand."

Rene turned her head abruptly away from Dan and looked outside her window. She almost laughed.

"You think?"

Dan checked his rearview mirror, then turned his head towards Rene.

"Rene, a month ago I had this worked out. Problem is, two days ago, in Rome, I got a call warning me not to trust anyone. I was told you were in danger—no matter what. They were going to kill us both after they got what they wanted. They are determined to send a brutal message. I could not take the risk of simply making arrangements on their terms, and just hope for the best. So, right now, my only chance is to pull you in until I can work this out."

Dan thought about other people close to him who could also be at risk. People close to him were in danger. He thought about his brother in Boston. He thought about the man he shot in Rene's hallway; he thought about the assassin he let go. He had to find his way out—fast.

Rene half listened; she heard the words come out of his mouth anyway, but she was back lost in a fog. Reality was crashing down on her.

She groaned; a man died in her hallway. All she wanted now was to wake up from her nightmare. She looked at Dan's hair again. She closed her eyes and lowered herself into the velour seats. His damp hair, of all things, brought home the reality that she was not dreaming.

Chapter 13:

June 12, 9:40 pm - Annapolis, Md.
The Yacht Club Parking lot

The Crown Vic rolled into the yacht club parking lot and pulled into to a spot along the bulkhead and adjacent to the boat docks. Dan looked over at Rene—her eyes were closed. He could see she did not want to move. Had he done enough to keep her out of the shadowy world of Vatican power struggles? If he had listened to the man in the book store in Rome, Rene would be free.

Dan stepped out of the car and looked back towards the parking lot entrance. As far as he could tell, he had not been followed.

He opened the back door to get the dog, walked around to the passenger's side and looked down into the car window at Rene, who was curled up quietly against the passenger side door. She was awake, but so not to startle her, he lightly tapped on the glass before opening the door.

He gently took her hand, and as she slowly stood up, she ran her hand through her hair, then reached out and took the leash from Dan. Standing by the car, the priest took both of her hands, and with Rene's body leaning wearily against the car door, Dan said, "You know Rene, I have never regretted becoming a priest, and I will be a priest until the day I die, but I have also never stopped loving you."

There was nothing for Rene to say, and she listlessly looked away toward the boats. Then without another word, all three headed to the docks, but not before Dan took one more glance back towards the nearly empty yacht club's parking lot entrance.

Chapter 14:

June 12, 9:45 pm - Annapolis, Md.
Rene Meets Tucker on "D" Doc

Tucker and Sanjay stepped off the boat and onto "D" dock—the restaurant was in Eastport, Annapolis, about a ten minute march across Spa Creek Bridge from the yacht club. As they made their way down the dock, Tucker looked towards the storm remnants; the high clouds and lightning were now over Tilghman Island, on the Maryland eastern shore heading south and east.

About half way down the dock, Sanjay subtly elbowed Tucker in the ribs. Tucker looked ahead and down the dock. A priest was moving towards them; he was walking swiftly and holding hands with a woman who was struggling with an anxious yellow dog.

Sanjay said quietly to Tucker, "I guess that's better than the alternative."

As the couple neared, Sanjay and Tucker were set to look away as they passed, but then Tucker did the unexpected—something he had not done in years—there was no explaining it. It was completely out of his character, but he looked. Some intangible, elusive force had drawn him to the stranger. Was it something as simple as the way she walked? Was it the strands of hair that seemed to bend and sway with the moonlight in a pleasing way? He wasn't sure, but he looked at the woman as she passed, and then, the last thing in the world he thought she would do—she looked back.

Passing by a dock light, their eyes met, for an instant or for a moment, it seemed longer. Then something odd happened, something stirred inside Tucker, something opened and came in and it reminded him of a distant past.

As she moved by, he quickly looked away towards the harbor. But without warning, the dog darted behind the woman, twisting her into a pirouette. The Retriever then stuffed his nose into Tucker's pants.

"No, Luke, no," the woman said softly as she tugged on the leash, "Sorry."

Tucker buckled slightly and as he was gently moving the dog's head aside, still crouching, he looked up at her and their eyes met again. Her twirling motion had caused a few more strands of hair to come to rest on her glasses—the slight muss called him back in. Their eyes locked. A fleck of something good had now slipped inside him without warning. It was so unexpected. Maybe that's how the feeling found its way in. A priest, a dog, a beautiful woman with mystery about her—to Tucker, none of it made sense. But most jarring was the "something good," that had slipped in, a real outlier that had no business on the boat docks. His guards were not on duty; guards that had stood watch, by his side for years, and protected him. But it was not simply the woman's beauty that had moved him. His sentries would have defeated that intrusion. No, it was her eyes that had stormed the walls with nothing more than a simple allusion of something found.

Rene gained control of Luke, and Tucker straightened up. But before turning away, she looked up at Tucker, and this time they both sensed something had happened. She quickly looked away and grabbed the priest's hand and headed to a boat further down the dock. As Tucker turned to look out towards the harbor, away from the couple, he inadvertently caught the face of the priest. Embarrassed by his recklessness, and hoping to disappear, his turning motion became abrupt and he madly searched for the lights on the Chesapeake Bay Bridge in the distance.

After the strange trio passed, Tucker could not help himself. Before starting down the dock again, he turned around and looked back at the woman hurrying to the end of the pier. Her silhouette in the dim moonlight was all he could make of her. As she stepped onto a boat, he sensed something beautifully strange about her.

Sanjay, surprised at Tucker's peccadillo, playfully grabbed him around the waist and wrestled him towards the edge of the dock and said, "You turned around? What was that all about Tucker? Listen, my man," Sanjay pointed towards the end of the dock, "that—I promise you—is none of your damn business."

Chapter 15:

April 1994 - Rwanda
Nicholas Alexi

Before the genocide in Rwanda, something very strange happened in a town called Kibeho. The Catholic Church claims the Blessed Mother appeared to six school children in 1981.

Kibeho is a small village in Rwanda, and on November 28, 1981, five months after an attempt on Pope John Paul II's life, the apparitions of the Virgin Mary at Kibeho began. A sixteen-year-old school girl, named Alphonsine Mumureke, was the first to see the Madonna. Alphonsine Mumureke described her encounter with the Virgin Mary to the press:

"The Virgin was not white as She is usually seen in holy pictures. I could not determine the color of Her skin, but She was of incomparable beauty. She was barefoot and had a seamless white dress, and also a white veil on Her head. Her hands were clasped together on Her breast, and Her fingers pointed to the sky. When the Blessed Virgin was about to leave, I said a prayer. When She left, I saw Her rise to Heaven like Jesus." Alphonsine Mumureke

Within days of Alphonsine Mumureke's visions, five other school aged children began to see the Blessed Virgin Mary, but what they saw and heard was not always beautiful—there were also warnings and foreboding visions of a terrible future, as well.

"The visionaries at Kibeho were shown terrifying glimpses into the future by the Virgin Mary. They were weeping and crying and the witnesses who crowded around the seers were left with an unforgettable impression of fear and sadness. If Rwanda did not come back to God, said the vision, there would be a 'river of blood.'" The warnings of the Blessed Virgin Mary were not just for

Africa. "When I tell you this, I am not addressing myself strictly to you, child, but I am making this appeal to the world."

Marie-Clare Mukangango, who was later killed during the atrocities, said the Virgin described the world as in revolt against God, the world "is on the edge of catastrophe."

After shooting the statue, Nicholas Alexi got back in the driver's seat, pulled out a map from the glove compartment, and studied the roads of the Lake Kivu region.

A flash caught his eye, and Alexi looked towards the rain line in the valley. The landscape in the valley was laced with a soft gray curtain of smoky rain and he watched the lightning move up the hills away from the church.

He picked up his field glasses from the dashboard—there was something out of the ordinary in the sky. Dozens of vultures—more than he was accustomed to seeing—were circling a farmhouse in the valley. Cattle, Alexi thought, and he looked to the ground, but what Alexi saw surprised him.

Below the mist, settled on the front yard of a farm house, were dead bodies. The dead were stacked in sloppy piles, and in the piles, bodies were twitching like sleeping dogs. Then from the driveway, a pickup truck, filled with young, joyful men, kicked up mud as it left the grisly crime scene. He briefly followed the truck, but after it turned towards town, his eyes moved back to count the dead.

Maybe twelve, he thought. Alexi looked back up to the gray sky, and watched the vultures circle patiently in the light rain, waiting for the carrion to come fully to rest.

As the thunder claps faded into rumbles, Alexi put the glasses down, fixed the static on the radio, and returned to the map. He was looking for directions to the soccer stadium, and he needed outs. Rumors of a massacre inside an aging concrete soccer stadium, fifty miles north of Gitesi in the town of Gatwaro were jamming the airwaves. Alexi was looking for escape routes, near the stadium, in case of trouble. Traffic jams were not an inconvenience in Rwanda; they were often a matter of life and death. An awful way to die, Alexi thought—ripped through a car window by a mob, then hacked to death with primitive weapons.

The worst part would be the waiting—waiting filled with terror—waiting for the first hands to come through the shattered windows.

Hearing the news on the radio, Alexi thought about his supply of guns and ammo. A lot of people were going to die in the stadium tonight, and Alexi was sure Idi would be eager to join the hunt. Idi was behind on payments but business would be good in Gatwaro. Alexi would add new customers and Idi would find cash at the stadium.

Short, blond, and tough as a hammer, the thirty-two year old Russian turned off the radio; he had heard enough. He knew what to expect. Idi and his men had a penchant for killing in bunches, and Alexi had a good feeling the Hutu, inside the church, would push north to Gatwaro to join the slaughter.

Alexi folded the map carefully, making sure to cinch the creases tightly, and slipped it gently back into the glovebox. Alexi looked at his watch, wedged his foot up on the dashboard, lit a cigarette, and shook his head thinking of the map that he had just finished mending.

"You see it everywhere you look," he thought, *"the sloppiness; it is the root of it all. The starving would end if the bastards understood that."*

Exhaling and moving his lips in a smoky whisper, he said to himself, thinking of Africa, *"Learn to fold a damn map properly, and your wretched children will stop dying."*

Alexi watched the smoke leave the van; he shifted in his seat; he was uncomfortable now—agitated. The sophistry of his revelation had tainted him with foolishness, and Nicholas Alexi suffered fools terribly. Nothing before him now, or all that he had seen in Africa, would ever change; he was sure of it. The starving, the cruelty, the killing, and yes, the sloppiness, was eternal and arrived each day with the morning sun. Fools, like young gazelle at rivers edge, die young in Africa, he thought.

After taking another draw from his cigarette, inhaling deeper this time, he tossed his head back with a quick lurch, held his breath and stared at the metal ceiling emptying his mind of the imprudence of hope.

He then waited for Idi and his men to come out of the church. He knew they would come shortly; Idi's radio was always on, and the news of the massacre would change the day's plans.

Chapter 16:

April 1994 - Rwanda
Inside the Church Rectory

Idi Kambana hissed at the young seminarian standing at the top of the wood stairs that led to the basement of the church rectory.

"Enough of this foolishness."

Idi was a big man, not tall, but three hundred and ten pound. He was slightly out of breath as he reached the top of the stairs. After reaching the top of the stairs, Idi dug his finger into Daniel Baronowski's chest and hissed again.

"Listen to me, priest." Idi spat hard towards Dan's feet. "No more of your games. Bring me that cockroach, or I will start putting heads on this floor."

As Idi pressed his finger harder, his bloodshot eyes bulged and his forehead flinched towards Dan. Now inches apart, Dan's view was swallowed up by Idi's protruding gums, enormous yellow teeth, and the pink moist film inside his lips. Idi barked deeply, a menacing staccato, "I know she is in this church. Give me that Tutsi, Monique Butare, now, or your nuns are going to die!"

Two of Idi's men had gone straight to the church and took five nuns hostage. Idi Kambana was on a fishing expedition, and his catch, Monique Butare, was tucked underneath a ledge somewhere on the church grounds. The five nuns were Idi's bait.

Dan was in Rwanda to research the Kibeho apparitions of the Virgin Mary for the Vatican, and he now felt like the walls were closing in. But there was no time for fear; lives depended on him keeping his cool, and for the moment he was relieved that Monique, and her little sister, had not been found.

Dan backed away from Idi. He made his way behind his desk; he wanted to get away from the hallway. In the hallway, a hidden door, behind a large cabinet, opened to the girl's hiding place.

Dan turned and faced Idi.

"We have searched everywhere, Idi. She left with her father one hour ago, and so I ask you, in the name of God, to please leave. This is a place of worship, not vengeance."

"Don't preach to me your lies. Her parents are dead. I have been to the house. I killed them myself; they are on their driveway. Monique's mother, father, her brothers—they are all dead, and Monique was not with them."

Dan's stomach dropped. It had started. He was sure of it. The country was beginning to bleed, and astonishingly, the apparitions of the Virgin Mary, at Kibeho, had predicted the bloodshed. The Kibeho prophecies warned of epic violence and a 'river of blood'.

But what now? Monique and the nuns were in real danger. With no real plan beyond hoping to get Idi out of the rectory, Dan decided to bluff.

"Idi, I don't know about that. What I do know is that Monique came here early this morning, about 7:30; she was scared; she wanted to know how bad things were going to get. An hour later she was picked up by her father and they tore out of here. Last thing she said was, 'Goma.'"

Dan's deliberate lie made Idi Kambana seethe. Idi knew the family well; he had been friends with the Tutsi family, before the uprising. He also knew where he could find Monique's father. Monique's father now rested on the steering wheel of his blue Nissan, parked in the driveway, with a bullet in his head. Monique's mother and her two brothers were dead as well; they were killed with machetes in their front yard.

It didn't take much to set Idi off. Lying to a man like Idi Kambana and getting caught was like doing jumping jacks in a hippo's nest—you are going to get stomped.

"You're lying! I killed the father myself."

Idi charged the priest with his machete raised high.

The young seminarian put up his arms, crossed his forearms and waited for the blow. This was not Dan's first rodeo in Rwanda. He had learned that life in Rwanda was cheap—often the price of a Yankee's baseball cap or a pack of American cigarettes. He was powerless; there was nothing he could do to stop Idi. This was probably it.

As Dan was rushing through a "Hail Mary" before he was hit, Idi swung violently, but intentionally missed his head by inches.

Idi, instead, struck the priest hard with the back of his hand.

"Enough of your games." Idi turned to Kagame and shouted, "Get me the nuns, bring them to me now!"

Kagame turned his walkie-talkie on and called the men who were gathering the nuns, but there was no response.

Idi swung back around and snapped.

"You want to play games with me? Let me tell you, priest, I play rough, and in my country, I always win." Idi licked his teeth, a tick of some sort, and the habit drew Dan back into Idi's gums.

"Take me to Monique, or I'm going to rape the America nun before I kill her."

Dan put down the urge to lash out; it would only infuriate the human hippo further. Dan finished his 'Hail Mary' then returned Idi's stare—he was not sure why, but he couldn't think of what else to do. He drove his eyes into Idi, as if staring down a wild animal. Then to his surprise, Idi backed off; his demeanor changed. Dan sensed it immediately. Had Idi gone too far, striking a man of the cloth? Rwanda was a very Catholic country. No, Dan quickly understood; Idi's hard edge eased because he wanted to drink. Idi was drunk when he arrived, and he wanted more booze. Noticing a small liquor cabinet, Idi moved towards the bar. Idi was not ready to kill—not yet.

The Hutu decided to take a break from his search. Idi was sure he would find the girl—it was just a matter of time. Idi lit a cigarette, then reviewed his choices in the liquor cabinet, patiently—rum, whiskey, gin, vodka, a decent bar, and now, it seemed, he had all the time in the world. He twisted the cap off a whiskey bottle, took a sip, then poured some in a glass. Idi turned and faced Dan and with almost a calm elegant air, he said, "You are a silly goat, Father Daniel. We will see how brave you are when I have my knife on your nun's throat. You don't know me very well, but I'm a patient man— a just man, even—a nun's life for the girl seems fair. One way or the other, I will find the cockroach."

Dan said nothing, waiting for Idi's next move.

Idi strolled over to the priest's desk and turned on the radio and continued to share with Dan his expertise on murdering the innocent. Idi was poking around, looking for soft spots, hoping to soften up the priest; find his weakness. He really didn't want to kill the priest, but he wanted Monique. He was sure one dead nun would force the priest to tip his hand, but he wasn't sure what the priest would do. Idi doubted the priest would put his feet up on the desk and watch him butcher five nuns—but who knows. Perhaps the priest would fight like a leopard until he had to kill him—a form of suicide by police—damn messy business. He wanted to tighten the screws a little bit, let the priest contemplate horror. A few good body blows and perhaps the priest would hand over the girl without a fight and get on with his life.

"Priest, you think you know all about God and heaven. You think you know what's in a man's soul."

Dan said nothing.

"Believe me, priest, nobody wants to die; no priest, no monk, no religious fanatic, no matter how convinced they are of paradise. Trust me, they don't want to die. That's what I have learned. They fear it. Everybody begs for their life. You learn this when you kill with a machete."

Idi walked back towards the liquor cabinet and pulled it away from the wall; he lightly tapped on the thin plaster board, listening for hollow spots. With the investigation complete, Idi turned back towards the priest and continued his talk.

"I have seen a lot on the streets of Rwanda, priest. I have seen a lot of horror, and our revenge against the Tutsi cockroach has just begun, and there is nothing you can do to stop it. So, do yourself a favor and give me the girl, or I will bring an unspeakable horror into this church. I will start with the American nun. I am going to kill her right in front of you. I am going to put her head on this floor. Do you understand me, priest? This is how I do my business in my country."

Dan didn't know what to say and again he stayed with his silence.

"I will give you a couple of minutes to think about it. But think of that America nun with her pretty white face in your hands, looking up at you with hope in her eyes, and the rest of her body on the floor at your feet."

Idi paused for a moment and looked up at the ceiling, thinking if Monique could be there, but he had checked the attic thoroughly, and the ceiling was much too thin. Idi turned around and walked back towards Dan. Then, standing by the desk, Idi spoke in a quiet voice.

"Hey, Priest"

"Yes, Idi?"

"I'll do it you know."

"What's that Idi? Do what?"

Idi turned his hands over and showed Dan his palms like he was holding a large melon.

"I'll put her in your hands; I'll put that American in your hands."

With his promise made, Idi threw back the glass of whiskey, and turned up the volume of the radio on the seminarian's desk.

After the President's plane went down, Idi's devotion, aside from murder, was the radio and from the airwaves came a tsunami of propaganda—the words never stopped. Idi loved the sound of the great man in the little box. The voices on the radio empowered Idi; they liberated him; made him invincible. The constant call for violence was intoxicating; it was like a drug to Idi Kambana; it was cocaine, and Idi could not get enough of it.

Idi Kambana kicked a chair towards his friend, Kagame, and invited him to sit down with a wave of the whiskey bottle. The two Hutu sat in silence and drank heavily, listening to the radio. The radio commanded all Hutu to kill quickly and without mercy. The man in the box rose to a crescendo.

"Seek retribution! Go to your homes and pick up your machetes, your rakes, and your hoes and take to the streets. Kill the Tutsi cockroaches and fill the rivers with blood!"

Idi smiled and moved his stumpy fat legs up and down like a child. "You hear that, priest? That's what I'm talking about, kill the cockroaches."

Idi dropped the whiskey bottle to the floor, saw there was no more bourbon, then reached over and grabbed the bottle of rum.

The young seminarian still felt the sting of the back of Idi's hand, but he was in no mood to turn the other cheek. Lives were at stake, and he now had a huge urge to take a lamp, the empty whiskey bottle, something, anything and pound Idi Kambana into unconsciousness. He also had a hunter's knife strapped above his ankle inside his sock. Despite his hopes and prayers, he knew Rwanda was a dangerous place, even before the Hutu uprising. The knife was always there.

Chapter 17:

April 1, 1994 - Rwanda
The Whistle

Down the hall from the rectory's parlor, and behind a cabinet, a doorway to a small bathroom opened to Monique Butare's safe room—her hideout. In their tiny room, Monique Butare had her hands on her little sister's mouth. One accidental cough, hiccup, sneeze, and Idi would open the door. Monique wasn't sure what Idi would do, at first, if they were caught; probably not kill her right away, more like rape and beatings.

Idi had courted her before the uprising. They had grown up together; he had been like a big brother to her. Not long ago, she remembered Idi helping her father gather up chickens that had escaped from their pen. She remembered his huge face beaming as he lunged and lurched for the fleeing hens. After the round up, Idi and Monique's family shared dinner that evening. But now everything had changed. Idi wanted to kill her. If he found her, he'd probably keep her in the trunk of a car until she died of dehydration.

Monique could hear Idi as if he were standing in the room beside her. She could also hear the radio's voice of doom, and she was thankful for the tireless noise. The incessant call to kill was, ironically, keeping her alive. The radio allowed the girls to breathe without being heard.

Idi Kambana took another big drink from the rum bottle and decided to get back to business.

He wiped his mouth.

"Okay priest," Dan noticed the cadence in Idi's speech had changed; he was getting drunker. "I am finished with your game of hide and seek. It's time to flush my little bird out of the bush."

Dan's stomach churned, seeing Idi stir.

"Listen to me, priest. Kagame, over there; he likes the American nun; he likes the way she dresses." Idi sniffled through his nose at his wit. "So we are going to start with her. Kagame is a little rodent but don't underestimate his love-making powers; I have seen his work—he is very passionate". At this, Idi and Kagame smiled; they grinned from ear to ear. Then, as quick as the smile appeared on Idi's face, it turned into a scowl and he shouted in anger—his quick staccato, "Do you hear me, priest? Do you understand what I am saying?"

Dan began to feel sick to his stomach. Idi was serious. People he loved were about to start dying.

"What's it going to be, Father? Is it going to be your five nuns or the cockroach?"

Dan was beginning to feel defeated; all he had were empty words.

"She's not here Idi. She's gone to Goma. Idi, please, in the name of God believe me."

Losing his patience, Idi walked over to Dan and knocked him to the floor with a heavy blow to his head.

Dan looked up at the ceiling; the lights seemed to turn on and off as he fought to stay conscious; he had to stay awake. He then thought of the nuns and the two hidden girls. He thought about his knife. At that moment he felt he did not have enough.

Idi bent down and pressed the machete blade against the priest's throat, and shouted at his side-kick, "Kagame! The nuns! Call the idiots, call them again at once."

Kagame, a Catholic Hutu, stood frozen, looking at the blade against the priest's throat. Idi, sensing no movement, erupted with a deep guttural demonic voice, "Did you hear me, fool! Bring me the bloody nuns now!"

Kagame jumped back on the walkie-talkie, and this time there was an answer.

With the menacing howl of "bring me the nuns," nausea overtook the two girls. Terrified and barely able to breathe, Monique's mind ran through her choices. Would they give themselves up if the nuns begin to scream, only to die slowly and violently themselves? Could they let the nuns die and stay silent? Would Father Daniel open the door for the killers? Who would he choose? Maybe Father Daniel would fight and lose his own life for them.

Monique's little sister began to wretch. Monique grabbed her hard and smothered her face into her stomach to muffle the sounds. Her little sister's body hiccupped, unable to control the heaving. Monique worried she might suffocate her little sister. She hoped she would pass out soon. As Monique held her own breath, an uncommon sound came into their hiding place from the window. Monique's eyes quickly moved to the window. From the window, hideous, high-pitched sounds came rushing in. It was the devil's song. Screams and cries from outdoors charged into the room and punctured the silence of their shelter.

Not far from the church, the Hutu gathered the young Tutsi children, of Gitesi, onto the steamy pavement by the town plaza. Wide-eyed terror poured from the desperate eyes of the condemned children.

A fourteen year old Hutu boy with a dull, empty face was the first to strike. He plunged his machete deep into an eight year old girl's shoulder, just missing her yellow bonnet. As she fell to the pavement her hat slipped away and her sweet smile vanished with her life. As he struck her again, the soft white dress offered no shield, and when the boy had finished, her pleasing smile was sad and still. It seemed as if the yellow bonnet's defeat had unleashed the rage. Mercilessly, the mob began to cut the children down by the hundreds. The baying sounds of horror cascaded through town, disturbing the manner of the damp spring day in Gitesi.

The genocide had begun. No gas chambers, no ovens, instead, machetes, spears, and knives would do the killing. Nazi Germany, with 20th century military precision, engineered their brand of genocide. The Tutsis were slaughtered, standing on their feet by the Hutus, wherever they were found. And by the time it was over, three out of every four Tutsis in Rwanda would be killed; over 900,000 lives—the largest loss of life in a hundred day period in the history of the world.

In the rectory, with the machete blade at his throat and with the call of "bring me the nuns" piercing his heart, Dan, with his strength returning, was set to reach for his knife. He had no choice. He would make his stand. Idi was going to kill him, the nuns, and eventually he would find the girls. He had to do something.

Idi was drunk, Dan knew that. He would have to move quickly. It was his only advantage. As soon as the nuns were brought into the room, he was sure Idi would look to them. Dan would quickly roll away from Idi. Idi's reactions would be slow. The delay would give him time to get to his feet. He would then plunge his knife into the back of Idi's neck. The three men with Idi? Well, if he got one more, he hoped the two remaining would simply quit, leave. The pickings were easy outside the church. He heard footsteps coming from the hallways. The nuns were brought into the room and lined up against the wall. Kagame quickly tore at one of the nuns clothing—the American—and he went to his belt. Dan watched Idi's eyes.

"Let's do it." But at that moment, the room went silent—dead silent. The man on the radio stopped talking and stillness overtook the room. Idi looked towards the radio, not towards the nuns. Idi straightened up and moved across the room towards the radio to investigate the silence. Dan's concentration had been thrown off by the sudden quiet. It had caught him by surprise. He now thought his lapse would lead to the fulfillment of Idi's promise. As soon as Idi put his hands on the volume switch, the man on the radio came back on the air—almost shouting this time. His easy mellow tone was gone, replaced with a frantic call for action.

"We have them surrounded. We have caught them, thousands of Tutsi cockroaches inside Gatwaro, inside the football stadium. Go there! All of you—hurry! We must cut them! Cut them! Cut them!"

Idi froze—blood lust and greed to kill in large numbers began to seep into his veins. The chant of, 'Cut them! Cut them! Cut them!' poured into his soul, and it suddenly changed everything. Monique could wait. She was just one cockroach. Idi listened to the man's call to kill. Idi let the sounds and words wash over him. He picked up the rum. He closed his eyes and took a little sip, almost politely, from the bottle.

"Cut them! Cut them! Cut them!" again the man on the radio shouted.

Idi then heard the whistle from outside the church rectory. The walkie-talkie attached to Idi's belt squelched and Alexi, a man of few words, came on.

"Massacre at the stadium—come now or I leave. I'll find better customers than you at the stadium."

Idi knew Alexi meant business; he knew he'd leave. He'd never heard the whistle before.

Opening his eyes, Idi stupidly looked around the room and up at the ceiling—Idi's drunken attempt at thoroughness; he took another drink from the rum bottle, much bigger this time. He wiped his mouth with his huge forearm and looked at the nuns—Spanish, Hutu, an American. The booze was beginning to temper his drive. He wanted Tutsi. He turned and glared at Dan, now standing. Idi walked towards the seminarian and put the machete under his chin.

"I want Monique Butare when I come back, or God help you."

He looked at Kagame and at the other two men standing by the wall next to the terrified nuns and gave them an authoritative quick upward tilt of the head. He clasped his right hand onto the underside of his left forearm and cocked his head towards the American nun. The men knew what to do.

They took the America nun and brought her over to the priest's desk. She began to scream. Dan lunged towards the men. One of the men let go of the nun and body-tackled Dan, knocking him to the floor. As Dan struggled to free himself, the Hutu holding the American nun violently jammed her arm onto the desk. Dan furiously tried to reach for his knife, but he was pinned down. He couldn't move; it all happened so fast. Idi stood by calmly and watched the activity. As Idi was taking a small sip of rum, Kagame, with one swift swing of the machete, severed the arm off the American nun, below the elbow. Idi barely reacted; his mind was now on the football stadium. Idi was finished with the nuns, and the church, and so he turned away from the bloody scene and strolled out of the rectory. The Hutu, seeing Idi make his way out of the rectory, let go of the nun and followed him outside.

As the men made their way towards the van, Nicholas Alexi looked away. He gazed into the side-view mirror, and stared at the heat rising from the damp pavement. He heard more gun shots up the road.

Idi opened the sliding van door and stumbled into the back bench seat behind Alexi. The engine was on. Kagame moved into the front seat, opened the glove box, and pulled out the map. Idi put the rum bottle between his legs, and with bloodshot eyes and a boozy tongue, began to shout instructions at Alexi. But before Idi finished, the Russian, without looking away from the mirror, told him sharply, "Shut up and close the door; the stadium is fifty-five minutes north."

Alexi then glanced at Kagame who was clumsily unfolding the map. Alexi winced at the man's carelessness, his sloppiness—he then shoved the gear shift on the steering wheel into reverse almost violently. Before driving off, Alexi looked for the statue in his rear view mirror. The head was gone and most of the fragments rested peacefully in the courtyard.

Alexi put his foot down hard on the accelerator, turned on to the main street, and headed towards the town square. As he passed through the town center, he began to run over dead bodies that littered the street, some larger than others.

A mile outside of town, as the van was crossing the bridge, over the river that fed Lake Kivu, Alexi looked along the river bank, and saw water churn and whirl. The source of the disruption of the quiet waters came from a crag overlooking the river. At the edge of the bank, men were standing with shovels in their hands watching a small bulldozer work dead bodies over the ridge. Alexi looked further down the river and saw bodies, like timbers, calmly float down the river. The drifting dead left a sullen trail, and the water now looked to Alexi like a river of blood.

"A river of blood." Those haunting words he remembered hearing before. The words had come from a child who sold him cigarettes in a market place, two weeks ago. The boy followed him around the market, nimbly darting around the crowd. The boy would not leave him alone. The child talked of "A river of blood"—he said it would come soon. The boy went on:

"*A tree of flames, bodies would be thrown into rivers—bodies without their heads—decapitated. There would weeping and crying and unforgettable fear and sadness and if Rwanda did not come back to God, there would be a river of blood.*"

Finally Alexi turned around and grabbed the boy's hand, gave him some money for cigarettes, and asked, "Who the hell are you? Who told you all this?"

The small boy told Alexi that a pretty lady from the sky had told him everything.

Alexi looked back at the river—the river of blood—then the image of the statue and the stone eyes from the church garden came back, and the horror returned and shot through him. To shake the image, he spat out the window and reached for his cigarettes, but it was not enough. The image of the piercing blue eyes blazed through his body. He saw the stone eyes blink again and the blood turn to tears—stone into flesh. Now fear and dread, rooted by the vision, began to infuriate him and he wanted to strike back—it had always been his way, it was how he confronted threats. Then from the back, Idi giggled and, like a paddle boat sight-seer, he nudged the man next to him and pointed to the activities along the river. Alexi heard the map next to him shake and crackle. He looked to the river's edge again, and saw two men pulling on a headless, dead man's leg. Other men stood by with shovels. The body had lodged itself underneath the bulldozer, slowing progress down. Another silly cackle behind the driver's seat enraged Alexi further. He was overwhelmed by all that was around him— death, violence, fear, hatred, carelessness, the vile of sloppiness—to Alexi it all melded into an uncontrollable horrific stew of filth.

Kagame, sitting next to Alexi, ruffled the map again, louder this time. Kagame was finished with the map, and as he was getting ready to stuff it back into the glove box—any which way, almost in a crumpled ball—Alexi pulled his gun from his holster and in one quick motion rammed the barrel under Kagame's chin and effortlessly pulled the trigger. He was now in control—blood and bone flew out of the open window, much of it finding the side view mirror.

Nicholas slammed on the brakes, hopped out of the van, opened the passenger door, and rolled the body out of the van and onto the road. Alexi looked at Idi with his cold eyes: "Learn how to fold a damn map, you stupid lazy bastard."

Idi looked back at Alexi, calmly took a sip of his rum, and paused for moment, thinking if there was anything to add. He looked outside the open door and saw something of value.

"Gimme the cap."

The gun blast from inside the van was still ringing in Alexi's ears; Alexi only saw Idi's lips move. He thought for a moment if he should shoot the fat man as well, but the fat man still owed him money.

"What?"

"The pygmy's hat, Kagame's Homer Simpson hat." Idi motioned with his hand. "Right there, there on the road."

Alexi bent over, picked up the cap, and tossed it to Idi.

Idi adjusted the strap, put it on his head, reached over the seat and turned on the radio. Alexi cleaned the mirror with the dead man's bandana. After picking up the map that had blown a few feet away into a drainage ditch, Alexi got back in the van. He took special care to fold the map neatly and placed it back into the glove box. Sitting squarely and erect in the driver's seat, Alexi took a quick glance down at his whistle, resting on his chest. Using his thumb, Alexi centered the whistle with a slight nudge, put the van in gear, and headed north to the football stadium.

Over two days, at Gatwaro stadium, ten thousand human beings —Tutsi—were massacred inside the soccer field. Bullets from AK-47s poured down into the ring all night long. Most of the Tutsi were killed the first day, and those that survived, ate grass from the bloody field that evening. In the morning, the Hutu returned to finish off the unlucky that had lived through the night. The unlucky survived only to see the horror advance into the stadium at sunrise, and again the Hutu began to cut all that moved.

Chapter 18:

June 12, 10:00 pm - Annapolis, Md.
Boat Yard Bar & Grill

At the Boatyard Bar and Grill, Annapolis's favorite hangout for sailboat racers, Tucker Finn and Sanjay sat silently eating their hamburgers in peace. After a few minutes of grazing, Tucker broke the comfortable silence.

"I got it. I remember now. I've met that priest before—briefly. I am not a hundred percent sure, but I think I know his brother; he's a good friend actually. I met the priest in Boston at a party when Bob got his appointment at MIT."

Sanjay looked up at Tucker blankly for a moment, said nothing, then went back to texting and eating.

"Sanjay, that was pretty odd back there on the dock, wasn't it? What do you think was going on with that woman with the dog? What do you make of all that?"

Sanjay, without looking up, said, "Forget it, Tucker. Let it go, that whole business on the dock never happened."

"No seriously. I don't think it is what you think it is."

Sanjay put his hamburger down.

"First of all, Tucker, that girl was not with a dog, she was with a priest. You do understand that, right? You understand the difference?"

"Yeah, so, what's your point? I sensed something, something that doesn't add up."

"My point is, just forget it. Look, my man, listen up; here's my real point. I've sailed more than halfway around the world with you and you have had every opportunity to meet some of the most beautiful women in the world; I went out of my way to make that happen, all the time, and now suddenly you nearly fall in the water over a girl that's holding hands with a priest. You're sick, you know that? I should have you committed. For over a year, I have had to endure your monologues on the love life of plankton and jelly fish, and now you want to talk about a girl sneaking onto a boat with a priest in the middle of the night. What the hell is wrong with you, Tucker?"

"Nothing, I'm just saying…"

Sanjay cut Tucker off before he could finish.

"Forget it, Tucker. Look, here's the deal. I am hooking up with Margot tomorrow, you know the one I met in Barcelona? I pick her up at Reagan Airport in the morning. She is bringing two of her friends—pick one, they are both unbelievable. So you are going to forget about your little encounter with mystery girl. You are going to go with me to the airport and we are going to pick them up together."

His point made, Sanjay took a big bite of his hamburger, chewing aggressively. Shaking his head, he went back to his phone, resting on the table.

"Something's not right. That's all I can say, Sanjay. I got a feeling on this one."

With his mouth full, Sanjay shot back, spewing hamburger.

"You're damn right, something's not right. Priests ain't supposed to be sleeping with hot women!"

"All right, all right, Sanjay, I hear you, let's forget it."

Again, Sanjay went back to his phone. Tucker stared straight ahead for a moment, then reached over and picked up his beer. But, before bringing it to his mouth, he thought about the silhouette in the dim moonlight back at the dock.

This time, Tucker's thoughts were not of the priest or whether or not he was Baronowski's brother, but instead he thought of the woman's eyes. He thought of the pretty woman with the dark hair, whose beautiful eyes in the moonlit sky seemed so strangely and perfectly right, at a moment when everything around her should have seemed so strangely and perfectly wrong. He also asked his sentries to stand down for the first time in years.

Sanjay, still looking down at his phone, shook his head, again. But this time, for different reasons. Sanjay, glaring at his phone, tapped his beer glass lightly with his fork to get Tucker's attention.

"Hey Tucker, something strange is going on in the financial markets; oil prices have just sky rocketed the limit."

Chapter 19:

Four Years Earlier - Zihuatanejo, Mexico
Tucker Finn on Land

A Lavern and Shirley re-run, dubbed in Spanish, was playing on an old RCA TV set inside Tucker Finn's dingy Aero Stream RV, when he finally came to terms with the fact that he was now a very wealthy man. Earlier in the day, at 12:45 in the afternoon before the news, he had been summoned out of bed by a loud knock on the door to his trailer. A Fed-Ex package required his signature.

After doing what he was told by the man in the uniform, tired and hung over, Tucker pitched the Fed-Ex envelope on top of the TV. Tucker shuffled a few steps towards the mini fridge, bent down and grabbed a longneck bottle of Corona. Tucker moved a couple of more steps across the trailer and turned the shower on. As he waited for the water to heat up, he took a long drink. With steam beginning to fill the trailer, he took his gym shorts off, stepped in, leaned his head against the flimsy plastic shower stall, and felt the hot water around his body. The shower felt good, and as his mind slowly cleared, his thoughts turned to last night's card game and the poker bully he ran into. Tucker was happy to rid the jerk of some of his money; probably year-end bonus money the mid-level executive should have parceled out to his staff that hated him. Tucker had gone to bed at 4:30 in the morning, with eight-hundred and fifty extra dollars in his wallet. It felt like a lot of cash; he had been living off bar tips and poker winnings for the better part of a year.

Tucker had forgotten how long it had been since he left the United States. He stopped thinking about it. It had stopped mattering months ago. He was called away from the United States to Mexico by a late night cable TV movie. Andy Dufresne gave him the idea. Zihuatanejo, Mexico was the beach town fugitive Andy Dufresne escaped to, after getting the best of

Samuel Norton—Warden of Sharshank Prison. Hearing Andy whisper to his friend: "Mexicans say the Pacific Ocean has no memory" settled it for Tucker Finn. The movie's ending was about the only thing in the world that ever made Tucker Finn happy—that and a poker game.

Tucker left the United States to drink, play poker, and forget. It is what he did almost every night and he was starting to get good at it—the drinking and the poker anyway.

He found, not to his surprise, that his doctorate degree from Stanford in statistics was a useful tool for a poker player, but what did surprise him was the peace he found in the cards themselves. They brought him comfort. He liked the touch of them, the gliding movement of the cards in his hands, the cascading sound of shuffling cards. But, in the end, it was really all about the numbers.

Numbers couldn't hurt you. He had learned that the hard way. They were reliable, predictable, and eternal. They were his friends. Getting lost in numbers helped him through the night. The card games, along with the heavy drinking, helped numb the pain and keep his mind off of Heather.

Tucker Finn's life in Mexico began after his wife, Heather, died of leukemia at the age of thirty-four.

The day the doctor told Heather she was feeling tired because she had leukemia, and that her pregnancy was not the cause of her fatigue, because she had lost her baby, Tucker Finn had taken the day off to paint a bedroom pink for their daughter, who was expected any day.

Before moving to Mexico, Tucker Finn had taught statistics at Stanford University. After marrying Heather, for the first time in his life, his life had purpose; it was bigger than just him; it mattered. Heather and Tucker traveled, entertained, had lots of friends, and they enjoyed each other's company immensely. It was when they were ready to start a family that everything changed.

After Heather passed away, he realized all he really ever had in his life that was good, was her. With her death, he lost everything—his soul, his heart, his dreams. He loved her, and to see her die slowly, left him clinging to a buoy in a running tide.

"Why hold on?" he had asked himself. "I'll let go and be with her."

But it was her fight to live, her will to ease the pain for those left behind, that made him feel shame. She would have none of it, and he promised her no self-pity ever again.

"Go find somebody," She would say. "Find love, start something new. You would want me to. I know it seems impossible to believe, Tucker, but I am at peace. God loves me, Tucker, I'm okay."

He saw in her eyes how much she loved him. He also sensed a great love in her heart, not meant for him, and that hidden love gave him comfort and gave him hope. She left him with her final wish.

"Promise me, Tucker, that one day, you will look to the heavens for answers. Maybe not now, but someday, take a few steps down a path with an open mind and an open heart. I think you will find something good."

Holding her in his arms, his last words to her were, "I promise."

After her death, he sold his house in Palo Alto, liquidated his retirement plan, and headed to the Pacific coast of Mexico. Heather believed God finds you when it's time, and Tucker Finn knew it was not his time. Not now anyway. All he wanted to do was get away. Everything around him in California reminded him of her. But before he packed his bags and left for Mexico, Tucker gave most of his cash, about $650,000 from the sale of his house, to two smart Stanford computer engineers; students he met in his statistics class. He told the two computer geeks; "Put it all on black fellas; I'm going all in."

After leaving California, Tucker moved into the Aero Stream parked behind the restaurant—shower, bed, TV with rabbit ears, fridge, no internet, no rent—home. All Tucker demanded from his landlord, Manny Menendez, was that the mini-fridge keep his beer cold.

He had arrived in Mexico with $25,000. Living for free in the trailer, with food and beer available at the restaurant, he noticed he had more cash at the end of each month than he ever had living in the States.

After about six months, Tucker began to enjoy his new life by the sea. He was in no hurry to get back to the United States. He still missed Heather every day, but in Mexico there were fewer reminders of his past.

His boss, owner of Los Amigos Bar and Grill, Manny Menendez, had turned into a great friend. Tucker thought Menendez was fat, ugly, and perhaps the funniest human being who ever lived. Tucker and Menendez would often turn the restaurant over to Menendez's brothers and the two would pack large coolers with beer, food, and bait, and head out to remote dunes to camp, fish, and look at stars.

Tucker's tan was deep, his hair a little grayer and, to his surprise, he felt fit from the late night boozy jogs along the moonlit beach. Menendez also liked Tucker because he had helped the bar become very popular with the ladies. It turned out that Tucker Finn was irresistible to vacationing single, divorced, and married women. Best of all, for the single Menendez, Tucker had no interest in any of it.

"You and your miserable numbers," Menendez would say, "Man, all you need to know is one plus one equals fun."

Tucker got out of the shower, dried off, got dressed, and opened the Federal Express package. He reached into the envelope and pulled out a stack of papers garnished with a Post-it note. The note said: "Thanks, Professor, we could not have done it without you."

Tucker peeled off the Post-it and read the first newspaper headline: "Google closes at $195.00 on the first day of trading."

In the package was a stack of news reports about the Google IPO. Tucker thought, *"Not bad."* One hundred and ninety five dollars a share sounded like a high price for a new stock, and he reasoned his investment had done well. He just had no idea how well. Tucker had exchanged e-mails from the restaurant's office computer with the founders on occasion, but he had a stack of unopened snail mail, including legal documents from Google stuffed in a grocery bag. He had not cared. Tucker Finn thought to himself that the boys had done alright. He tossed the documents back on top of his TV. He was hungry—the rest of the mail could wait.

Tucker walked over to the restaurant and noticed a truck with thirty day tags parked in front of the restaurant. Manny had his head under the hood. Manny popped out as soon as he heard Tucker's feet shuffling across the ground as he neared the restaurant.

"Check it out, Tucker. Nice ride, eh! It's loaded—Chevy Silverado pickup. It is hot!"

Tucker wondered what in the world was going on.

"Tucker, give me some lovin', my man...What do you think of the truck?"

"Menendez, if that's your truck, then I want a damn raise."

Reaching into his pocket, Menendez pulled out a piece of paper.

"Look, Tucker, take a look at this letter I got from Google."

Menendez read the note out loud, "Dear Mr. Menendez, Tucker Finn has spoken well of you in the past. He says you're friendship and generosity has been a very special blessing to him. Enjoy."

Menendez said to Tucker, "Thanks buddy."

Tucker scratched his head, and decided to go back and read some of his mail; a sandwich could wait.

Unbelievable, Tucker thought as he was opening his old mail back in his trailer. Six hundred and fifty thousand shares of Google—Tucker's buy-in was at a buck a share, and now it traded near $200 per share —the stock would soon reach $500.

Tucker thought, "You don't need a PhD in math to calculate that he was now worth one hundred and thirty million dollars."

Sipping on a beer, he slowly looked around the trailer, his eyes paused for a moment on the portrait of "Our Lady of Guadalupe," a small water color he had recently purchased, and said to himself, "I got the rent paid anyway."

Tucker walked back to the restaurant to get his lunch.

Tucker saw that it was quiet, a couple of customers sat in the booths. He noticed Menendez behind the bar tossing his keys in the air and bragging to one of his brothers. Tucker made his way around the bar and, with a smile on his face, snatched the Silverado keys in mid-flight.

"Look, Menendez, you got your truck and so, not only do I want a damn raise, I want a new fridge as well."

"Right, and I want Halle Berry to marry me. Tucker, come clean with me; what's up with Google and you? You have something going on with those suits?"

Tucker took a hold of Menendez's shirt and eased him away from his brother.

"Menendez, two things—first, I did okay, and if you need anything let me know, and second, if you open your mouth I will kill you."

Menendez looked at Tucker and understood. Tucker looked at Menendez, and was thankful Menendez was his friend—he trusted his friend.

"Okay, deal. You said anything, right, Tucker."

"Yeah, that's right, anything."

"Okay, I need a ham and cheese on white and a tuna on wheat toast for that table over there, Gracias. Oh! And one more thing."

"Yeah, what's that?"

"Buy yourself a new shirt; that one stinks."

Pinching the material away from his body and giving the shirt a quick glance, Tucker dismissed Menendez with an easy wave of his hand. Tucker grabbed a cold beer out of the ice bucket, kicked the swinging doors leading back to the kitchen and did what he was told. Standing in the kitchen, pressing the toaster down, he thought of Heather.

"I miss you so much, right now, and I hope you are listening. First, yes, I will help your little sister and her kids, and no, I will not buy the house in New Mexico without you. But really, Heather, what am I supposed to do now?"

Chapter 20:

Rene and Dan stepped into the main cabin of a forty-two foot trawler docked at the end of the pier at the Annapolis Yacht Club. Dan took the gun out of his holster and put it under the navigation table. He moved to the starboard side galley and snatched two water bottles from the boat's refrigerator and handed one to Rene. He put the other on the table, reached into a cabinet and took out a plastic red bowl, filled it with water and put it on the floor for the dog. Dan then went forward to prepare Rene's bunk in the forward cabin.

Rene thanked Dan as he went by. She snapped opened the plastic bottle and drank it all without putting it down; the stress of the night had dehydrated her. After finishing the bottle, she stood up and walked over to the galley and poked around; it was her habit on unfamiliar boats. She opened drawers and cabinets, then opened the refrigerator. Two apples rolled out. The fridge was stuffed to the gills.

"Hey Dan, are we going to Tahiti? You have food here for months."

Dan was still fixing the linen in the forward berth.

"What's that, Rene?"

"Food, you have food for a month."

Dan popped his head back into the salon.

"Yeah, don't worry about that. This is going to end soon. We are going to be fine."

Dan went back to his chores.

Rene looked around the cabin, her eyes settled on the navigation table and thought of the gun; she then stepped outside onto the back of the boat to survey the night sky and get some fresh air. She looked up to find the moon, and as she fixed her eyes on the sky above, something puzzling worked its way into her thoughts.

She had left the cabin to clear her head, to get away from her nightmare, to think of the boat race; to think of Wharf Rat, her brother, and the guys on the bay, but to her surprise, the man on the dock—the stranger—was the first thing that came to her. In her thoughts, she saw him bend down to move Luke gently away. She thought about his easy smile and his friendly eyes. She liked how it made her feel when she thought about the moment, and she was surprised that she liked to replay the encounter in her thoughts.

Rene took a quick look down the dock then stepped back into the salon. She sat down on the bench seat by the settee, leaned back, closed her eyes, and reached under the table searching for Luke's head. Luke was happy, curled up, and sound asleep.

Dan had been planning his escape for months. He believed they were safe for now. The boat belonged to a friend, who had inherited the boat from his parents. The boat was untraceable back to Dan.

Dan opened drawers to make sure Rene's clothing had been stored. The boat had been provisioned by the yacht club staff. Dan finished his chores and headed back to sit with Rene, but he stopped, abruptly, in the companionway. He saw Rene, lying down with her eyes closed, and the emotions of the rehearsal dinner—the night he will never forget—came to him. He never doubted his decision to become a priest, but looking at Rene, seeing her so vulnerable, the sense of something lost shot through him from head to toe. Dan shook his head, crossed himself, said a prayer and moved into the main cabin.

"I know it doesn't change anything, Rene, but I am very, very sorry about all this."

Rene barely heard Dan, or she did not want to hear it. Her off-shore racing mindset was kicking in. Rene knew "Sorry" was not going to help reef the mainsail, in middle of the night. Somebody had to go forward to the mast; it just had to get done. They needed to start solving problem; start looking for a answers and a way out.

"Dan, if we find your Indian, will that make this all go away?"

Chapter 21:

Darcy and Tim scurried out of the office while Bob Baronowski continued to ignore the department chair's tantrum. Jim Cromwell shook the papers frantically in front of Bob's face.

"Bob, the Virgin Mary? Some town I can't pronounce? Apparitions? Look Bob, I've gotten complaints from your students, and I don't know for sure, I haven't spoken with legal yet, but you may be violating religious discrimination rules of this school, maybe even breaking the law. This is a public university."

Bob didn't look up; he stared into his computer screen and said, "Leave, Cromwell, leave right now."

"Bob, what the hell are you up to in your class? Look at these complaint letters I have gotten from your students. I can't ignore this any longer."

Bob pressed a few keys to pull up his e-mails; Bob then addressed the department chair as he continued to look at his computer monitor.

"You're a chicken sandwich Cromwell. Why don't you remind those students that I am a tenured professor here, and I run my class any way I damn well please."

Jim Cromwell sat down at Bob's desk and tossed the complaint letters on the desk.

"Okay, okay, Bob, I'll start over. Call me curious. Now please, tell me what does this Virgin project of yours have anything to do with probabilities and statistics? You are the most brilliant professor in this department, and I would like to know why you are wasting your time with this nonsense?"

Bob finally looked up.

"Jim, only because I like you is why I am still talking to you right now.

Don't ever come into my office with this kind of crap again. Got it?"

"Okay, fine; I hear you."

Bob looked at the department head for a few seconds without saying a word; and then the math professor said, perhaps, the last thing Jim Cromwell ever expected to come out of his star professor's mouth.

"Jim, do you believe statues cry?"

"What? No…What?"

"You heard me. Do you think statues can cry—you know, weep?"

"No, of course not!"

"I do. I believe they cry, even bleed. In fact, I know they bleed and cry. In 1973, a Catholic nun in Japan, Sister Agnes Sasagawa, reported receiving messages from a weeping statue of the Virgin Mary. The statue wept, off and on, for over six years. Other nuns, at the convent, reported seeing the statue tear and bleed as well. They saw the tears, they touched them, and they told their superiors about it. The weeping statue episode is an immensely well documented event. Former Pope Benedict XVI, when he was a Cardinal, accepted the findings as authentic and I am willing to bet my endowed chair that your nuclear physicists across campus can't explain what happened."

"Ah, for Christ's sake, Baronowski."

"Just shut up and listen to me, would you?"

Jim Cromwell leaned back in his chair.

"This better be good, Bob."

" Jim, of all people, Justice Scalia, is haunted by a case of weeping statues—he brings it up in speeches all the time. The incredible event that he is attached to took place, over the course of a year, on the outskirts of Washington, DC, in the Arlington Diocese of Virginia, a few years ago. In his speech, Scalia talks about a priest from Lakeridge, Virginia, where statues of the Blessed Virgin Mary, would weep in his presence."

Jim Cromwell looked at Bob Baronowski with a blank stare. Bob continued with his talk about weeping statues.

"Thousands of people, in Lakeridge, Virginia, testified to seeing the statues weep. Soon, reporters for The Washington Post, CNN, and a host of other media ran down to the sleepy suburb, to cover the story. The story quickly made national news after the statues wept on camera, right in front of the reporters. They were dumbstruck, and nobody had an explanation. The mystical events that took place in Virginia are unprecedented. I have spoken with a graduate of Harvard Law School—an eye witness to the events—who told me the statues wept in his home when the priest, at the center of it all, would come over for dinner. The Harvard Law grad told me the statues wept in his hands—dozens of times. Hundreds, if not thousands, of credible people saw the statues weep, and to this day, the supernatural event, known as the 'Seton Miracles,' has never been explained. Justice Scalia won't let the case of the weeping statues go. Scalia chides the press for not demanding answers to explain how statues could weep right before their eyes. He mocks the secular world's mindset towards unexplained supernatural occurrences, saying, disdainfully, 'the wise do not investigate such silliness,' and so, Jim, I have decided to investigate the "silliness" of a strange religious event in Medjugorje because, quite frankly, I don't have an answer to explain what's going on in that town—not yet."

Jim Cromwell slouched in his chair. He thought about the letters on the desk. The idea of beginning the monumental waste of time of responding to the complaints from his "outraged" students, and going through "proper channels" was too depressing to even think about. But crying statues, apparitions, the Virgin Mary? Bob was giving him no choice but to start grinding through the process.

"Bob, I don't know—this project of yours—the religious subject matter. I'm going to have a problem with this. I need to get back to these kids who have complained."

"Okay, Jim, forget that. Here's the deal. The JFK assassination, the moon landing, Roswell—what do they all have in common?"

Cromwell moved slightly in his chair, showing a sign of life. Cromwell really wanted Bob to give him something. He wanted to walk out of the room satisfied that his friend hadn't gone off the deep end. He needed to be sure Bob hadn't turned into some kind of evangelizing religious nut. He wanted his math professor, in control.

"Conspiracies, the lunatic fringe, government secrets, that kind of thing, whatever, I don't know."

"Wrong, Cromwell; what the JFK assassination, the Roswell incident, the moon landing, and all of the other so-called Government cover-ups have in common is that, in the end, the conspiracy theories are all debunked by math, probabilities, and statistics. You've seen the JFK documentaries. They are awfully compelling. The circumstantial evidence is very convincing, but ultimately you know in your heart somebody would have talked—evidence would have come forth. The statistical improbability of keeping a secret with so many people involved in intricate plots is the primary reason most reasonable people don't believe in conspiracy schemes. Last year my students calculated the statistical probability of NASA faking the moon landing. The kids laughed their heads off when they saw the number. They actually named it. They call the number 'Tranquility,' not for the obvious reasons, but because it rhymes with infinity."

Cromwell thought "okay maybe we are getting somewhere"; Bob was back on the subject of math, but where was he going, he still wasn't sure. He looked at the e-mails on the desk.

"Sounds like fun Bob, but this town, M-e-d-j-u-g-o-r-j-e, apparitions?"

"Right, Medjugorje. Jim, this thing, this town, the mysterious events called apparitions occurring there, are really fascinating to me, and my students, as we peel away the layers; we can't crack the nut. I have some students who are obsessed with it. They are determined to solve the mystery—a spiritual, religious mystery. Some of my kids told me the problem was becoming bigger than a math problem. Some are going back to church, Mass, even confession."

Cromwell picked up the letters off the desk, leaned back in his chair, and again waved them in the air.

"That's part of the problem, Bob."

"Jim, tell your religious bigot friends to get a life."

Cromwell straightened up in his chair and leaned forward.

"Look, the fact of the matter is, religion makes a lot of people uncomfortable."

Bob slammed his fist on the desk and said, "That's the whole freaking point!"

Bob shot up from his desk and took Nicholas Taleb's book, <u>The Black Swan</u>, off a bookshelf, then rifled through some pages.

"Listen to this, Jim."

"We love the tangible, the confirmation, the palpable, the real, the visible, the concrete, the known, the seen, the vivid, the visual, the social, the embedded, the emotional laden, the salient, the stereotypical, the moving, the theatrical, the romanced, the cosmetic, the official, the scholarly-sounding verbiage bullshit, the pompous Gaussian economist, the mathematicized crap, the pomp, the Academie Française, Harvard Business School, the Nobel Prize, dark business suits with white shirts and Ferragamo ties, the moving discourse, and the lurid. Most of all we favor the narrated.

Alas, we are not manufactured, in our current edition of the human race, to understand abstract matters—we need context. Randomness and uncertainty are abstractions. We respect what has happened, ignoring what could have happened. In other words, we are naturally shallow and superficial—and we do not know it."

Bob snapped the book shut.

"We are naturally shallow and superficial—and we do not know it—you hear that, Jim. Now, the guy who wrote this book made millions of dollars trading complex derivatives, betting against Wall Street. He does not consider himself a Wall Street trader, but a skeptical empiricist, a philosopher, a statistician, a professor. His financial success came only after he determined that academia and Wall Street had lost their minds with their complete adoration of mathematical models as a bullet proof means to managing portfolio risk. Many of these models, incidentally, were designed by your hot shot friends in this department. Wall Street came to believe that these models had hedged away all portfolio risk, on gigantically leveraged assets, that were extremely difficult to value. It became a religion, with its own doctrines of infallibility. Push a button on a computer and watch the earnings pour in and the stock prices rise. That was all there was to it. Nassim Taleb concluded that a Black Swan event, a high-impact, hard-to-predict event, was occurring before his eyes in the banking industry. He didn't predict the market collapse, the so called Black Swan event, because by definition you really can't. He simply recognized, soon after the market began to decline, that trillions of dollars of leveraged assets were propped up by nothing more than math equations. Nassim saw that the Wall Street emperors had no clothes, and went short. He bet his entire firm's capital, then watched the implosion of our financial system—at least a trillion dollars' worth of losses. More money was lost in a year than the banking industry, cumulative, ever earned—in their history. The point is, Jim, not that he got rich, but rather he challenged the High Priests of Wall Street and the politically correct goons at elite universities by thinking for himself. He stood up to intense ridicule, but, in the end, his work has humiliated the so called best and the brightest—ruined careers of Nobel hopefuls. He is now considered one of the great thinkers of our generation. One of his remaining goals, in life, is to have the King of Sweden request that the Nobel Prize committee stop giving its award away to economists. What this all means, Jim, is that I am teaching my kids to think for themselves and I am telling them that unless they do, they will remain, as Mr. Nassim Taleb says, 'Shallow and Superficial'."

Bob pulled his glasses down to the end of his nose, and stared at the Department Chair to drill his point home, and just as Cromwell was about to speak, Bob cut him off with a raised hand.

"So, if my students want to investigate a strange religious phenomenon having to do with the Mother of Jesus Christ, then so be it, and if they are going to catch hell from you, so much the better; because, then they know, they are on the right track. You need to understand this is hugely interesting to me and to my students from a mathematical point of view."

Cromwell put the letters back down on the desk.

"Okay fine, Bob, but give me a little something—background, whatever—so I sound like I have looked into this matter."

"Okay, Jim. Six people, thirty years ago—they were but children at the time—growing up in a communist village, in Yugoslavia, called Medjugorje, claim they saw the Virgin Mary in an apparition, in a vision. No big deal, right? The problem is these six children, now adults, four women, and two men, maintain, that they continue to see the Virgin

Mary. A couple of the so-called "visionaries" say they still see her daily. They say they talk to her. They say she comes directly from heaven. These six people, universally described, even by the visionaries themselves, as ordinary and unremarkable, in both intelligence and personality, have for three decades stuck by their claims. They have withstood intense pressure from the communist party, and segments of the Catholic Church to recant their story and to say the whole thing is one big outrageous lie. The 'seers' have been poked and prodded during their apparitions, by scientists and doctors. They have been subjected to meticulous medical examinations by world renowned psychologists. Their conclusion: can't explain it, and the shrinks don't think they are lying. They have been asked relentlessly, by the local Bishop and communist officials, at the time, to admit the whole thing is made up, but they won't, because they say they can't, and because they say EVERYTHING IS TRUE. They say, 'We see what we see.'"

Bob stopped and looked for Jim Cromwell's reaction.

"That's all fine and good, Bob, but come on, despite what you say—it's a hoax—a fraud.

"Jim, we started with the assumption that Medjugorje was a hoax – but right now we have no evidence of that."

"Well, look harder; it cannot be that difficult find.

"Jim, understand what would be required to maintain a fraud of this magnitude. Six children, unrelated to each other, one as young as ten, all would have to agree, or be convinced, to fabricate an enormous lie and maintain that lie perfectly, without any denial, for thirty years—a lie so spectacularly conceived, that it would manifest itself into a gigantic religious movement that now has put the Vatican into a fit on what to do about it all. Millions of Catholics swear the apparitions have changed their lives. The idea that six school-aged kids invented a profound religious movement, that the Vatican and the communist party couldn't suppress, is absolutely preposterous. Additionally, Jim, as I said, there has been an incredible amount of medical examinations, on these kids, designed to detect a fraud. We actually have measurable data, and this is exactly what makes the case of Medjugorje, the case my students are working on, so unique and important. For the first time in history, we have an opportunity to scrutinize religious mystics who have been willing to submit themselves to exhaustive medical and scientific examinations. Most private revelations of the past have been prejudicially dismissed by modern thinkers as cases of hysteria or fraud. But with Medjugorje, we can actually apply science to determine the cause of alleged private revelations. Today, with Medjugorje, skeptics need to deal with concrete empirical evidence, instead of simply proposing preconceived reductionist theories about mystical experiences. Cromwell, the apparitions in Medjugorje have been subjected to more medical and scientific investigation than any alleged supernatural event in the history of the human race—including polygraphs, neurological examinations, psychiatric tests, electrocardiogram, blood pressure, and heart rhythm examinations. The tests have shown that the visionaries were NOT lying or hallucinating, nor were they in any epileptic or hypnotic state during their daily ecstasies but, indeed, experiencing something unexplainable, beyond the boundaries of scientific understanding."

"Alright, Bob, alright—but look, my friend, your project, to me, sounds more like something for the medical school—not the math department."

"Fair enough—okay—now here's the math problem. We are attacking this puzzle with an application of Bayes' Theorem."

Bob stood up and moved to the chalk board.

"Jim, here's the deal."

$$P(H|D) = \frac{P(D|H)\,P(H)}{P(D)}$$

As Bob slapped the equation onto the chalkboard, Cromwell started to see where Bob was going.

"Okay, I am beginning to see the picture. It's Bayesian probability. Your H is the hypothesis, which, I guess, is that the conspirators and visionaries are lying, and D is the data which includes the scientific and medical examinations and other data you choose to include."

"You got it, Jim. In our model, the Bayesian interpretation of probability can be seen as an extension of logic that enables reasoning with uncertain statements, such as the claims the visionaries are making. To evaluate the probability of our hypothesis, we are specifying some prior probability, which is then updated in the light of new relevant data. The Bayesian interpretation provides a standard set of procedures and formulae to perform this calculation."

Jim was now relieved—at least he had a way to respond to the e-mail complaints in the short term.

"Good lord, you've been one busy bee on this thing."

"Call it a labor of love."

"Alright big fella, looks like you can keep your day job for now."

"Jim, there is one other thing I ought to tell you."

"Yes, what's that?"

"Confidentially, the Vatican has asked me to look into this, for now, somewhat informally —please keep that intel to yourself."

"The Vatican?"

"Yes, it seems that powerful people in Rome have just woken up to the fact that millions of Catholics are captivated by claims that the Virgin Mary is appearing at Medjugorje. The Virgin Mary is also giving important messages to the visionaries and the visionaries say that the messages are meant for the world. The messages are urgent. In the messages the Virgin Mary is pleading for the world to return back to God. The Vatican has no explanation and they are not sure what to do. They are not in control."

Cromwell considered everything he had just heard. He was going to let it all go. He had heard enough; he had what he needed.

"Okay, Bob, keep me posted on this; let me know what you find out."

Cromwell got up from his chair and tossed the e-mails in the trash can and started walking out of Bob's office.

"Hey, Jim."

Jim turned around

"What?"

"It's kind of spooky."

"What's that?"

"It should have leaked by now – the fraud or some explanation, but I have nothing. I don't have an answer – I have no explanation-nobody does."

"Okay, what's your point?"

"What if it's true, the supernatural event—I mean, like it's really happening? That these kids really see somebody who comes from another world, from an eternal world, a world beyond ours that they call heaven?"

Jim turned back around and walked out of Bob Baronowski's office into the hallway without saying another word.

Chapter 22:

A bellhop opened the backdoor of the Mercedes Benz. Father Roberto Indelicotta stepped out of the car, and looked towards the Italian mountains and briefly thought of obscure monks and obedient priests who, over the centuries, had carved out simple lives in the woods and foothills of the Italian Alps. Such faith, he thought; faith built on the rock of Peter. He thought about his Church, his faith today, and in the clear air he understood—Vatican II—over time, had eroded his faith in the Catholic Church like a river cutting through a canyon. He turned back around and handed the bellhop, who was holding the hotel's door open, five euro, then walked into the restaurant and headed to the outdoor terrace.

As Roberto took his seat, Beckett threw down another glass of champagne, filled his guest's flute, and refilled his own.

Roberto looked across the lake; he did not look at Carl Beckett as he spoke.

"We need Warwinka. It needs to happen tomorrow. It may be our last chance. Tomorrow evening at six o'clock, in Washington, DC, on the campus of Catholic University, Warwinka will be giving a lecture to the United States Conference of Catholic Bishops. It will be easy to get to him."

"Hold on, Roberto; we agreed to get the Codex first, and I don't have it—not yet. Father Baronowski still has it. A meeting has been arranged, and the priest has agreed to hand it over. I will have the Codex de Rio Grande as soon as I land in DC, tomorrow – it will be waiting for me at my hotel."

"I am telling you Carl, we need to make arrangements for Cardinal Warwinka, now, even if we have the Codex."

"Warwinka can wait. I got enough on my plate. Warwinka is not my problem, he's yours."

"Carl, I've got bad news, there is a rumor in Rome that Cardinal Lombardi protected a pedophile priest when he was Bishop of Sienna. This could spell disaster for our cause of ending the apostasy of Vatican II. The details are not clear. The New York Times is working on a piece that they intend to run in two days. We may be able to keep it quiet, so don't blow a gasket just yet, but Cardinal Peter Warwinka's prospects, to become the next Pope, have been greatly enhanced."

"Forget the New York Times; nobody believes those atheists, anyway. But what is your concern with Cardinal Warwinka? No one I talk to thinks he is on the fast track to become Pope."

"Carl, you are not talking to the right people; Warwinka has been gaining support. He has a lot of friends in Rome."

Carl Beckett straightened up and moved forward in his seat; his relaxed manner was now diluted. Beckett thought Cardinal Lombardi had been framed; some Vatican conspiracy to destroy his career was at work.

"What, in the name of God, is happening in that screwed up city? I am sick and tired of those heretics having their way in Rome."

"Easy Carl, I think we will be okay. Cardinal Lombardi is a ferociously ambitious prelate—more than likely he will crush the rumor, and anybody close to it, but time is running out. I don't need to tell you he has a fiercely loyal constituency, but if a Papal Conclave is formed now, the College of Cardinals—to elect Cardinal Lombardi under this cloud—will be faced with selecting a Pope, who could potentially be a public relations disaster if the rumor turns out to be true. They may quickly turn to Cardinal Warwinka."

Carl Beckett slumped in his chair. "You have got to be kidding me; this is outrageous. Cardinal Lombardi's a great man, and now you tell me Cardinal Warwinka is next in line. This is terrible news. "

"I understand, Carl—it's bad."

"I didn't think Cardinal Warwinka was even papabile, after his recent troubles in the press."

"I know, Carl. It is hard to imagine a Roman Catholic Cardinal saying that the Church should perhaps rethink its position on gay relationships. He seems to have a pathological fixation with sex. And he has been a high profile supporter of Medjugorje. But make no mistake; Cardinal Warwinka is without question papabile. Do not underestimate his strength."

"Indellicotta, do you hear what you are saying? He will destroy the liturgy. Centuries of traditions will be swept away and his obsession with the poor is an embarrassment – he degrades the Church at every turn and he ridicules the sacred past with his behavior."

Beckett spun away from Roberto. After a moment Beckett turned back around and said, "Good Lord, Indellicotta that man is a heretic with his support of Medjugorje."

"There are a lot of people in Rome who disagree with you Carl. His supporters look around and see a dying, withering Church and a vacant spiritual landscape. Catholics in Europe are even now de-baptizing themselves. Because of this, Cardinal Warwinka's followers say it is time for a new way and Medjugorje and the Virgin Mary are a big part of that new way."

Carl Beckett had heard enough.

"A new way?! The problem is not that we need a godforsaken new way. We don't need the Virgin Mary and her miracles and apparitions; what we need is a return to the traditions of the Catholic faith which made the Church great in the first place. The Catholic Church is failing because it is in a state of apostasy and you know that."

"Carl, I agree with you, but despite what you are saying, you will find this hard to believe, but Cardinal Warwinka has a lot of support, precisely for his role as defender of the apparitions of the Virgin Mary. He wants to make the Virgin Mary the star of the Church; he wants to rebuild the Church with the Mother of God as the preeminent conduit to Christ. In many ways he wants to put a woman's face on the Church. He wants to make the Virgin Mary the "Mediatrix" of all graces – officially. He wants to establish it as the "Fifth Marian Dogma." The rumor is he seeks to make it an infallible Church teaching."

"You mean to tell me, he has support in Rome because he believes in apparitions of the Virgin Mary?"

"Yes, Cardinals are ready for his position. He is unafraid to battle the secular world with stories of miracles and the supernatural, including apparitions of the Virgin Mary. He does not bow to the demands of a godless press who ridicule any talk of the supernatural. He has also been critical of the Roman Curia, the governing body of the Vatican. He holds them accountable - calls them worldly, bureaucratic and timid. He says they often turn faith into a secular academic endeavor. Warwinka talks about miracles, the Devil, and the supernatural all the time and when he does, priests, bishops and Cardinals come alive. The young Cardinal, by embracing mystical spirituality, represents a new way into the future – a new evangelization if you will."

Beckett jumped in.

"What a bunch of bull. What we need is a Pope to teach the faithful to dread the loss of heaven and to fear the fires of hell. Priests have got to get back to scaring the hell out of people – it keeps people in line; it's worked for centuries. Instead what do we get, we get Warwinka who believes we should bend our knee to the tooth fairy and to six children. Damn it, Roberto, I am getting sick to my stomach."

Carl Beckett gulped down his champagne and reloaded his glass.

"Now Carl, Cardinal Lombardi's outlook to be elected Pope is greatly enhanced without Warwinka. It may take a month of black smoke during the conclave - but it may be enough time to clear his name."

"We need to stop this Roberto. Let me tell you something if Warwinka becomes Pope it's over. The conciliar progressives, the elites, and their politically correct happy crap, will have finally won."

"I couldn't agree with you more, old friend; it's why we need the Fatima secret – it will prove to the world the failures of the modern Church."

"Look Roberto, as I see it, without a return to the strict infallible dogma that salvation can only be gained through the Catholic Church, which Vatican II emphatically rejects, the light of the Church, guided by the Holy Spirit for two thousand years, is going to darken further. I am beginning to sense that we may have entered into the final stages of the Church's transformation. The Church is mutating into the Beast, before my very eyes. The sacraments are becoming meaningless and without the sanctifying graces of the Holy Sacraments the path to the Heavenly Father is closed, we know that, and if we stay on this path it could be lost forever – Christ will be separated from man. The once eternal body of the Roman

Church will be altered into the mortal body of the Creature – the Creature of a New World Order. The faithful will unwittingly pray to the Demon – a diabolical disorientation will overcome the faith. Satan will have defeated Christ if we don't do something. We must choose sides. Either we are for God, or we are for the Devil. Cardinal Lombardi MUST be Pope! There is no other possibility."

Father Roberto nodded his head.

"I understand your words only too well. In the full realization of my responsibility to God and to my Church, I am ready to take any measures necessary to guarantee the legitimate apostolic succession."

Roberto picked up his glass and emptied the drink and turned back towards the mountains. As Roberto took in the view, a surprising calmness came over him. He felt peaceful for the first time in months. The pains in his stomach and chest eased, and with the pain gone, he realized that the ache and soreness were always with him. The Demon inside him was at peace.

Carl Beckett looked across the table at Roberto and saw that his eyes were closed. Beckett pulled out his phone and called Nicholas Alexi. As Carl Beckett let the phone ring, he tapped his fingers on the dining table to get Roberto's attention.

"The gates of Hell will not prevail, Father Roberto Indellicotta, not on my watch. I will have the Codex tomorrow—the Fatima letter will reveal everything—the errors of our faith. The Fatima letter will reveal the truth. The dogma of our faith will be preserved."

"I understand, Carl."

"Now, about Cardinal Warwinka, Roberto—do you want to take him hostage until we have a new Pope, or should I just have him shot?"

As the Demon rested, Roberto felt free for the first time in months. He thought of the girl—Sofia—he would see her tonight, and it would be a good night.

"He needs to be eliminated, Carl; he is young; he will continue to evangelize. He will outlive Cardinal Lombardi; a permanent solution is vital."

Chapter 23:

This New World has been won and conquered by the hand of the Virgin Mary. Our Lady of Guadalupe is often considered a mixture of the cultures which blend to form Mexico, both racially and religiously Guadalupe is sometimes called the 'first mestiza' or 'the first Mexican.' In the Journal for the Scientific Study of Religion, Mary O'Connor writes that Guadalupe brings together people of distinct cultural heritages, while at the same time affirming their distinctness.

Before Tucker left Mexico to sail, he would often find himself in the middle pew in an empty church on Saturday afternoons.

Tucker would come to the Catholic Church, not to pray, but to be close to Heather; to think about her, to talk to her. It was quiet and peaceful. He would close his eyes and be with her.

A few weeks before the Google news, Tucker was standing outside the church when he noticed a little girl handing out small pamphlets. Tucker took one in his hand and glanced at the little magazine—on the cover was the familiar image of "Our Lady of Guadalupe." He put the pamphlet in his back pocket and walked into the church and sat down. His thoughts turned back to Heather. His first thoughts were always the same -was he going to miss her forever?

Twenty minutes later, as he got up to leave, the church pastor walked into the church to tend to some chores. For some reason—perhaps the pamphlet the little girl had given him had jogged his memory—but at that moment, he remembered Heather's words, "God will find you when it's time."

Something told him, now was the time to begin the walk, start down the path.

Tucker took the small pamphlet out of his back pocket and calmly waved it towards the priest.

"Hello, Father, do you have a moment?"

Somewhat surprised, the priest turned around to answer the voice. For the past year, Tucker would quietly enter the church, sit by himself, then, as he left, he would drop twenty dollars into the offering box. The priest had grown accustomed to the stranger's peaceful Saturday afternoon visits.

Pointing to the cover of the pamphlet, Tucker took a few steps towards the priest.

"Father, I have seen this picture of 'Our Lady of Guadalupe' all over Mexico, she seems to be so important to everyone here. I made a promise to my wife a few years ago, and I was wondering if this woman in the picture could help me keep my promise?"

"A promise?"

"Yes, I promised my wife that I would look to the heavens one day. Start down a spiritual path."

The priest smiled, and quickly walked past Tucker, gesturing with his finger to follow him into his office. In the office, the priest handed Tucker a small booklet with a picture of "Our Lady of Guadalupe" on the cover.

"Start with this; it is a book about the apparitions of the Virgin Mary that took place in Mexico a long time ago, it is a magnificent story—it will help you begin your journey. I recommend you learn all you can about the miracle of the tilma; do some research into the miraculous painting of the Virgin Mary. The famous portrait that you see all around Mexico – the original painting– you must understand was painted, not by human hands, but by God. Understanding this will help you. The miracle, of the painted Virgin, has helped many people."

Tucker took the book from the priest and casually flipped through the pages.

"Thank you Father, I'll read it carefully and maybe next week we can have a talk."

"Yes, splendid. Stop by next Saturday, this time."

After the conversation, Tucker thanked the priest, then walked outside to the parking lot. He leaned against his car, stared at the image of the Virgin Mary and opened the book.

"My dear little son, I love you. I desire you to know who I am."

Tucker was almost startled at the simple words spoken by the Virgin Mary to the peasant Indian—Juan Diego. The words unexpectedly touched him. The words from Mary were simple, yet seemed to say everything that needed to be said. Tucker immediately sensed something good. The words were modest, loving and theoretically, anyway, came directly from heaven—no dogmas, or abstruse rules—this was a good start—perhaps a God he could do business with. He continued reading the Nican Mopohua - the aboriginal telling of the Virgin Mary's personal evangelism to the indigenous peoples of the Americas.

"My dear little son, I love you. I desire you to know who I am. I am the ever-virgin Mary, Mother of the true God who gives life and maintains its existence. He created all things. He is in all places. He is Lord of Heaven and Earth. My son (Juan Diego) the least, Call me and call my image Santa Maria de Guadalupe."

Tucker closed the book and headed back to his trailer. Back home, he popped open a beer then walked down to the beach as the sun was setting. He sat down on the sand, looked up to the furthest points in the sky, and listened to the ocean's timeless slow rumbling chant. He dreamed he was Juan Diego meeting Mary, the Mother of Jesus, in the hills of Mexico.

"My dear little son, I love you." It was the first time in years he had dreamed of a beautiful woman whose name was not Heather.

Chapter 24:

June 12, 10:00 pm - Milan, Italy
Malpensa Airport

Waiting for his plane that would take him back to the United States, and with a plan in place to deal with Cardinal Warwinka, Carl Beckett's thoughts returned to his missing ship. Sipping on a short glass of Johnnie Walker Black, in the executive club, at Milano Malpensa Airport, Beckett searched for more news on the whereabouts of the Arctic Mariner. By now the United States Navy had to know something strange was happening in the Strait of Hormuz. His best guess was his freighter was just miles outside of Iranian waters.

Beckett checked his watch; he would be boarding soon and still no word from his point man on the ship. He would be in London in two hours. From there, he could not get out of London until 4:30am, putting him in Washington, DC, a little after 6:30 in the morning.

Beckett called a few CIA contacts—they were alarmed, but like him, they knew nothing.

What Beckett could piece together was that Russia and Israel were in a dispute—Israel was accusing Russia of smuggling weapons to Iran and Russia had accused Israel of high seas piracy. What the United States Navy planned to do was anybody's guess. Carl Beckett finished his drink and headed to the airline gate. By morning he hoped things would be clearer.

He was not in control, and he hated the way it made him feel. As he walked down the nearly empty jet bridge, Beckett looked at his watch—in five hours he would be somewhere over the Atlantic Ocean and the Codex, by then, would be waiting for him in his hotel room. Focus on the positive, focus on things he could control.

Chapter 25:

"Dan, if we find your Indian will that make this all go away—I mean, if we locate the canyon where he is buried?"

Dan gave Rene a puzzled look—then remembered dinner.

"For sure, it's the key to everything."

Rene sat up and stretched her arms, then reached for the book on the table that was causing all the trouble—the book about Medjugorje.

Dan watched her put her head back, and run her hands through her hair—a habit of hers he had always found attractive.

Rene opened the book and shuffled the pages.

"Dan, I take it this book is the cause of your troubles, but before we get into that, I need to know when did you turn into a secret agent; a real life James Bond, 007. You just shot a man dead...in my house."

"Rene, that man came into your house for one reason and one reason only. I did what I had to do."

"Dan, what you need to do is tell me what the hell is going on, and I mean everything."

"I'm looking for something."

Rene sneered at Dan.

Dan quickly sat down beside Rene and took the book out of Rene's hand and opened the back cover. Inside a small gap in the book binding was a folded document—a pictorial with an old weathered appearance.

Dan carefully pulled it out and handed it to Rene.

"It's a codex, Rene, and that piece of paper in your hand is our ticket out."

Rene unfolded the document. The pictorial had the aged, brown and yellow crinkled look of an old pirate's treasure map.

"It looks like the Codex Saville."

"It is supposed to look like the Codex Saville—it is based on that. The artist of this pictorial calls it the Codex de Rio Grande. Take a good look at it, Rene. Take your time; any thoughts you have could be really helpful. I am stuck in the mud."

"Dan, right now, I don't really care about your religious relic."

Rene slid the Codex across the table towards Dan.

"I need to know why I am in this mess? Your mess. I know what you said in the car, but that does not explain everything."

"All right, I'll start from the beginning."

"Please do."

"Four months ago, this Codex was given to me by a stranger in Rome. It was actually shoved into my pocket, and from that day, enemies of the Church want this and they are willing to kill you and just about anybody close to me to get their hands on it."

Rene shook her head then picked up the Codex.

"Now I am really confused. Here it is; just give it to them."

I can't; they will kill us both anyway."

"Maybe I'll take my chances without you. I mean nothing to your Church."

Rene looked at her purse on the table; she had Luke with her. She could call a cab and just disappear for a while.

"Rene, hear me out; maybe you will understand better."

Rene reached under the table and gave Luke a scratch. She decided to hear Dan out. She then crossed her arms firmly. After a moment, she turned one palm over.

"Proceed."

"This all started six months ago. It started after a close woman friend of Pope John Paul II died. She had known the Pope for over fifty years; she was at his bedside when he died; she was at the hospital, in his room, after he was shot. They visited often, secretly, just the two of them. She was a mystical presence at the Vatican. No one asked about their friendship. They would talk for sixteen hours a day. Nothing funny went on, but she was known as his soul mate. They had identical views of history and faith. Not long ago, powerful members of the Roman Curia learned she had a letter, but not just any letter; it is a letter that is believed to contain the greatest secret in Catholic Church history. The letter is known as the "Third Secret of Fatima". It is unclear how she got it, the rumor is she either stole it from the Pope's apartment or the Pope just gave it to her for reasons that are unknown. But before she died, she put into place a mechanism to ensure the Fatima letter would remain in the hands of clerics who were loyal to Pope John Paul II. Her death, six months ago, put into motion a race to find the letter, and this document is a coded map, that she created, which gives directions to where the Fatima letter is hidden. The problem is, I haven't decoded it yet."

Rene tried to follow Dan, but it seemed like a bunch of inside the beltway jargon. Vatican, Fatima, secrets? She also decided to leave the whole question about the Pope and the woman alone—what did it matter to her?

"Fatima? Portugal? You're talking about the apparition of the Virgin Mary?"

"That's right, but forget that; you want to know how we ended up here, right?"

"Right."

"First, believe me when I say all of this was forced on me—literally. It all started in a book store in Rome. I was in the back, doing research, when a stranger pushed me up against the bookshelves and said, with a tormented look, 'Father Daniel, the Catholic Church needs you—find the Fatima letter; this Codex will show you the way.' He then stuffed the Codex into my jacket pocket and said: 'Don't follow me, or people you know will die.' I was frozen for a moment; I could not believe what I was hearing. Then I asked him how he knew my name. He didn't answer; he just let me go and ran out of the store. I followed him outside. I saw him in the middle of the street - a busy street, Via La Spezia. Just as I was about to go after him, he stopped and turned around and yelled: 'Father Daniel, remember: the Church needs you. You have been chosen.' I took a few steps towards him, but, as he continued to stare at me, he stepped backwards right into an oncoming bus. The bus was probably going thirty-five miles an hour."

"Dan, that's horrible. What did you do? "

"I didn't know what to do, really. I thought of his warning not to follow him, but I couldn't just leave the man lying there in the street like that. I cared for him, gave him his last rite. I waited until the EMT got there. I decided not to tell anybody about the encounter in the book store. I told the police only that I was a witness to the accident. Had I listened to the stranger and not followed him, you would not be with me right now. Nobody would have known I had the Codex. The dead man wanted our exchange to be a secret. It all happened so fast. But I couldn't just leave him dying on the streets."

"I understand, of course you couldn't."

"Anyway, police records had my name in the accident/suicide report and the thugs you met this evening, and the people they work for, have been after the Codex, ever since."

"Dan, one thing I don't understand is, why me? Who told you my life was in danger?"

"Soon after I was given the Codex, I was approached by a few of my colleagues. They asked me if I knew anything about a document the dead man had been carrying. I didn't say anything, but I had a bad feeling. I didn't know what to do with the Codex, at first; I sensed it was something important. I felt, sooner or later, I would be approached by someone, who I trusted, who could tell me what to do with the Codex; or that over time, I would understand better its significance. Then one night an anonymous letter was slipped under my door. It was shocking, Rene. The letter let me know that people I cared about were going to start dying, if I didn't turn over the codex. Your name was at the top of the list. By then, I had had it. I went to my Superior, and I told him everything— about the Codex, the stranger, the book store, the suicide—all of it. In a meeting with my Superior, my hair stood up when he said, 'Father Daniel, the Church needs you; you have been chosen. It is too late now; you must find the files— the Madonna files—it contains the Third Secret of Fatima. You must find it before the others do. The Codex will lead you there.' He handed me a list of ten clerics that the Pope trusted. My Superior then said, 'It is up to you, Daniel. Get the Fatima letter to one of these men.' I was staggered, and incensed that you and other innocent people had been pulled into some kind of conspiratorial Catholic plot, and I let him know it. But after speaking my mind, I understood why the stranger in the bookstore threw himself under the bus. I suggested, to my Superior, I was going to do the same to save you—to keep you out of it. In the meeting, my Superior told me it would not matter. He said, he had been told you would be killed anyway to make an example. He said we would both be killed if I gave up. They wanted to make sure the trail ended with me. So you see, Rene, even if I left the Church, they would have come after me and you, I am afraid. I have no outs; they made sure of that. Now, if we find the letter and get it back to the people I trust in Rome, then, and only then, will we be free—but there are a lot of things I don't know right now."

"Do you know who is behind all this?"

"I have my suspicions. There are people in the Vatican that have extreme views; they are not obedient to the Church and to our Pope. These people believe they are doing God's work; they believe the Pope is the Anti-Pope. Look, Rene, we could run, but I don't want you to live that way. I believe, if we find the letter and get it back to Rome; ninety-nine percent of the motivation to harm us will disappear. And don't worry about the one percent—I have a plan for that as well, which includes taking the roof off the Vatican, if I need to find out who is behind all this."

Rene slumped in her seat; she didn't know what to think or what to say, what could she say? She dropped the Codex onto the table. All of a sudden, she knew, she had been pulled into something much bigger than anything she could have imagined. The way out, now seemed more distant than ever. She was in deep.

"Well," she thought, "the dream of saying 'I do' to the question, 'till death do us part,' to the man sitting next her seemed, ironically now, to have a good chance of coming true."

Chapter 26:

June 13, 8:00 am - Washington, DC
Mandarin Oriental Hotel

Carl Beckett touched down at Dulles Airport at 6:40 in the morning and was in his hotel room by 7:30. He had slept on the plane, but was still tired as he drank tea, in his hotel room, waiting for the Under-Secretary of State to arrive. He had scheduled the early morning meeting long before his ship went missing.

Beckett's room, at the Mandarin Oriental Hotel, overlooked the Potomac River title basin and the Jefferson Memorial.

Beckett took another sip of tea and walked over to the balcony on the fourteenth floor, and gazed towards the river. After a moment, he turned around and looked back at the coffee table—the Codex was not there! The Codex de Rio Grande was nowhere in the room—he didn't know where it was and he had not heard a word.

That the Codex was not in his room was shocking to Carl Beckett; he was sick about it. The Codex should have been in his hotel room by now, and, like the Russian cargo ship, it was missing and no word. Beckett had to accept both operations were out of his control—compromised, as the DC suits liked to describe such predicaments.

It had to be a simple delay—an easy explanation would be forthcoming; he had made sure the penalty for noncompliance was sufficiently harsh. His freighter was another story. The ship, escorted by mercenaries working for Carl Beckett, had been missing for three days.

The ship was not just any Russian tramp freighter. Far from it; the Arctic Mariner was, in fact, carrying the most lethal cargo in the world.

The rattle and hum of plastic on wood startled Beckett out of his trance—the phone, shimmering on the teak coffee table, called him back into the room. He picked up the phone and read the text message.

"We've lost the priest, and he has the woman."

Carl Beckett looked at his watch and put the phone back down on the table. He wanted to cancel his meeting with Ben Dirkson, the Under-Secretary of State for Public Diplomacy and Public Affairs. Beckett had asked for the meeting. He wanted assurances that the United States Government was taking recent intrusions by the Russian Orthodox Church into Russian state affairs, including the military, seriously, but the agenda now seemed perfunctory. Beckett wanted to be alone. He had one hundred million dollars of his money tied up in the smuggling job. There were new complications on top of already extremely delicate matters; Father Baronowski still had the Codex, and his boat was missing.

Ben Dirkson was a fundraising superstar for the Republican Party, and a man who had the newly elected President's ear, but Dirkson had no real operational authority or power as far as Beckett knew. Beckett had a big mess on his hands, and he doubted Dirkson could help—he was greatly annoyed that he was on his way.

Beckett picked up his phone to cancel; he needed to talk to his point man on the Arctic mariner, George Tela, and find out what the hell was going on. He put the phone back down on the table and thought to himself,

"Hell with it. I'll see the useful idiot, maybe he can do something. The ball needs to get rolling. I need to clean up the Arctic Mariner mess."

Beckett found himself with few options, and the fact that Ben Dirkson was one of them, was troubling—a real sign of weakness.

Beckett's Iranian sting operation had been in the works for two years. A one billion dollar payday was the prize if the missiles made it to Iran. Russian mafia, business partners with Beckett's group, had contacts with Iranian officials who were willing to pay top dollar for the weapons of mass destruction. Beckett's contribution was not only big, upfront money, but it was also Beckett's team that convinced the Russian gangsters that their ties to the CIA would keep the U.S. Government out of the way.

It took George Tela two years to persuade the Russian gangsters that hardcore neocon's at the CIA did, in fact, want missiles to get to Iran. And now with the newly elected President in place, the timing of the sting could not have been better. The new administration was swept into office promising to go to war against Iran if they did not end their nuclear weapons research program. The President of the United States, Jack Murphy, defeated the incumbent by beating the war drums. It had turned the election. The President had a mandate to be harsh with Iran, and if Americans wanted war against Iran, by god, the President of the United States was going to bring the heat. The President was drafted to rock and fire. Beckett believed he was doing the United States a giant favor. This time, when the U.S. goes to war, weapons of mass destruction will be found.

As soon as the President won the election, Carl Beckett put into motion his own version of the Gulf of Tonkin "incident" – the "incident which started the Viet Nam war. If the missiles made it to Iran and the Russians' received a wire transfer from the Iranian Government, the gangsters and the Russia military officers could keep their share of the money. The White House and its hawkish National Security Council would then be notified of the smuggled nuclear missiles. With nuclear missiles in Iran, the United States would have no choice but to act swiftly and launch a massive attack.

But the plan was in jeopardy. None of his field operatives knew the whereabouts of the ship; Beckett didn't even know if his boat was still floating. A few of Beckett's lower level contacts, at the CIA, were aware of the plot from the beginning, but not until the ship made landfall in Iran were top officials to be notified.

Beckett was flying blind, and it made him hugely uncomfortable. The only news he was getting was from a couple of shipping industry periodicals. The shipping rags were reporting rumors that the Israeli "Mossad" had discovered missiles onboard the cargo ship. For all Beckett knew, the United States Navy had boarded the Arctic Mariner and seized control. By now the entire United States defense apparatus including the CIA, NSA, and Homeland Security, were aware that something strange was happening in the Strait of Hormuz.

He couldn't believe he had not heard from his guy on the Arctic Mariner, George Tela. It was very likely he was dead.

Chapter 27

Like posting for a watch on a cold stormy night, Rene cleared her mind and focused on what needed to get done. Dan needed help.

Rene took the Codex back from Dan—it was folded in three.

"Okay Dan, it is a script, a Codex like you said—it's a pictorial calendar of some kind, and like I said it looks vaguely like the Codex Saville. They keep the Codex Saville at the Smithsonian."

But was it the Codex Saville? She wasn't sure—the pictorial calendar was filled with dozens of images, illustrations and dates. She did not remember the Codex Saville having so many drawings.

"Okay, Dan, there is a lot going on here; what are we supposed to do with this?"

"The Codex tells a story—in code. The coded messages are designed to answer a riddle that will tell me where a set of files are hidden—The Madonna Files. It's small, only a handful of documents, mostly secret letters of Pope John Paul II—his views on the Virgin Mary, including his views on Medjugorje, but most importantly, the file contains an original letter—a letter known as the Third Secret of Fatima."

Rene was fixed on the word "code," and missed Dan's mention of a "riddle".

"Dan, I am familiar with Native American pictorial calendars, and I know a little bit about the original Codex Saville. It illustrates Aztec history from 1440 to 1557. It is called the oldest book in America—the original is in the Smithsonian at the American Indian Museum. It is best known for a drawing of the Virgin Mary."

"That's right; it is a lot like it. The original was discovered by Marshall H. Saville, a staff member of the Museum of American Indians in Peru in 1924. Historians believe the Aztec drawing of the Virgin Mary is conclusive evidence of the Blessed Mother's spiritual and cultural influence on the native population in Mexico. It is worth noting, Rene, that just months before the apparitions of the Virgin Mary in Mexico, Aztecs worshipped human sacrifice on a grand scale. The presence of the Virgin Mary quickly built a bridge between two worlds—the old and the new—and within a few years, millions of Aztecs converted to Christianity."

Rene continued to study the Codex; she quickly had her own ideas. The Codex had subtle and not so subtle differences to the original in the Smithsonian. She noticed now there were major alterations, the geographic regions had been expanded, years had been added, and there were three ships she had never seen before on the original.

"Dan, this Codex looks like the original. Right here is the drawing of the Virgin Mary, the church bell, and the Catholic Saint, but now I see there are big differences; different years, and look here at these two bell towers—they belong to Mission San Antonio de Valero, a former Roman Catholic mission—it's now a ruin; it's the Alamo—and look here; there are drawings of square riggers, black slaves, and references to the American Civil War."

"That's right Rene – that's all accurate."

Rene studied the beginning of the Codex, paying particular attention to the three square rigged ships—then she glanced at the ending—it looked like activity along the Mexican /American border—it did not make any sense. She hoped Dan had made some progress because right now she had no clue.

"Dan have you narrowed down the location of the Madonna Files; have you made any progress?"

"The files are somewhere in the Basilica of the National Shrine of the Immaculate Conception, in Washington, DC; that much I know."

"How do you know that?"

"In Rome, my Superior told me that I would find the Madonna Files and the Fatima letter in a great cathedral. He handed me a note that said "Worthy are you to receive the scrolls and open its seal". He said I would find the Madonna Files there. I had no idea what the note meant at first. I thought it was about me, that I was "worthy" to search for the secret letter, nothing more. But it turns out, after a lot of researching "great cathedrals", I found the words are written on top of the southern dome of the National Shrine of the Immaculate Conception – one of the great cathedrals in the world. So Rene, what I know, right now, is the Fatima letter is inside the Basilica, in Washington DC, but to determine its exact location, I need to find a painting of the Virgin Mary, The problem is that there are hundreds of paintings of the Virgin Mary inside the National Shrine, and to find the one I am looking for, I need to solve the riddle."

This time, Rene heard the word riddle.

"A riddle? What do you mean a riddle?"

Dan pointed to an area on the Codex about mid-point.

"You can't read it, not without a magnifying glass, but it is right here. The words stream together in a meandering fashion in a pattern that follows the Rio Grande River along the Mexico/Texas border."

Dan took a small piece of paper out of his jacket pocket and handed it to Rene.

"Here, read this."

Rene took the small note from Dan.

They protest and dismiss me, yet my son they adore
He loves me like no other but they choose to ignore
With blood and tears, a trail has been made
I cry with the memory of the last one they laid
Find the canyon, where my child is buried
And there you will find a painted young virgin named Mary

"The painted young virgin named Mary, that's who we are looking for?"

"Correct, we know the riddle is speaking of a painting of the Virgin Mother, that's clear, but the trouble is, where do you start? Right now the only thing I have to go on is 'Find the canyon where my child is buried, and there you will find a painted young virgin named Mary.' I think that line refers to the last Indian killed by the U.S. Government—where he was buried, because the lines before that refers to the 'Trail of Tears,' the sad episode – a horror really - of America's participation in the ethnic cleansing of Native Americans. I think the location of the canyon where the last Indian was killed will tell us where we need to go in the Basilica."

Rene, put the note down and picked up the Codex, and thought about the riddle—The painted young virgin named Mary. The word, "painted," jumped out at her. She glanced again at the small drawing of the Virgin Mary. Rene ran her hand through her hair, then returned her attention back to the three square rigged boats—where the Codex begins—Dan was focused on the end of the story, on the, "last one buried."

"Dan, the three boats, right here at the beginning, they look like three crudely drawn square riggers. Like a lot of things on this diagram, the ships are not on the original Codex Saville."

"Yes, I know that; I've looked at that. It's Columbus's fleet. The three ships depict the first encounter between the New World and the Old—when the Spanish explorers first met the indigenous population, and we are looking for the end of the trail of tears—we are looking for the last Indian killed."

Rene put down the Codex.

"This is not making any sense to me; you are talking about 'The Trail of Tears.' I am a history professor—I don't see the connection: Trail of tears, Virgin Mary, and the Catholic Church?"

Dan put his finger on the small note.

"Look here. Look at these three lines."

They protest and dismiss me, yet my son they adore
He loves me like no other but they choose to ignore
With blood and tears a trail has been made

Rene shrugged her shoulders.

Dan continued and said, "First understand, the words, 'protest,' 'ignore,' and 'trail they have made,' are meant to reference Protestants and Evangelical Christians, and their treatment of Native Americans—the word 'protest' is a direct reference to the Protestant religions and the word 'ignore' refers to the faith's devaluation of the Virgin Mary. Their liturgy, their faith, ignores her."

Rene gave Dan another shrug of the shoulders; she had no idea what he was talking about.

"The riddle, actually the entire Codex, is making the point that Protestants and evangelicals who 'ignore' the Virgin Mary, yet 'adore' Jesus Christ, were the ones most responsible for supporting the politics that legalized ethnic cleansing of American Indians that led to the Trail of Tears—one of the ugliest chapters in American history. Rene, this entire Codex is a push back, of sorts, by the Pope's friend who created this Codex, against the prevailing orthodoxies of American history—and Christianity, for that matter. This Codex is a retort, with a Marian twist, to what is known as the 'Black Legend'—the demonization of Spanish Catholic settlers in the Americas invented by the English. The creator of this Codex believes the Virgin Mary played a vital role in the early history of the Americas – a much greater role than people understand, and the Pope's friend pulls no punches in blaming the Protestants for the shameful treatment of American Indians. You know the story of the Trail of Tears—the U.S. military, after the United States Congress passed the "Indian Relocation Act in 1831, expelled Native Americans throughout the South, from their homeland, with little regard for dignity or life. Families were pushed out of their cabins at gunpoint. The war against Native Americans would last until the end of the century; the trail of tears and ethnic cleansing would end, if we are to believe this Codex, with the last Indian killed, by U.S. soldiers, buried somewhere in a canyon in the Southwest. Rene, the theme that runs throughout this pictorial is that Catholics, because of their deep devotion to the Virgin Mary, treated the indigenous population more humanely than Protestants who were establishing the United States."

As Rene listened to Dan, she was also getting a hunch—Mexico, the painted Virgin, the square riggers.

"Dan, let's go back to the three ships for a second."

"Ok, sure, the three ships—they are the three boats that discovered the Americas, Columbus's fleet. Look right here, they have the names written under each vessel in very small print."

"That's what I thought."

Rene picked up the Codex and looked at the riddle—the name of the three boats took her mind back to her high school Spanish classes and her elementary school history books.

"Dan, I think I may have something for you. Maybe those boats are more important than you think. Work with me on this. Let's start with Christopher Columbus—his boat—the name of the boat he captained when he discovered America?"

Dan looked at Rene like she was crazy.

"You know the name of the boat, Rene."

"I know, but just name the boat. It will help to sound it out."

"Okay, Santa Maria."

"Right. Santa Maria, Saint Mary, the Mother of Christ. To many, she is better known as the Virgin Mary; am I right?"

"Yeah okay, Columbus sailed on the Santa Maria; everybody knows that."

"No, Dan, think of it differently, Columbus sailed on a boat named the Santa Maria, but Santa Maria is really the Virgin Mary, right? He sailed on a boat basically named 'Virgin Mary.'"

"Yes, okay, I will buy that, but we are looking for the end of the trail of tears."

"Forget that for a minute; now, the two other boats—their names?"

"Come on, Rene."

"Okay, fine."

Rene got up and grabbed a pen and note pad off the navigation table, and wrote down the name of the three boats and sat back down.

"As you know, Dan, the two other boats with Columbus were named the Pinta and the Nina. The Nina, Pinta, and the Santa Maria made up Christopher Columbus's fleet. We all know that, right?"

Rene jotted some additional words down on the piece of paper.

"Now look here."

Rene moved the note pad over to Dan and pointed to the words on the piece of paper.

"The English translations of these Spanish words are…"

Pinta = painted, Nina = girl or young woman assumed to be a virgin, and Santa Maria = the Virgin Mary

Dan shrugged his shoulders.

"Yeah okay, so?"

Rene took the note pad and placed it just below the drawing of the Virgin Mary that was illustrated at the top of the Codex.

"Dan, this drawing, at the top of the Codex, looks a lot like 'Our Lady of Guadalupe.' See how the head tilts forward? In fact, it looks a lot like the drawing on the original Codex Saville. Historians agree that it is a picture of 'Our Lady of Guadalupe', right?"

"Yes, that's right."

"Okay, 'Our Lady of Guadalupe'—the original painting in Mexico, is a portrait of the Virgin Mary, right?"

"Yes, yes, of course."

"Finally, we are getting somewhere. The Catholic Church claims, if I am not mistaken, the portrait of 'Our Lady of Guadalupe' was created supernaturally by God, literally painted by God; the key word here is 'painted'—painted by God. Am I right?"

Dan was scratching his head, trying to figure out where Rene was going.

"Yes that's correct. The miracle associated with 'Our Lady of Guadalupe' is that of a supernaturally formed painting of a young girl, about fifteen or sixteen years old, known as the Virgin Mary. The miraculous painting of the Virgin Mary was revealed to the Bishop in Mexico, by the peasant Indian Juan Diego."

Rene stood up quickly, and took a few steps into the galley area, opened refrigerator. and pulled out a bottle of water.

"Dan, do you understand what you just said? Do you hear what you are saying?"

"No, not really, what?"

"Come on Dan! The riddle, you just answered your own riddle; don't you see? The Santa Maria, the Pinta, and the Nina, Columbus's fleet translated into English literally means a painted young virgin named Mary. The painted young lady who is named Mary—the virgin you are looking for, Dan, is Our Lady of Guadalupe."

Dan took Rene's note pad and put it under the last line to the riddle.

Then you will have found the painted young virgin named Mary....
Pinta = painted, Nina = girl or young woman assumed to be a virgin, and Santa Maria = the Virgin Mary

"Rene, I cannot believe this."

Dan read Rene's note again to himself slowly and just shook his head.

The painted young virgin named Mary—Columbus's three ships together translate, incredibly, into a perfect description of 'Our Lady of Guadalupe.' And it was the Virgin Mary, in Mexico, who would inspire the conversion of millions of indigenous Americans to Christianity. It seemed impossible. How could it be? Was it just one great providential coincidence? Or was it a mysterious sign that had been under the world's nose for centuries?

Dan finally spoke up.

"This is completely mind boggling, and I agree with you—this must be the answer to the riddle; I really do, but I still wonder about the last Indian buried."

"Dan, at the Basilica, an exhibit, a chapel, is there anything there that honors 'Our Lady of Guadalupe'? There must be a painting of her in the Cathedral."

Chapter 28:

June 12, 6:00 pm - Boston, Ma.
The Professor's Office

A short, stout, man wearing a finely pressed outback shirt with a whistle around his neck, stood outside Professor Bob Baronowski's office, gently tapping on the door frame.

Bob looked way from his computer screen and at the figure standing in the door way.

"Hello, sir, what can I do for you?"

The man stepped into his office and stood there without saying a word.

Bob tried again.

"Hey nice whistle—old school, shiny and chrome; are you a coach here on campus?"

"No, sir."

"Okay, how can I help you? Who are you looking for?"

The man at Bob's door finally explained himself in a thick Russian accent.

"Yes, I was in area for business and my son tells me this best school in America. He says you best teacher. You see, my son is in Russia and he want to come to America to study mathematics. He is excellent student. You are Professor Robert Baronowski right?"

Bob put down his coffee.

"Guilty as charged, I'm Bob Baronowski. Come on in and have a seat. You've come along way; the least I can do is welcome you to MIT. What can I do for you today? How can I help your boy?"

"Yes, perhaps so, perhaps you can help my boy. He is in Moscow, in elite High School #135. Very good school. He want to apply to school here at MIT."

"I would like to help but, honestly, I'm really not the guy you need to start with. I don't have any pull around here, believe me. I can give you a couple of names and phone numbers—department heads, admissions; they would love to help you. Have you checked MIT's website?"

Bob reached into his desk drawer, pulled out a directory and scribbled down some numbers.

"Me? No. My son, yes, perhaps."

"By the way, what's your kid's name? If I get lucky and see his application I can put in a good word."

"Sergi, Sergi Brezhnev, like the great leader of the Soviet Union. Brezhnev was a great man for my country, don't you think?"

"That was a long time ago, sir. Here are some phone numbers and the web address. Take this, but go ahead and tell me a little bit about your son. What's he interested in?"

Nicholas Alexi reached over and took the Post-it note and put it down on the desk without looking at it.

"Mr. Professor, I have problem right know with school—my son's school."

"Yeah, don't we all? Take a look at this place, it's falling down."

"Mr. Professor, I have problem with my son's school for different reason. You see they teach religion in school, no more communism, now they teach- Jew, Muslim, Orthodox. Soviet Union, before, never teach religion."

As Alexi was finishing his sentence, he stood up and walked back to the door.

"Mr. Professor, I have sensitive subject to inquire, may I shut the door?"

Bob suddenly got an uneasy feeling. The man he was talking to, he realized, was a complete stranger who seemed to have no interest in mathematics whatsoever. Soviet Union? Communism? Religion? Where was this guy going?

"Sir, why don't you just leave that door open, that's school policy.

Alexi ignored the professor's request and quietly shut the door.

Chapter 29:

June 13, 8:25 am - Washington, DC
The Mandarin Hotel

On September 8, 2000 Larry King interviewed President Vladimir Putin.

Larry King: There is much talk about Vladimir Putin and religious faith. I'm told that you wear a cross. Is that true? Are you religious?

Vladimir Putin : As regards to wearing cross, earlier I never had one, but then my mother gave me a cross and when I visited Israel she asked that I have a blessing there at the Tomb of Lord. I did so and now it's with me always.

Carl Beckett had been funding a private army of action junkie mercenaries for years. His soldiers existed in a lawless, borderless frontier loosely affiliated with the CIA, and George Tela, Beckett's commander on the Arctic Mariner operation, was head of the force.

But Carl Beckett did not green light the Arctic Mariner operation to satisfy a junkie's need for action or for the money. Carl Beckett wanted to do battle with the Russians. He had been itching for a fight. By organizing a conspiracy to undermine the relationship between the United States and Russia, diplomatic relations, Beckett hoped, would take a major hit. The trust factor among both countries would plunge and Russia would move to the front pages of American media with the narrative that Russia could not be trusted. To Beckett, Russia was the one true enemy. Russia had always been the enemy—not just the enemy of the United States, but the enemy of God, the enemy of the Catholic Church. The Virgin Mary at Fatima had singled out Russia repeatedly, and warned the world of Russia's errors. Until Russia is properly consecrated to the Immaculate Heart of the Virgin Mary by the Pope—Russia would continue its errors, deepen the schisms, and threaten the Catholic faith and the United States of America.

Oddly, though, despite his long held beliefs about Russia, something about Russia was starting to bother him—he had to admit to a certain truth—he could no longer ignore the evidence; Russia was in the midst of a mysterious religious awaking. The Orthodox Christian faith in Russia seemed to be experiencing a baffling revival.

To Beckett, under Vladimir Putin, the Russian Orthodox Church's incursions into government affairs had grown deep, and ominous and he did not know what to make of it.

With each passing day, Putin was praising the virtues of the Russian Orthodox faith. The Russian Government was funding restorations of Orthodox Cathedrals with public tax dollars. Putin's inaugural ceremony was attended by black-cowled patriarchs armed with Holy water and incense. Bishops were regularly seen at military installations, including nuclear missile bases, conducting religious ceremonies, chanting prayers, burning incense, and sprinkling holy water on weapons of mass destruction. Carl Beckett could not get past the visual—Russian priests sprinkling holy water on nuclear missiles. The United States press would lose a lung protesting, if they discovered that Catholic priests were invited onto U.S. military bases to sprinkle holy water on atomic bombs. Carl Beckett was convinced the Russian Orthodox Church and the Russian State were establishing an unholy alliance.

Beckett picked up a magazine resting on the coffee table, then stepped back out onto the balcony. He was going to make Ben Dirkson read the magazine out loud—every word of it. The State Department was clueless about what was happening in Russia. Russia was becoming an Orthodox Christian theocracy and nobody in Washington was paying attention.

Beckett looked at the magazine's headline: "Russian Nuclear Submarine Aleksandr Nevsky Named after Russian Saint". The subtitle read, "Fitted with Orthodox chapel" It was the sixth military chapel consecrated into the Russian fleet. Just last week, the Russian military unveiled a new weapon—a squad of parachuting priests. Russian Orthodox chaplains have joined the Russian Air Force and have been trained to assemble mini churches, decorated with icons of the Virgin Mary that can be airlifted into battle.

A loud knock on the door startled him. It was Ben Dirkson. Beckett opened the door and let the Under Secretary of State into his hotel room. He had met Ben Dirkson, many times at political fund-raising events. Beckett had been a huge donor to the President and Ben Dirkson, a fundraising honey badger for the Republican Party, considered Carl Beckett the big Tuna.

Dirkson sat down quickly, and immediately started bragging about important people he had recently met and asking Beckett for tickets to the next year's Oscars. Beckett, annoyed and uninterested, moved his chair slightly to improve his view of the river, but Dirkson's head, decorated with an impossibly full head of hair, was an obstruction and it bothered him greatly. He, again, thought of asking the Under Secretary of State to leave.

As Ben Dirkson droned on, Carl Beckett tuned out. All Beckett wanted to do was look out of the window and think about his next move, but instead, with his view ruined by Dirkson's hair, Beckett found himself examining the Secretary's features: his hair, teeth, his perfect shoes, his White House cuff links. Beckett thought he must spend more time grooming his hair then monkeys do picking nits at the Zoo. How is it that after billions of years of evolution, this dope, this particular species of life, plays golf with the most powerful creature to ever walk the face of the Earth? Then it occurred to him, men like Ben Dirkson—you see them everywhere in Washington, DC—all seem to be "cut from the same cloth." Beckett thought of the phrase, "Cut from the same cloth" and winced at the cliché. Just looking at Dirkson had dulled his senses. He was uttering banal clichés to himself and he hated himself for it. Beckett was certain the turn of phrase was part of Ben Dirkson's frat-boy lexicon. The first time he met Dirkson, his manner of speech, his perky "You bet" clubby dialect, of the privileged, had bothered him. The good old boys, if anything, knew how to put people in their place. Putting his tea down, Carl Beckett stood up, moved towards the window, and interrupted the Under-Secretary.

"Look, Ben, knock it off already with your sales pitch. Your President has enough of my dough; it's not why I asked you to meet me here today."

"Sure, Carl. You bet; ball's in your court."

Beckett stood up and looked at the paddle boats on the tidal basin and resisted the urge to have Ben Dirkson fired on the spot. But Beckett had another idea. If he didn't hear from Tela soon, he was going to have to go further up the food chain to keep his plan intact. He was now going to see if Dirkson had any real pull with the White House, or was he just a fund-raising whore. Maybe Dirkson could, in fact, help.

"Ben, that Russian tramp freighter—the Arctic Mariner—news reports say it was heading to Iran, the news says the boat has disappeared. European press is all over this story, and they are reporting that there could be nuclear weapons on board. Where the hell is that ship? Did it sink? Did the U.S. torpedo it? "

Dirkson didn't see Beckett's question coming and it made him uncomfortable. Beckett was a hot head and when he didn't get what he wanted he could be difficult. Dirkson had been briefed on the Arctic Mariner incident, on his way over to his meeting with Beckett, by his good friend, Pat Allen, Director of the National Security Council. Dirkson knew intimate details about the Arctic Mariner, but he had to maintain confidentiality.

"No can do, Carl—off limits—classified, chief."

Of course, Carl Beckett knew what was on the Russian tramp freighter; but he wanted to see if Dirkson was in the loop, before he asked him for a favor. Beckett, now figured out that Dirkson could help—Dirkson had the President's phone number—the President would take his call—but in order to get Dirkson to do his bidding, he needed leverage.

Beckett baited him. "That's a bunch of bull, Dirkson. You're bluffing. You don't know what's on that ship. I'm hearing storm clouds are building on this. I'm hearing Russia is involved— Iran, Israel, nukes. You're out of the loop on this one, aren't you?"

"Sorry, Carl, not to pull rank, but you are on a need-to-know basis. I am sure you understand."

"Cut the crap, Dirkson, you don't know what is on that ship. You're a poser. How the hell would you know anyway—far as I can tell your job at State is to make sure guests at White House dinners know which fork to use."

Beckett turned away and looked out of the balcony window.

"Damn it, Ben, I'm not sure what good you are to me anymore. I pay you to get me answers."

Dirkson shifted gears. It was time to lie. It was Washington, DC's favorite pastime—lying to people's face. By lying to Beckett, he would not divulge State secrets, and he would keep Beckett on his good side.

"Carl, I can tell you this confidentially. There are no nuclear weapons on that boat and no SS-300 surface to air missiles—all just rumors. The Arctic Mariner is carrying two million dollars of timber from Norway. That's all I can say. The story will blow over in a couple of days."

At first, Beckett was surprised to hear Dirkson's confident reply; maybe he was out of the loop. Then Beckett understood and thought to himself: "B-I-N-G-O. *What a lying rat.*"

Dirkson could have manned up and said nothing, but instead he chose to lie. Beckett would have respected him more had he just kept his mouth shut, but instead Dirkson, lied right to his face. He was shameful. Ben Dirkson is lying right to his face while asking him for favors.

"Timber, that's a bunch of horse hockey. Timber my ass!"

"I know what I know, Carl. Carl, it's my job to know about these things. Let's leave it at that, and if this is what this meeting was all about, well then, this meeting is over."

Carl Beckett knew where Dirkson stood—he was lying. But, in Washington, so what—it was the culture—what mattered most was access and power, and he could still use him. He needed the President of the United States to either get the Navy to stand down, if they were involved, or get the Israelis off his boat. He needed Dirkson to make a call to the

President, but He needed leverage over Dirkson. Beckett didn't think Ben had it in him to simply call the President of the United States to do him a favor, considering the enormity of the situation. The only way he could motivate Ben Dirkson to make the call would be out of fear, and Beckett had learned over the years how to do that. He needed to threaten Dickson's career. He needed Dirkson to tell him State secrets, then blackmail him. Beckett thought his investment in Dirkson was about to pay off. He had funneled his campaign contributions to Ben Dirkson because he knew he was a weak man who also happened to have the President's ear. Beckett had an idea.

"Oh, come on, Ben. I think you are lying to me, but forget it. Keep your little secret. You're a heck of a good American. You should be proud of what you do for this country."

"I am, Carl. You bet I am."

"Let's forget the freighter for now. Tell you what—you got your tickets, but don't push for seat assignments, ok?"

"Hey, Carl, that's terrific; Babs is going to be thrilled. Thanks, and sorry I can't be more help on the Arctic Mariner situation, but as I said there is not much to it anyway. I hope you understand."

"Sure, I do."

Carl Beckett then noticed Dirkson look at his watch and it irritated him, but he went on, "Forget it, Ben, let's drop the Arctic Mariner for now; it is just the tip of the ice-burg anyway. The Arctic Mariner is just a symptom of the disease. I've been warning you about Russia, for at least a year, and I am here to tell you, we have a serious problem in Russia. It's not communism we have to worry about in Russia anymore, but rather it is a rising theocracy in that country that will pose problems in the future and nobody is paying a damn bit of attention."

"What are you talking about Carl."

"Do you know that Vladimir Putin, wears a cross around his neck? That he waits in line in the cold to kiss ancient relics of the Virgin Mary? That elementary schools in Russia are now required to teach religion and classrooms are to be adorned with portraits of Jesus Christ and other sacred items? Ben, do you know that Russia is naming submarines after Russian Saints, and nobody at the State Department thinks it's a big deal—nobody. Russia was a communist, atheist nation just a few years ago."

Carl Beckett picked up the foreign policy magazine and tossed it onto Dirkson's lap.

"Dirkson, do you know Russia is installing Orthodox chapels inside nuclear submarines?"

"Wait, Carl, take it easy. Who did you talk to at State?"

"Ben, it's always "who" with you "suits". I am not interested in crucifying anybody at State. It doesn't matter 'who?' What matters is, you have a serious problem. Are you going to listen to me or not?"

Ben Dirkson looked at his watch again.

"Yeah, sure."

Again the watch. Carl Beckett looked down at the floor and shook his head. Beckett had planned to come down hard on Ben Dirkson, anyway, but his anger was going to be an act. But with Dirkson peeking at his watch, He was now truly steamed. He was ready to unload. Asking for Oscar tickets and money while lying to his face was bad enough—but like a prostitute, Ben Dirkson, having turned his trick, was now looking for the door.

Beckett glared at Ben Dirkson, and then at Dirkson's watch. But Beckett kept his cool, and in a friendly tone, he asked Dirkson about his watch – the watch would get things rolling.

"Hey Ben, that's a hell of a nice looking watch you have there, I think I saw one like that last week when I was in Milan—at the Pisa Orologeria. It's beautiful; I almost bought one—Submariner, right?"

"That's right."

Ben lit up, he was now in his comfort zone—shopping, spending money. "Here, take a look." Ben snapped the watch off his wrist and tossed it to Beckett.

Beckett stood up and admired the watch. He held it up towards the light, then walked over to the balcony.

"I'm guessing six grand, maybe a little more. What do you think? Is that about right?"

"Yes, something like that, Carl. I know a guy who can get you a great deal on one." He reached into his wallet. "I have his card; jeweler right here in town."

"That's good to know; maybe I'll check it out."

Carl Beckett then casually tossed the watch over the balcony, and without bothering to see it hit the pavement fourteen stories below, he charged towards the Under Secretary of State.

Chapter 30:

Alexi closed the door to Bob Baronowski's office, then slowly turned around and stared at the professor for a moment, and said, "Dr. Baronowski, do they teach religion in this school, here at MIT?"

Without waiting for an answer or invitation, Alexi went back to his seat and sat down, which surprised the professor. Bob now wanted the stranger out of his office immediately.

"Look, sir, I don't know where this is going; you have the phone numbers of people who can help you. I would start with those. They can answer those types of questions. Frankly, I don't think I can be of any more help. I think you have what you need."

"Mr. Professor, do you believe in God?"

Bob rolled his eyes.

"Okay, sir, there is nothing more I can do for you. I am done with this conversation. I am busy and I am going to have to ask you to leave, right now. Have a good day."

Alexi didn't budge.

Bob stared him down with raised eyebrows and a dismissive look. Bob was starting to get angry.

"I said, Mr. Professor, do you believe in God?"

Bob stood up behind his desk.

"Look, Brezhnev, or whoever you are, I would like you to leave right now; and if you don't, I am going to have you escorted out of here."

"Mr. Professor, my son believes in God, and he is friends with filthy Jews. It is very wrong. So it is important for me to know. Do you believe in God?"

Bob finally blew his stack and pounded on his desk.

"It's none of you damn business; now get the hell out of my

office—now!"

Alexi pulled out a knife.

"I asked you if you believe in God, and you are not answering me."

"Jesus Christ." Bob thought. He quickly sized up the stranger. Bob weighed two hundred and thirty five pounds and rarely was he physically intimidated, but the guy he was facing was a raving lunatic holding an incredibly lethal-looking knife in his hand. Bob quickly looked around the office to see what was in reach to use as a weapon or shield.

Then, more calmly, hoping some kind of response—an answer to his question—would alleviate the sudden crisis.

"Look whoever you are, about God—yes, no, I don't know, maybe. I am getting closer, but quite honestly I just don't know about religion—maybe. How about a maybe."

"Well, Mr. Professor, it's time for you to find out."

With the speed of a magician, Alexi threw the knife into Bob Baronowski's chest, then quickly pulled out another. Alexi charged the professor like a panther and with the heavily serrated knife, he opened Bob's throat.

Chapter 31:

June 12, 10:45 pm - Annapolis, Md.
The Codex Decoded

"Dan, in the Basilica is there a chapel, any kind of room dedicated to 'Our Lady of Guadalupe'?"

Dan nodded his head.

"Yes, as a matter of fact, it's the most popular chapel in the entire church."

Dan continued to think about Rene's discovery.

Then you will have found the painted young virgin named Mary.

Pinta, Nina, and the Santa Maria. Columbus's fleet, the names taken together, no doubt spell out "Our Lady of Guadalupe"—what a remarkable coincidence, he thought—but then maybe it wasn't a coincidence, perhaps it had all been divinely established. The names, of the three ships, utilized in that providential first voyage were truly PROPHETIC!! The Nina, Pinta and Santa Maria, the names mystically prefigured the apparitions of the Virgin Mary. The ships names foretold the miraculous picture of the Virgin that would lead to the conversion of the New World—it was more than any imagined coincidence. For Dan, everything began to fall into place.

"Rene, this is really incredible, the Madonna files must be at the chapel dedicated to Our Lady of Guadalupe at the National Shrine."

Dan stood up and gave Rene a big bear hug.

"The Virgin Mary of Guadalupe has to be the answer."

"But what about the last Indian buried, Dan, are you sure this is the answer to the riddle?"

"I don't know, maybe at the chapel I will find more clues, I just don't know."

Rene saw Dan look at his watch.

"Are you going now?"

"Not sure."

Finally, he had a destination. The riddle had been answered, at least he hoped so. He was close; at least closer. Go now? The Church would be open, but what if the trail didn't end there. What if there were additional clues found at the Guadalupe chapel? He would have to snoop around, in the middle, of the night with a flashlight, like a cat burglar. Even though his position, at the Vatican, gave him the power to examine every square inch of the Basilica, no questions asked, he did not want to bring attention to himself. He picked up the little note he had been carrying with him for months.

"In the canyon where my child is buried."

Was there more to the riddle? It didn't matter, really; he would go to the Basilica and chase the lead down, regardless. Dan looked at his watch again.

"Rene, I'll stay here tonight; I'll leave in the morning."

He picked up the Codex and considered all its the riddles and codes. Dan found himself thinking about Pope John Paul II's friend and her message. She had a story to tell and the Pope was probably involved. The Pope's friend would not have acted without his approval. Dan sat back down and turned the Codex back towards Rene. There was still something nagging him, a part of the riddle – "The canyon were my last child is buried."

Maybe Rene could pull another rabbit out of her hat. Maybe if he shared his thoughts on the Codex, it could lead to fresh insights; perhaps, it would lead to answering the riddle more fully.

"Rene, this Codex is not just some kind of treasure map. The Pope's friend felt it would be the last chance to tell an important story, and, by the way, I do think the Pope was involved. They both wanted the treasure hunters, those searching for the Fatima letter, to understand some deep truth about the Virgin Mary, about Guadalupe, and about Christianity in the New World."

Rene could see Dan was hopeful and with the changed atmosphere in the cabin, her curiosity as a history professor, perked up.

"Okay, what do you think this Codex is trying to say?"

"Let's go back to the picture right here of the Virgin Mary—it is clearly Our Lady of Guadalupe. An amazing thing happened after the Mexican apparition occurred, and before the Trail of Tears took place in the United States—Indians and Spanish came together to form a new race—they were called 'Mestizos.' There was co-existence. Early Catholic settlers and the indigenous populations knew the Virgin Mary, from the start, as the dark virgin, the little brown one."

"Dan, I read that some people think the Virgin Mary's portrait in Mexico is a symbol of racial harmony—the Virgin Mary's skin tone is a perfect blend of white, brown and black."

"Exactly, Rene, exactly, that is so important. She appeared as a Mestiza—a blend of Indian and Spanish. The skin tone of her hands were diverse shades—one darker than the other."

Rene looked at the Virgin Mary drawn on the Codex.

"She looks peaceful."

"Right, Rene, she does look peaceful. That's part of the message of the apparition—peace and racial harmony. In Rome, I studied the Codex intensely; I had secret meetings with experts. We concluded that the dominant theme of the Codex is about race.

"Dan, in the back of my mind, I have always wondered why the United States has such a different racial profile than the rest of the Americas. Why do North and South Americans, including Central Americans, look so different? It is as if the United States had purged the Indian blood from it's genetic make-up."

"Rene, believe it or not, your observation is sadly rooted in the Bible and the Protestant theology of Sola Scripitura—by scripture alone."

"What do you mean by that, Dan?"

"Protestants believe the Bible is God's word, and as you know, the Bible is chalk full of racial references, including frequent mentions of 'masters and their slaves.' Even Jesus talked about that almost casually. To Protestants, slavery was effectively sanctified by God. In Bible racial dominance was a common theme. The Catholic Church, on the other hand, is a sacramental religion—the old cliché is: Catholics don't even read the Bible. The Catholic Church is all about the Holy Mass. In addition, the Church introduced its own interpretations of Christianity, including Marian dogmas. These elements of the Catholic faith allowed for flexibilities, and it was the Mother of Jesus Christ who had a huge impact on the racial profile of the New World."

"What do you mean by that?"

"The Virgin Mary—the 'ignored one,' Rene, is why North Americans and South Americans look so different. Very few people are aware that Christopher Columbus and his crew were deeply devoted to the Virgin Mary—a female religious figure, obviously—but not so obvious was that the female figure on the Santa Maria was dark skinned—she was a 'Black Madonna.' Fewer still are aware that each night, at sunset, the crew sang songs to the black skinned Virgin Mary—they had a statue of her. When Columbus made landfall his men sang the last prayer of the Holy Rosary - the 'Salve Regina.' The first Christian prayer recited in the New World was a song about the Mother of Jesus Christ. Understand, Rene that Christopher Columbus was not bringing Christianity to the New World, but rather he was carrying with him a strand of Christianity defined by a devotion to a dark skinned woman. Some historians believe this eased integration between the indigenous population and the Spanish colonists who settled there. Right from the beginning, Spanish friars built schools and churches; provided medicine, and farmed, side by side, with the local native people. The first Protestant settlers in America, on the other hand, shunned the Virgin Mary—they ignored her, if you will. When Protestants and evangelicals were forced to confront the Virgin Mary, usually only at Christmas, she was portrayed as a pale faced Northern European. There was no place at the table, or the church, or in the homes for a dark skinned Madonna, in the puritan and white world, of Southern evangelical Christians and New England Protestants. And this fact set the stage for the racial horrors that would define the United States, for the next two hundred years

"Hold on a second, Dan; let me add something to that, a piece of American history I had never considered before—it's a remarkable coincidence, really, but who knows, maybe there are no coincidences. It is interesting to consider that Columbus came to America, on a boat named after the Virgin Mary. The Protestant English, on the other hand, first settled in America on land they called Virginia, named after another virgin—the virgin Queen of England—Queen Elisabeth I. Of religious significance, the first move of the Queen of England was to establish the Protestant church which would challenge the supremacy of the Catholic Church in England. Dan, it is kind of strange, to think, that men in the Americas fought religious wars for over two hundred years, unwittingly, fighting on behalf of two virgins—a Protestant virgin and a Catholic virgin."

"Rene, that's a great observation, but it is more relevant than you may think. Following the apparitions in Mexico in 1531, as millions of Aztec Indians were converting to Catholicism, the most significant period of the Protestant Reformation in Europe was taking place at the same time. Millions of Europeans left the Catholic Church between 1532 and 1538—ironically, to a large degree—precisely because of the Catholic Church's excessive devotion to the Mother of Christ. Protestant Reformation was not only a rebellion against the authority of the Roman Pope, but also against the devotions to the Virgin Mary. To Protestants, devotions to the Blessed Mother are not scripturally sound. Protestants feel the Virgin Mary's role in Catholicism was based on legends and dogmas that were simply invented by Popes and obscure Cardinals in Rome. Protestants, on the other hand, believe in Sola Scriptura—Scripture alone—that is, only the Holy Bible revealed God's word. That the Pope would elevate the role of the Virgin Mother—willy-nilly—was, in the end, the real-deal killer for Christians who broke away from the Catholic faith. Mary's role in the redemptive process of human souls, widely promoted by Catholics, convinced many Christians that the Catholic Church had moved so far away from Biblical teachings that, finally, the Church was viewed by many as a heretical cult."

Dan let his words settle. He looked at Rene; he could see her wheels were turning. Dan picked up the Codex and his thoughts drifted back to Rome and the quiet nights of his research. He put the pictorial back down, got up and walked over to the refrigerator, and pulled out a Gatorade. The full meaning of the Codex was becoming clear. Again Rene's insights were helping.

As Dan stood by the icebox, Rene wanted to solve the riddle, more than ever. She wanted to know where the *last Indian killed by the United States was, in fact, buried.* It had to be significant. She held the Codex up in the air and gently waved it at Dan; she wasn't done.

"But what about these other drawings, Dan, the Alamo, the Mexican-American War, and African slaves, the Civil War? What is the point of all theses illustrations? How does it all connect to the painted young lady named Mary. Maybe there is more to all this. Maybe we still need to find the last Indian and the canyon where he is buried."

Chapter 32:

Carl Beckett, just inches apart from Dirkson and gesturing aggressively with his pointing finger, exploded.

"Dirkson! Don't you ever, and I mean EVER, look at your watch again when you are in a meeting with me! And, don't you ever lie to me again! Listen to me, Dirkson, I know you are lying; so tell me what is on the Arctic Mariner, or I am going to make it my life's work to destroy you."

Ben Dirkson looked like an oncologist had just told him he had six months to live. He looked sick.

"You owe me this one. Jesus Christ, after all I have done for you, and this administration—I made you in this city."

Ben was sick to his stomach. He knew, right away, Beckett had caught him lying. But how did Beckett know? Right now that was a secondary concern, more importantly Dirkson knew Carl could and would hurt him. Beckett made a huge investment for the President in Florida, and Carl Beckett had heaped mountains of praise in letters to the President. Carl Beckett's support was what got him his job, in the State Department, in the first place. Beckett could turn off the money spigot at anytime - blackball him. He would be worthless. Carl Beckett was right, he could ruin him in Washington, DC.

Beckett watched Dirkson squirm in his seat. He knew Dirkson would probably sing, but Dirkson's pettiness and vanity would have to come first.

"Damn you, Beckett, you son of a bitch, I can't believe you just tossed my watch off the balcony. You're going to buy me a new one, take that to the bank, you jerk."

Dirkson moped for a minute, then stood up.

"...Jeez...Damn you, Beckett."

Beckett knew Ben Dirkson was breaking. He was going to spill his guts. Dirkson was now his prison snitch, and once he revealed State secrets, Dirkson was his.

"Now, what's on that boat, Ben?"

"Okay, listen up, and if this goes past this room I will have you shot. You want to know what's on the Arctic Mariner—I'll tell you what's on the Arctic Mariner - state of the art nuclear missiles, Beckett—that's what's on the Arctic Mariner, missiles. Russian mafia is behind it, as far as we know, and the boat was headed to Iran. The ship was stopped a hundred miles from Iran. Israeli Mossad are on the boat. Israel's security service had been tipped off and they took control of the ship. Right now, Carl, the situation is very tense; nothing has been resolved. The US Navy is on the scene. The White House is trying desperately to keep this entire matter quiet. One big problem—organized crime might not be the only ones behind the incident—we now think it may be the Russian Government, or an inside job by the Russian military—it's all very fluid, a lot of moving parts. Also, satellite recon tells us a Russian carrier has changed direction and is steaming, at full speed, in the direction of the Arctic Mariner's position."

"Jesus Christ," Beckett thought. *"There's no time; if the Russians or American's board the Arctic Mariner, my plan is finished, not to mention my one hundred million dollars is gone."*

Carl Beckett had to get Dirkson to call the President. The Navy has to stand down, and he needed to get the Mossad off the Arctic mariner. The Arctic Mariner has to make Bandar—Abbas before the Russians get on the scene.

Carl Becket sat down and poured Ben Dirkson some tea. His prison snitch had done well. He was impressed—Dirkson was in the loop—even better. Now it was Beckett's turn to ask for a favor. As Beckett began to refill his cup, the phone buzzed inside his coat pocket. It was a text message.

"Idi Kambana has the African girl."

Chapter 33:

Dan, with the refrigerator door still open, responded to Rene's question and said,

"Maybe, Rene, maybe we still need to find the canyon—it is very possible that's the answer to the riddle."

Dan then held up his Gatorade bottle.

"Thirsty?"

"Some water would be great; Luke needs a fill up."

Dan tossed an unopened bottle to Rene, opened the Gatorade for himself and took a sip.

"Rene, let me get some air—clear my head for a minute."

"Sure."

Dan stepped outside and looked up at the stars that were starting to appear in the sky. He had studied the Codex for months in Rome. But only now, was he beginning to understand the full meaning of its message, perhaps the Pope's message, and the message in the Codex was beginning to shock him.

With the Codex, Dan suddenly saw a unity of the Mexican apparition with other major Marian apparitions of the twentieth century. At Fatima, the Virgin Mary warned of atheist Russia. This warning was followed by World War II, the death of millions in Russia and China, at the hands of state sponsored atheism, and the genocide of six million Jews engineered by the godless neo-paganist racist regime of Adolf Hitler.

At Rwanda, the Virgin Mary warned of "A river of blood." Rwanda was followed by Medjugorje. 'Our Lady of Medjugorje' came to Yugoslavia in 1981. Her words of, "Peace, peace, and only peace," were discounted and in 1994, the most horrific act of genocide on European soil, since the Holocaust, took place in the region. One hundred thousand people were slaughtered in appalling, ethnic violence. Ominously, the Medjugorje apparitions are still ongoing and the Virgin Mary continues to issue warnings.

Before today, Dan had believed that 'Our Lady of Guadalupe' was different—that the apparition did not come with warnings. The apparitions referred only to the conversion of the native people, and an end to pagan rituals and human sacrifice, nothing more—but now, he saw things differently—very differently. The call for racial harmony, by 'Our Lady of Guadalupe', was the crucial message; a message that was embraced by millions of indigenous dark skinned Americans south of the Rio Grande, but suppressed in the United States. The Virgin Mary was kept away, and what transpired north of the Rio Grande would be horror for Native Americans, African Americans, and the six-hundred thousand young men who died fighting in the American Civil War over the right to own slaves. Fatima - genocide; Kibeho -genocide; Medjugorje - genocide; now Guadalupe. Dan now understood, the message attached to the Mexican apparition was black and white.

He walked back into the salon, reached into a cabinet and pulled out a bag of peanuts, then sat back down and slid the Codex toward Rene. The apparitions of 'Our Lady of Guadalupe' had come with a powerful message—the message of racial harmony—and the priest wanted to let the Georgetown University History Professor know what he was thinking.

"Rene, let's take a quick tour of the Codex. I think you will find it interesting, and maybe this will help with the riddle; you see this date here—December 6, 1810."

"Yeah, I saw that, okay. What about that date?"

"On that date, a priest named Father Hidalgo, known as the 'Father of Mexico,' introduced a decree to abolish slavery in Mexico. Earlier that year, Hidalgo had led a group of peasants in a revolt under the banner of the Virgin of Guadalupe. Around that same time, 'The Father of Texas,' Stephen Austin, brought slavery to Texas from Arkansas. A few years later the new President of Mexico, Vicente Ramon Guerrero, who was black—his father was of African descent, a little known but historically momentous fact—freed all slaves in Mexico, including the territory of

Texas. Stephen Austin ignored the new abolition laws and continued to own slaves in Texas, and it was Austin's commitment to own slaves that would lead to the battle of the Alamo. Think about that for a second, Rene—think about the irony. The Alamo, today, is a considered a great symbol of American bravery and heroism, but the reality is Americans fought Mexicans, Catholics let's not forget, at the Alamo to protect their "right" to own black slaves - a "right" that Mexicans had outlawed. It is ridiculous, Rene, the history we are taught in American schools. 'Remember the Alamo', good lord, Rene, just what is it that we are supposed to remember?"

Rene shook her head; she had not thought of American history from that point of view. She looked at the Codex—what else was it trying to say?

"Okay, Dan, from the Alamo, if you follow the Codex along the timeline, you see here references to the Civil War, slavery—what do they have to do with the Virgin Mary and the Catholic Church? I guess it all is leading somewhere—presumably to the 'last Indian.'"

"That's right; that's the path I went down—that's how I ended up at Wounded Knee—but it was a dead end."

"But, Dan, I don't get the connection. What does all this have to do with the Catholic Church?"

"Okay, you see right here, Rene, the year 1846—the start of the Mexican-American war? And right there, you see a reference to General Ulysses S. Grant."

"Ulysses S. Grant? You're kidding me, right? The Virgin Mary and General Grant?"

"No, I am not kidding, and we can see how the dots are connected when we look at the origins of the Mexican-American war, which Grant fought in. Many of the military leaders, on both sides of the American Civil War, had fought as junior officers, in the Mexican-American war, including Ulysses S. Grant, George B. McClellan, Ambrose Burnside, Stonewall Jackson, James Longstreet, George Meade, Robert E. Lee, and the future Confederate President, Jefferson Davis. General Ulysses S. Grant was a young war officer under General Taylor during the American invasion of Mexico."

"I know all that, but that is not helping me."

"All right, but I am not sure if you knew that General Grant believed the Mexican-American war was the most unjust war in world history, and he said that America's war with Mexico had brought about 'God's punishment' in the form of the American Civil War. As you know, Rene, the American Civil War, with six hundred thousand dead, was one of the bloodiest wars of all time."

"Dan, today the number would be seven million dead—seven million American young men - boys."

"A chastisement, Rene. The American Civil War was an epic, epic, chastisement. Nobody ever thinks of it that way, but, my God, the scale of carnage was monumental—what else can we call it."

"Agreed, but the dots, are not still connecting."

"It starts with Columbus bringing the Virgin Mary and the Catholic Church to the new world. This was soon followed by the Virgin Mary revealing herself to a poor dark skinned Indian in Mexico, which led to integration among races in Mexico. In the United States, Protestant leaders in the north and Evangelical Christians in the south, on the other hand, had different views of race, different interpretations of the Bible, and of course very different views of the Virgin Mary's role in Christianity and the consequences of failing to heed the Virgin Mary's message of racial harmony would be enslavement of African blacks, the American Civil War, ethnic cleansing of the American Indians, the Trail of Tears, and the near extermination of a race whose remnants are found today mostly in isolated reservations and in Indian casinos. The United States would be defined by racism and violence against people of color for over two hundred years. The plain fact is that it just did not happen in colonies settled by Catholics in the New World. The ugly truth, Rene, is that American evangelical and Protestant leaders left the blood of Native Americans on the killing fields and kept the blood of Indians away from their veins. Spanish friars on the other hand invited Indians into their churches. North of the Rio Grande, we have a population free of Indian blood; and south, we have a mixed race of people – white, brown, and black who love a painted picture of a miraculous Virgin."

Rene leaned back in her seat, and thought about Dan's words. She thought about 'Our Lady of Guadalupe'—the painting—what a beautiful image: humble, peaceful, a young woman, black, white, brown—she thought of Buddha and the Dahlia Lama and now, in her mind, the peaceful racially harmonious image of the Virgin suddenly had no equal. Dan said the image was painted by God. Why not painted by God? The image now seemed perfect. She thought about her own lectures on the Civil War, six hundred thousand dead—six hundred thousand boys. So much violence, so many wasted young lives—for what? Fighting over the right to own slaves? A God's punishment? Who knows? Perhaps Dan was right on that account. Rene's thoughts began to drift, the word violence made her think of guns; she looked at the navigation table—Dan's pistol—and now the reality of her own condition slowly returned. She thought of the man that was shot and killed in her home. She found herself getting sad again. The drive to answer the riddle seeped out of her. Rene reached underneath the dinette table, searching for something to comfort her. Rene needed Luke. Dan noticed Rene drift away. He had seen her glance towards the navigation table. Dan sensed that Rene had heard enough for tonight. Dan took Rene's other hand.

"We are going to get through this, I promise. We are closer to a way out now, thanks to you."

Rene's thoughts moved away from the religious intrigue. Another wave of reality passed over her. Dan, it seemed, had found new hope, but now her own life came crashing down on her. Was it the touch of Daniel's hand—a reminder of things lost?

She looked around the boat.

What am I doing here? She retraced the evening and her first thoughts turned to the mirror in her bedroom. Why the mirror? A man had just been shot in her house. Why would she think of the mirror first? Rene thought of the eyes she had seen in the mirror—her eyes—she thought of the lonely edges. Was the mirror whispering to her about a wasted life?

Was she going to die as the lonely person in the mirror? It was bad enough to die, but die alone? That word again—lonely.

She looked blankly at the navigation table across the companion way. Then, unexpectedly, the man on the dock came into her thoughts, and that feeling came back to her again—a good feeling. She could not believe it but, she had to admit to herself, she liked it when she thought of him—why? Was the man she bumped into on the dock just at the right place at the right time? Was he some kind of fantasy "lifeline" to her in a desperate situation? She thought of him bending down to Luke and looking into her eyes. She liked how it made her feel. She liked his eyes. He seemed nice, but there was more to it than that, she thought. A little spark of life came into her as she thought about the stranger with the deep tan and the friendly smile. She looked out of the window of the main cabin and looked down the pier at the other boats. She wondered if he was staying on one of the boats. Maybe he had been leaving. She wondered if she would ever see him again.

Rene looked towards the parking lot and saw two men walk past the security gate. It was him—maybe—he was heading back to the docks with his friend. She watched the two as they stepped on to "D" dock—her dock—and suddenly thoughts of an old recurring dream came to her. In the dream is a dark endless highway. The dream seemed to last for hours. The dream would make her melancholy. In the dream, she would drive for hours—she would be the only car on the road, and her only wish was to see headlights coming her way, coming towards her. As the two men made their way along the dock, she thought of the dark highway, and this time she could see a faint headlight. This time, maybe something was coming her way. She slowly pulled her hand away from Dan's.

She turned and looked at Dan. His head was down; he looked like a weary bull, near the end of the fight. She now felt sad and sorry for him. The poor man must be ready to tie an anchor around his neck and jump. She wanted to lighten the mood before she turned in.

"Don't worry about it, Dan, I trust you; and don't worry about me. I will be fine, and honestly, I was ready for some time off anyway; I was planning on taking a vacation. I made up my mind this evening after having dinner with you. So here I am, on a boat—on vacation—all expenses paid, even."

She closed her eyes and reached down underneath the table again, looking for Luke's ears.

"And one of my favorite things to do on vacation, as you know, is to sleep. And right now, Dan, I'm exhausted. I think I am ready for bed."

She laid there with her eyes closed for a minute, and as she was about to get up to go find her bunk, a "ding" went off in her purse—it was a text message. She raised herself slowly and took the phone out of her purse, then leaned back down.

Dan was jolted out of his thoughts with the unexpected phone noise.

"I called Monique earlier tonight. I think this is from her."

She read the message to herself. The text message was from American Indian Studies Professor, Shane Costoff, from Georgetown University.

May 17, 1896—The last Indian killed was an Apache. His name was Adelneitze. He was shot by the 7th Calvary of the United States Army 10 years after Apache war leader Geronimo surrendered for the last time. Two other Apache women were killed in the last skirmish. The last Native American Indian was killed in an area which straddles the Arizona-New Mexico border and continues on into Mexico—The exact location is called...Guadalupe Canyon.

Rene could not believe it—there was that word again—Guadalupe. The last Indian killed by U.S. troops was in Guadalupe Canyon, a canyon named after the Virgin Mary, right on the Mexican-American border. It seemed impossible. Rene just shook her head.

"Hey, I think I found your Indian, and look at this; this is incredible, the last Indian was killed by the United States Calvary in 1896 at Guadalupe Canyon. Guadalupe Canyon, Dan—the Codex begins with Our Lady of Guadalupe—Pinta, Nina, and Santa Maria—and the trail ends with the last Indian killed in Guadalupe Canyon, right along the Mexican-American border—right along the Catholic-Protestant divide, you might say."

A chill shot through Father Dan Baronowski; but not because he had found where the last Indian was buried or because of the astonishing connection.

"Rene, did you say you called Monique Butare?"

"Yes, I called her just before you came over. Why?"

Chapter 34:

From the cockpit speakers, the song, "Hallelujah"—a song written by Leonard Cohen and mournfully performed by Eric Nielson of Denmark, played quietly as the morning dew slipped away. The humidity and temperature had dropped from last night, and the morning sun and sky were pleasant. The docks were quite. It was Tuesday morning and Tucker Finn was sitting in the cockpit having breakfast alone, reading a book on Portuguese Man of War.

"Anyone unfamiliar with the biology of the venomous Portuguese man-of-war would likely mistake it for a jellyfish. Not only is it not a jellyfish, it's not even an "it," but a "they." The Portuguese man-of-war is an animal made up of a colony of three separate organisms working together.

Tucker, as was often the case after making landfall following an ocean passage, found himself abandoned by his crew. The Captain, Tom Conway and his wife Deb, the boat's chef, were off on morning errands—to the grocery store to pick up provisions and to the boatyard to schedule routine maintenance and repairs.

Sanjay had also gotten an early start to the morning. In a hurry to upgrade his digital toys, he was off to the Apple store near Reagan Airport. Sanjay had not been able to convince Tucker to go with him. His plan was to gear up, then head to the airport to pick up his friends flying in from Spain. Though Pilar's communication and computer technology could guide a rocket to Mars, Sanjay liked gadgets and he liked to buy stuff.

Tucker put his book down to listen to his favorite part of the song, and as he turned his face towards the sun, he saw the woman and the dog making their way down the dock. She passed his boat and headed towards the clubhouse and parking lot with the dog leading the way—the yellow lab was more confident this time.

Her hair blew across her face, and she took her free hand and brushed it back from her sunglasses. She was wearing jeans and a navy blue cotton sweater over a white tee. As he watched her walk towards the parking lot, he thought of last night's chance meeting, and the good feeling came back. He shook his head. He thought of the priest, and Sanjay's advice, and picked up his book, but not before one last peek. Standing by the edge of the parking lot, she turned back towards the docks. She lifted her sunglasses onto her forehead, looked up to the sky, closed her eyes, and took in the morning warmth. Tucker, with his book now back on his lap, took in her simple elegant beauty.

After a moment, he closed his eyes. A song from one of Tucker Finn's favorite albums, "Mermaid Avenue," began to play in the cockpit. The song, "At My Window Sad and Lonely," was written by Woody Guthrie and arranged by the Alt-rock band, Wilco. Jeff Tweedy started in on Guthrie's song:

At my window, sad and lonely
Oft times do I think of thee
Sad and lonely and I wonder
Do you ever think of me

Every day is sad and lonely
And every night is sad and blue
Do you ever think of me my darling
As you sail that ocean blue

Ships may ply the stormy ocean
And planes may fly the stormy sky
I'm sad and lonely but remember
Oh I'll love you till I die

As the song came to an end, he took another look towards the parking lot and saw that she had not moved—she was now texting with one hand on her cell phone, and her state of grace had completely vanished. She seemed tense. She yanked the dogs leash then dropped it to the ground, and put her foot on the lead so she could text with both hands. Finished, she quickly ran her hand through her hair and anxiously stared at the phone. After a moment, she again pounded her thumbs into her phone. She looked at the phone again, but this time with anger, or was it fear? Then, she dropped to her knees—she was on the ground.

Tucker quickly looked towards the end of the dock for the priest, but in an instant he jumped off the boat and onto the dock and raced towards the woman. By the time he reached her, she had righted herself, but she was now sitting down on the pavement, with her head down, and her hands around her knees.

"Are you ok?"

She didn't say anything. He picked the phone up from the ground and now he found himself annoyed. He thought about Sanjay's lectures. Maybe Sanjay was right, this woman was now making a spectacle of herself in his club's parking lot—he'd never seen her before, or the priest. Who are these people? He looked at the phone in his hand. What the heck, he thought; let's see what all the fuss is about. Tucker read the text message.

"We have Monique Butare. Tell the priest to bring us what is rightfully ours; we will call back at 11:30. If our instructions are not followed precisely, she will disappear."

Rene saw Tucker reading the messages and she quickly came to her feet. Her first instinct was to grab the phone, but instead she let him read it. What did it matter? The whole world could read it for all she cared. Put it on a blimp in lights and fly it over New York City. Her life was upside down, inside out, whatever you wanted to call it. She had no control. To Rene, there was no longer any right or wrong. She was numb and defeated.

Tucker was taken aback by the threatening message.

"Let me get you to the police right now Ms..."

At the sound of the man's voice, Rene's resolve momentarily stiffened. Something inside her rose up and spoke to her—survival instincts kicked in. Now it was about saving Monique—and finding a way out of her nightmare. She knew Monique would die if Dan did not cooperate. People had already died in her home, and the people holding Monique most certainly knew about that. A chill went through her as she sensed that her best friend, Monique, would be dumped in a marsh, never to be heard from again if the abductor's demands were not met. She also knew that the man standing beside her had no idea of the complexities of her situation. Hell, she figured, to him, the whole charade was nothing more than a drug deal gone bad, but she didn't have time to explain. Who would believe her anyway? Dan had been right on that score. She did not want to go to the police—not yet. Dan got her into this mess, but something told her, despite everything, Dan was the only one who could get her out, and he held the ticket to Monique's freedom—the Codex. There was also something about the man holding her phone in his hand that somehow made her feel safer, more at ease.

"No, please, please. Monique Butare is a friend of mine. Please, believe me, but right now, I can't go to the police. It is important that this is handled quietly. I know you saw me with that priest last night on your dock—it's not what you think. I need to talk to him, the priest; he'll know what to do."

As Rene was trying to put on a strong front, a tear began to run down her cheek.

Tucker was a little surprised by her tears, but he was more surprised by what he did next—he took her in his arms. He held her gently. She put her head down on his shoulders and her tears turned into a soft cry.

After a moment, she moved her head back slightly and looked up at the stranger. Seeing his face, she thought of last night, just before she went to sleep. The word came back to her—"lifeline". Rene's life was completely undone, and yet, she felt something comforting that seemed out of place. Was she losing her mind? Maybe she just needed somebody, something—anything, hope—she was desperate after all, that had to be it, but there was more to it than that. She felt something good—now she was sure she was losing her mind, but the feeling was there—something new, something hopeful.

Tucker met her eyes and he was drawn in again like he was last night. Their eyes held each other, but this time, rather than look away, a force urged them both to stay together. Something had started, something happened, and as their eyes searched deeper for answers, suddenly, from the parking lot—a voice.

"Hey Tucker, you're back, great to see you."

A club member was walking towards them.

"Have you got time for some crab soup a little later?"

Tucker Finn let go of Rene, and turned towards his old friend, Dave Floyd.

Before Tucker could speak, Dave took note of his intrusion.

"I'm sorry, Finn, I didn't mean to…"

"No, no, 'Floyder,' its fine; good to see you buddy."

Tucker, reluctantly came back to the world.

Tucker shook Dave's hand, then glanced back at the woman he had just embraced and realized he did not know her name.

"Hey, Dave, uh, look, I would like you to meet a friend of…"

Rene, on cue, jumped in. She put her hand out and introduced herself as she shook Dave's hand.

"Hi, I'm Rene, Rene Estabrook, nice to meet you, Dave."

"Very nice to meet you, Rene."

Dave took a little extra notice of Tucker's female friend, but quickly returned his attention back to his lunch invitation.

"How about it Finn; how about the two of you join me for lunch around twelve-thirty? I would love to hear about your passage."

"Thanks, Dave but Rene and I have lunch plans already. Let me give you a call a little later."

"No problem Finn. Oh, and you're doing the race Saturday right?"

Tucker had promised his friend, as he was crossing the Gulf Stream, he would race with him if he got in on time.

"I'm in Dave. I'm in."

"Good, dock call at 8:30 a.m. See you, then."

Dave Floyd turned around, took a few steps towards the club house entrance, then stopped.

"Hey, Tucker, do you know whose dog that is over there sniffing around the dumpsters?"

Tucker looked at Rene, then up at the sky and after a big sigh and a shake of the head he walked over to the dumpster and picked up the leash.

"Thanks Dave, I'll take it from here; I'll see you Saturday."

As Dave headed into the club, Tucker handed the leash to Rene.

"Let's get you back to your boat and hear what your friend, the priest, has to say."

Chapter 35:

Idi Kambana worked for Carl Beckett in his personal security department, and somewhere in Washington, DC, Idi was enjoying a reunion with Monique Butare.

Shortly after the massacres in Rwanda had ended, Beckett found Idi Kambana in a Hutu refugee camp in Goma, a city in the Democratic Republic of Congo that bordered Rwanda. Beckett went to Rwanda after becoming obsessed with the idea that Rwanda, during the genocide, was quite literally, Hell. He believed Rwanda was a place where one could experience the fundamental nature of the afterlife – the afterlife faced by condemned souls. He believed it would deepen his faith. To Beckett going to Rwanda and meeting the men who killed on an epic scale, was like taking a trip into a modern day "Heart of Darkness".

But going to Rwanda had not been just a sightseeing trip; he also turned his trip into a money making venture thanks to a young executive who worked for him. George Tela, his rising star, had developed a business plan to help the United Nations distribute food inside Hutu refugee camps. The United Nations contractor, Médecins Sans Frontières, after a dozen of their workers were killed by Hutu gangs needed help. Médecins Sans Frontières, called the refugee camps in Goma "the messiest humanitarian quagmire ever—a revision of hell."

The clever George Tela had taken special notice of the U.N.'s willingness to hire contractors prepared to take risks but perhaps with "lesser reputations," to carry out relief work. Tela quickly launched "Lesser Reputations, Inc." to make deliveries. With the business up and running, visiting Goma became a tax deductible business trip for Carl Beckett, and after learning that nobody messed with George Tela's trucks, because of Idi

Kambana was in charge of security, Beckett hired him on the spot. Beckett needed muscle and Idi was just the man he was looking for.

Idi Kambana sat on the sofa, watching Sports Center, waiting for a phone call. He was waiting for instructions from his boss. Idi was muscle. Idi liked it that way—not too much thinking, it was the way it had always been since Carl Beckett brought him to America. Idi had texted Rene, but he was only doing what he was told to do. Monique sat in a chair next to Idi, with her hands, feet and mouth, tightly taped. Monique's eyes said it all. She had seen so much death before. She knew how quick and easy death could come.

A commercial came on, and Idi stood up from the sofa and looked down at Monique. Two hours earlier, Idi Kambana, without too much difficulty, got into Monique's house and within minutes, he had her neatly taped up. He hadn't seen Monique in twenty years, and now he had an urge to talk.

"I'm going to take the tape off of your mouth, okay, but I don't want you fussing, I don't want noise, you understand what I mean? I don't want to have to hurt you."

Monique nodded her head.

Idi took off the tape as gently as he could.

"There you are, is that better?"

Again a nod of the head, but fear filled her eyes.

"How have you been Monique? It has been a long time."

Monique couldn't read where Idi was going with his subdued and quiet manner. She raised her taped hands over her head and first gave Idi a shrug before speaking.

"Things could be better, Idi."

"Yes, I understand, I am sorry. I have to do this. It is what I do to make the money. Now Monique, I took the tape off because I want to ask you something, something about Rwanda. I still think about you and the time in the church. I want to ask you about 1994, the time of the genocide, the day of the Gatwaro massacre. Were you in that church that day? We looked everywhere for you in there. Where did that priest put you, anyway?"

Monique didn't know what to say. His question instantly brought back the horror, her dead family, but she still sensed something different in Idi,—a tone. It was strange the way he took the tape off of her mouth, but she still could not trust him. What was there to trust? She wondered if the question was loaded. She wondered if she said the wrong thing, or somehow embarrassed him or made him feel incompetent—that she had out foxed him—it would spell doom. Maybe he was looking for a reason to hurt her, but after a moment, Monique spoke. She was powerless and had nothing to lose.

"There was a small door in the rectory hallway, hidden behind a large cabinet. The doorway was in such a place that it would not seem natural that a door would be there that would lead to another room, but honestly, I am not really sure why you missed it. God had his reasons that day, I suppose. I prayed a lot—the Rosary, a lot of Our Fathers. It got me through so much."

"I don't know about that Monique—about God—but what I do know is, you're lucky that Russian was such a pushy man. Mean as a rattlesnake, that guy; he waits for nobody. I think I would have found you without him. I didn't want to really kill the nuns, but I can't say I wouldn't have. I know one thing; I would have burned the church down, had he not blown that whistle. I had a lot of hate back then. I guess you could say that Russian saved your life."

Monique said nothing, but it did seem Idi had things on his mind and wanted to talk. She now believed, from the moment he learned that he was to take her hostage; he had done a lot of soul searching.

"Monique, I killed a lot of men back then, in Rwanda, a lot of men—for what? We believed we would get the money; they promised us banana farms—that's what they told us. God, looking back on it, it was so horrible. Evil overtook our country, Monique; evil overtook the Hutu people—so horrible, that's all I can say. You're lucky you have a God to pray to, he will never forgive me. I am sorry for what I did to my country, to the people, to the Tutsi." Idi put his head down, "to what I did to your family."

Monique looked at Idi, almost tenderly, with sorrow.

"Idi, before the genocide, do you remember the chickens that got away after the storm at my house, when you helped my father and you had dinner with us?"

Idi looked at Monique and smiled.

"That was a nice day. I remember it well. It was the first time I saw you differently; you were not a bratty little girl. I noticed how pretty you were. I felt like I could not speak to you, after I discovered my feelings. I remember I could not wait until dinner was over because I was so nervous. But that night, at my home, I remember thinking that I could not wait to see you the next day. But of course that was before the genocide."

"I saw something nice in you too back then. You seemed to have a kind heart."

Idi, pinched his lips, shook his head, and looked up at the ceiling. He stood up and turned his back on Monique. The words, "kind heart," intended for him, nearly made him weep uncontrollably. He gathered himself, and turned back around.

"I killed your mother, your father, two brothers. I killed them with my hands and then I came looking for you in the church, that same day, to do the same. How can you say that? Kind heart? My job here, today, is to leave you in pieces in a swamp."

Chapter 36:

Carl Beckett had to get the President of the United States to allow the Arctic Mariner to make it to Bandar Abbas, Iran's largest seaport, and Dirkson was his only shot. He had one hundred million dollars of his money tied up in the operation and a place in history. Beckett now needed to tell Dirkson his side of the story. Carl Beckett sat back down and gave Ben Dirkson an earful.

"The Arctic Mariner is my ship, Ben. It's my operation. It's a sting against Iran. My men are on that boat and, you have to trust me on this one, but, they indirectly work for the United States. The men on board the Arctic Mariner have ties to the CIA. That ships needs to get to Iran—with the missiles on board."

Dirkson was dumbfounded.

"What are you talking about Carl—you're ship?"

"Dirkson, that's my ship. Now listen to me: the United States has been picking a fight with Iran for years. I don't need to tell you that, but the U.S. has been going at Iran like an old man with an inflamed prostrate and a weak stream. Jesus Christ, we need to get serious about their nuclear weapons program. Everybody in your Administration wants the Arctic Mariner to get to Abbas. Everybody at the CIA, the Neocons in the White House, the National Security Council, the American people, the Evangelical Christians who voted in the President to kick the hell out of Iran, want that boat docked in Iran. I need you to call the President and let him know all about this sting operation. America's security, and the security of our allies, is at stake. This is a great opportunity for the United States."

Dirkson could not believe what he was hearing. Dirkson felt he was now sitting in a room with a man who may have just masterminded the greatest crime in history. Dirkson did not know what to think.

As usual, Dirkson thought about his needs first. Was he criminally liable?

"Carl, you say the CIA knows about this?"

"Not the top guys. This operation was meant to be rogue, but to answer your question, the CIA is tangentially involved."

Ben Dirkson stood up slowly and walked out onto the balcony. Out of curiosity, he looked down to the pavement, wondering if the Rolex had withstood the impact. He turned around and faced Beckett. Beckett was right on two counts—first, he could ruin his career with a phone call; and he also agreed with Carl Beckett that it was time to rid the world of the Iranian nuclear menace—for good. He also figured he had wiggle room legally, in that the CIA was somehow involved. What would it hurt? He wasn't part of the crime. Calling his friend, Pat Allen, head of the National Security Council, and telling him what he knows would absolve him—to a degree—of any legal ramifications. It would be up to Pat Allen to turn Beckett over to the FBI, if that is what he felt like doing.

"Okay Carl, maybe there is somebody I can call, but first you got to tell me what is going on."

Carl quickly outlined the details of his entire operation.

After hearing all about Beckett's elaborate scheme, Dirkson decided he would do something.

"All right, let's do it. I'll call Pat Allen, head of the National Security Council."

"Good idea, Ben, let's call Pat Allen."

Chapter 37:

June 13, 9:30 am - Washington, DC
The White House

National Security Council Chairman Pat Allen sat at his desk in the west wing of the White House talking with an admiral about the Arctic Mariner incident which had moved up the chain of national security disturbances. Pat Allen's phone on his desk buzzed.

"I'll take the call."

The National Security Director sat up in his chair.

"What do you mean you know something about the Arctic Mariner? What the hell do you know that I don't know? We just talked an hour ago".

"There is something you need to know. I am calling to tell you that the Arctic Mariner is a CIA operation, but it's rogue – top CIA officials know nothing about it. The operation is designed to get nuclear missiles into Iran, at which point the United States Government was to be informed. The organizers of the sting expect an aggressive response by our military. The plan's objective was to have the United States Navy blow that ship up in port followed by the destruction of Iran's nuclear reactors and research facilities."

Pat Allen leaned back in his seat, rubbed his face and thought about what Ben Dirkson was telling him. Pat Allen's Neocon credentials and his obsession to attack Iran made Dick Cheney look like a peacenik. He had formed the President's Mideast policy and the policy's aggressive stance against Iran had been the deciding issue in the election.

"You knew about this operation, Ben?"

Dirkson paused a moment and looked over at Beckett.

"No, Pat, I just learned about it. The news reports of Mossad boarding the Arctic Mariner prompted phone calls to me from people who are close to the situation."

"That's too damn bad, for a minute there, I thought: out of nowhere, you really grew a pair. So what do you want me to do?"

"I recommend we let the freighter dock in Iran. Back everybody off—Mosaad and the U.S Navy. Once in port, you will have weapons of mass destruction on Iranian soil; you will have all the political fire power you need to move forward to fulfill the American security objectives of demilitarizing Iran. You can then bomb them back to the Stone Age."

Ben waited for a response. He looked at his phone. There was a long silence on the other end. The ill feeling, the sinking stomach, returned. Holy hell, he thought, had he just confessed to participating in a conspiracy that could send him to jail? Ben thought of his wife and his children.

"Hey, Pat, are you there?"

"God Almighty, Ben, you old son of a bitch! Yeah I'm still here, and I have to tell you I cannot believe what I am hearing from you—this is genius. We have had this one drawn up for some time now, but nobody had the stomach to green light it. I salute you, Ben Dirkson. This is fan-freaking-tastic. Now listen to me very carefully. We never talked; you understand that? I'll take it from here."

Ben Dirkson pressed end on his cell phone and looked over at Carl Beckett.

Beckett could not get a read on Ben Dirkson—the moment of silence made him nervous as hell. For all he knew the next words out of his mouth would be that FBI agents are on their way over.

"He likes your plan, Carl. Pat wants the Arctic Mariner in Iran more than you do."

Carl Beckett slumped in his chair, hugely relieved. He slowly worked his way out of his seat and made his way across the room to shake Ben Dirkson's hand.

"Well, I'll be damned, you made it happen."

"Carl, I have no idea what the President of the United States is going to do with your boat. I'm just telling you the head of the NSC seemed motivated to get that boat into Iran."

After shaking Ben's hand, Beckett walked over to the balcony and looked down.

"Hey Ben, let me have that jeweler's number of yours. And look, I can't promise you seats next to Leonardo DeCaprio, but I'll sure try. Let me know when you want to be in California for the Oscars and I'll have my jet pick you and Babs up anywhere—bring the kids."

Chapter 38:

June 13, 8:45 am - Annapolis, Md.
Tucker Meets the Priest

Rene, walking side by side with Tucker, turned her head towards him.

"That man back there, Dave Floyd, he called you Finn?"

Tucker Finn stopped in his tracks and faced Rene.

"I'm sorry, Rene." Tucker put his hand out. "I'm Tucker Finn."

Rene saw the friendly smile again and took his hand and smiled back.

"Nice to meet you, Tucker Finn. Do you prefer Finn or Tucker?"

"Tucker works fine."

They resumed their walk down the dock; Luke leading the way. Tucker didn't want to hurry; he was still trying to sort things out. He wondered where it would all lead. Was he being a fool? Probably, but something told him it was right to be walking with this woman he knew nothing about.

"Rene, your friend—what's your friend's name—the priest?"

"His name is Father Daniel Baronowski."

Tucker again stopped.

"Baronowski, really? Father Baronowski, I knew it. I thought I recognized him last night. He is Bob Baronowski's brother, isn't he? Bob's a friend of mine. We got to know each other over the years at math conferences."

"What? You know Bob?"

"Yes, I do. I know him well, in fact."

Rene grabbed Tucker's hand and started pulling him down the dock, double time.

"Let's move it, Tucker Finn. We need to talk to Dan, now."

Dan was on the phone, speaking with Catholic University, working out details on a dinner meeting with Cardinal Warwinka.

Before leaving Rome, he had set up a meeting with the eminent Cardinal. Cardinal Warwinka was a good friend and was on the list of men Pope John Paul II trusted to handle the Fatima letter. He was starting to see some light. As he was nearing the end of his conversation, he moved to the navigation table to get his car keys, and his gun—he was ready to go to the Basilica, but just as he put the keys in his pocket he felt the boat gently sway. Rene was back. He put the gun away—she did not need to see the gun, more reminders of the violence from last night. He looked out of the main salon window. Rene was back, but she was not alone.

Tucker and Rene walked into the main salon of the boat; Luke made his way to his spot under the settee.

Dan first looked to the navigation table—he should have grabbed the gun. Dan kept his cool, but he was enormously surprised to see Rene walk in with a stranger. Was he a cop?

"Monique's in trouble, she's been kidnapped."

Tucker took Rene's phone out of his pocket and handed it to Father Dan.

"You need to read this text message."

Dan was still reeling from the fact that Rene walked onto the boat with a complete stranger.

"Are you with the police?"

"No. Father Baronowski, I'm a friend of your brother, but more importantly, I suggest you read the text message on the phone."

Dan read the text, then dropped down on to the dinette seats. Shocked by the news, Dan looked blankly at Rene first, then at Tucker Finn.

Tucker spoke up.

"I know your brother, Bob. He's a friend of mine, and I think you and I actually met a few years ago in Boston when Bob got his appointment at MIT."

Tucker turned towards Rene and spoke to her as much as to the priest. "Look, I don't know what is going on here, and personally I think you need to go to the police, but Rene tells me that won't work—not just yet. Father Baronowski, I like your brother, and so if you need help, I have real capabilities in kidnap recovery. I understand sometimes it's best not to involve the police right away."

Dan sized up Tucker; he didn't remember meeting him in Boston, but he was definitely at his brother's party. Dan looked at Tucker, lowered his eyes and slowly shaking his head he said, "You don't want any part of this, Mr. Finn. You need to walk away now. The people involved are ruthless."

Dan then looked at Rene.

"I didn't think they would go after Monique so quickly. I did not think they would widen the net; not right away. I thought I had time. I am so sorry."

"Forget being sorry, Dan. What are you going to do about it? They have Monique, and I guarantee whoever has her knows you killed one of their guys last night."

Tucker jumped back in with calm authority.

"Now just a minute; please listen up. As I said, I have expertise in kidnap recovery. Kidnapping is a big danger sailing offshore. Remote waters and exotic lands—those were my primary destinations—and those waters are chock full of pirates, kidnappers and drug runners—bad guys. My security team is the best in the business. They are former Navy Seals."

He looked at Rene. "I can help."

"Mr. Finn, as I said, I am not sure you want any part of this. Like Rene said, I had to shoot a man last night."

Rene spoke up, this time at Tucker.

"Tucker, I appreciate all that you are willing to do. I don't doubt for a minute that you mean what you say."

Rene then turned to Dan.

"Dan, we need to give them what they want. This Vatican cloak and dagger business is over. Give them the Codex. They will be calling in one hour. I will deal with things once you give them what they want, and once Monique is free."

"You want to run for the rest of your life, Rene?"

Rene spun around hard, unable to look at Dan.

Tucker Finn turned towards Rene; she seemed broken and scared, and now a waterfall of thoughts tumbled through his mind. Heather, Mexico, drunken tequila nights, his promise, the lonely Southern Oceans, he felt something rush through his body. Why was he on this boat with a priest and a strange woman who was already making him feel changed? Maybe this was all meant to be. Maybe now was his time. Time to stop running away; it was time to run towards something. He looked at Rene and something told him he needed to help. The need to bring comfort to someone was now overwhelming. It now seemed that helping Rene and the priest was less about them and more about his own redemption. He knew, now, he really had no choice.

"Father Baronowski, I think I can get your friend out; do you want my help or not?"

Rene searched the table in the salon looking for the Codex. She was ready to take matters into her own hands.

Rene turned back towards Dan.

"Dan, they have Monique. For the last time, other than handing over the Codex, what are you planning to do about it?"

"Hold on, Rene, hold on. Let me think about this."

"Think? No, Dan, your time is up!"

Rene moved towards Dan and stuck her hand out.

"I want the Codex."

Tucker took a step in between Rene and Dan and spoke with authority.

"Father, Rene—I have a crew here in Annapolis; they are ready on a moments notice—I really can help you."

The tone in Tucker's voice instantly changed the atmosphere in the boat – at least for Rene. She instinctively trusted her new friend's hopeful, confident voice. She also knew hope was all she had right now. Her determination eased and she lowered her hand.

Rene again saw the pain in Dan—he was on the rocks. Rene knew Dan would do anything to help Monique.

Dan let Tucker's offer hang in the air. Dan knew his own words, "Let me think," were empty; he sounded weak. He also knew he had nothing.

His plan was a train wreck. Rene was on the run and now Monique was in trouble. He needed help, desperately. That's all there was to it. Rene was right; all Dan really had now was trading the Codex for Monique—but even that would not guarantee their safety. Dan really had no choices. He was going to take Tucker Finn up on his offer.

"Mr. Finn, are you sure you want to be a part of this?"

"I do, but it will make things easier if you just call me Tucker."

Dan looked up at Rene. Rene nodded her head.

"Alright, Tucker." Dan stood up to shake Tucker's hand. "It's a deal. And please, call me Dan; it's now your show."

Tucker gave Rene a quick glance, pulled out his phone and started dialing.

Chapter 39:

June 13, 9:00 am - Washington, DC
Reagan National

As Sanjay was pulling into Reagan National to pick up his friends, he answered Tucker's call.

"What up, Finn Man? I...Whoa! Wait a minute." Sanjay yelled out of his car window, "Sorry about that chief."

Sanjay returned to the phone: "Hey, Finn, don't drive with a 4G on your lap, or you gonna hurt somebody. This new iPad is awesome—bought you one too."

"Sanjay, look buddy, I need you back here now, we have trouble."

"What?" Sanjay looked up at the airport signs; he was looking for Delta.

"My man, I'm picking Margot and her friends up at the airport, like, right now. They're standing outside waiting for me."

"Tell them to take a cab, put them up at the Pentagon City Ritz. Tell them to go shopping or something. I need you now. You can see them later."

"Come on, Finn."

"Seriously, I need you big time. I will explain when you get here. There's real trouble and I need your talents."

Sanjay tossed the iPad onto the passenger's seat, slowed down as he read the airline arrival signs.

"It's that priest and girl, I guarantee it."

"Well, something like that, but they are fine. They are with me right now."

Sanjay, pulled the phone away from his ear and gestured like he was going to throw it out of the car window.

"Damn, Tucker; I told you to stay away from that."

"Sanjay, they…I mean, I need your help, really; there's been a kidnapping."

Sanjay was all fun and games most of the time, but he could tell Tucker meant business. Tucker never asked Sanjay for anything.

Sanjay looked up and saw the Delta sign.

"On my way, be there in forty minutes. See you."

Sanjay drove right by Margot and her friends, without stopping. As he passed his friends, Sanjay smiled and gave the universal thumb and pinky, "call me," sign to the three dumbstruck women.

Tucker was glad Sanjay was on his way back. When there was a job to do nobody was better than Sanjay. Sanjay could go from zero to a hundred faster than anybody Tucker ever knew. And for Sanjay—old habits die hard—his hacking skills had been finely tuned on the open waters of the Indian Ocean. He was state of the art.

Chapter 40:

Tucker hung up the phone.

"Father Daniel, I mean Dan, my friend Sanjay will find Monique Butare, and I have a lot of confidence, my team will get her out."

"Tucker, how are you going to find Monique? I don't see it. How can you be so sure?"

"Let's just say Sanjay is good at what he does. I'll let him explain when he gets here."

"All right, Tucker, like I said, it is your show."

"Now, Dan, I need to cut to the chase. Quite honestly, it should have been my first question and excuse me, Father—but just what the hell is going on? Rene says you have something the kidnappers want and they are willing to kill for it."

"Tucker, why don't we sit down and I can fill you in on everything."

Tucker's mind moved ahead, understanding what he had committed to do.

"Dan, let's go to my boat. Sanjay will go straight there, and I want to brief my security team."

"Show me the way, Tucker."

Dan picked up the Codex from the table and followed Tucker out of the cabin with Rene. Rene and Dan, for the moment, relaxed. Trust, hope, and a little confidence were in the air.

Rene stepped onto Tucker Finn's boat and was blown away—not because Pilar was a rich man's toy—she had seen lots of those before—but rather, she could tell Pilar was world class. Pilar was no floating condo; Pilar was a boat you could trust; she was a boat that had seen a lot of the world.

Father Dan was most impressed with the boat's name.

"Pilar, that's Hemingway's boat's name—it was a Wheeler 34; he kept it in Cuba. Did you know the name 'Pilar' comes from a Marian apparition—took place in Spain."

"You know, Dan, you are the first guy I've met who knows that whole story."

Tucker took his phone out of his pocket.

"Just a second, Dan, I want to call my security team."

They were having breakfast two blocks away from the yacht club at Middleton's Tavern, across the street from the Annapolis town dock better known as Ego Alley.

"Yes, Tucker?"

"Vin, we have a serious situation—kidnapping—it's a friend. I'm waiting on Sanjay to see if we can get a GPS position on the captive's location."

"Do you have an ID on the hostage?"

"Just a second, let me hand you over to Father Daniel Baronowski."

The priest took the phone and gave a detailed description of Monique.

Dan handed the phone back to Tucker. Vin was still on the phone.

"Hey, Tucker, we'll head back now, and let me know when Sanjay has the location."

"Roger that."

The pieces for the rescue operation were now set in motion. It was now time to find out what in the world was going on.

"All right, Father Dan Baronowski, why don't you tell me what is going on? And why no police? I'm sure you have your reasons. What is this thing they want?"

Rene, who was standing by the companionway and looking up to the top of the mast, turned toward the two men and said, "Yes, Father Daniel Baronowski, why don't you tell Mr. Finn your story."

As Dan was putting the Codex on the cockpit table, Tucker's phone rang—it was Sanjay.

"Hey, Tucker, turn the TV on. There is some messed up stuff going on in the Middle East, in the Persian Gulf off the coast of Iran—markets are freaking out. Looks like a Russian aircraft carrier, an Israeli destroyer and an American navy ship are in some kind of Mexican standoff."

Sanjay loved financial markets. On the ocean, he spent weeks writing code to help him trade stocks and commodities.

"How far away are you, Sanjay?"

"I'll be there in ten minutes."

"Okay, Sanjay, I'll check it out. See you in few minutes."

Tucker hated managing his money, and so he gave Sanjay a big chunk of his to look after. Dan was accustomed to Sanjay's financial updates.

Dan looked anxious. He had no idea what the phone call was about.

"Is there a problem? Does your friend think he can get a location on Monique?"

"He didn't call about that—he called about something else, some situation off the coast of Iran—Israel, Russia U.S. Navy. Sanjay said it's churning the world markets up pretty good."

Tucker picked up the Codex carefully. To Tucker, it looked like an antiquity—probably some priceless piece of rare art—kidnappings were always about money.

" This, I take it, is what the fuss is all about?"

Chapter 41:

June 13, 10:10 am - Annapolis, Md.
"D" Dock Aboard Pilar

Dan watched Tucker inspect the Codex De Rio Grande.

"Tucker, the people who have kidnapped Monique want what you are holding in your hand."

Tucker put the Codex back down on the table.

"What's keeping you from handing over the ransom? Sometimes it's just easier that way."

There was a long pause. Rene and Dan looked at each other. Rene then said, "Go for it Dan, tell Mr. Finn why you won't hand over the codex."

Dan explained everything as best he could - Fatima, conspiracies, secret letters, the Virgin Mary – the crisis of faith, but what really got Tucker's attention was that some people inside the Vatican believe the Pope is a fraud, a heretic and that the Catholic Church is in a state of apostasy.

"Dan, are you telling me that some people inside the Vatican think that an evil force—Satan—literally is somehow taking over the Vatican."

"I don't know, Tucker. Some people are absolutely certain of it. Is the Third Secret of Fatima about Satan ascending to the top? Who knows? Maybe, it's possible. I do know one thing, there are evil people in the Vatican who want that secret and are willing to commit murder to get it."

"So, Dan, how about you? Is the Church withholding something? Are they lying about Fatima and the third secret?"

"Tucker, I need to find the files. I want to free Monique; I want Rene to believe that there is a way out. I will let the Church decide. I need to get to the Basilica as soon as possible. The only way I see an end to all of this is to get the Fatima letter into the hands of people I trust, and one of those men is Cardinal Warwinka and he is here in Washington."

Tucker's security team– they were two of the best in the world - former Navy Seals, Vin and Susie, came down the dock, stepped on to the boat and told Tucker quietly, they would be prepared and to let them know when Sanjay had a location.

Chapter 42:

June 13, 11:00 am - Annapolis, Md.
Sanjay gets "Phreaky"

"Tucker, what's up?" Sanjay hopped on to Pilar.

Tucker quickly made introductions.

Sanjay glanced at Tucker with a slightly irritated look, turned towards Rene and Dan and reached out to shake their hands.

"Nice to meet you both."

Sanjay looked at Rene and smiled faintly, almost shyly. He was caught off guard by her beauty. But he recovered quickly.

"Where's that nice dog of yours, Rene. I was really hoping to see him. I miss dogs; it's nothing but fish and birds with Tucker. Other than a junk yard dog in Cape Town, I haven't seen a real pet in about a year."

Rene had to smile. Sanjay had that effect on people.

Tucker pulled on Sanjay's shirt.

"Sanjay, we have a very serious situation. Father Daniel and Rene have a friend who has been kidnapped."

"Right—sorry, Tucker; sorry, Rene, Father. Have the police been contacted?"

"No, Rene and Dan think we need to keep the police out of it for now. I learned my lesson in South America, so I agree."

Sanjay said, "With all due respect to everybody, but is this really your business, Tucker, seriously? Do you even know these people?"

"Fair enough, Sanjay—but I'm in. These folks need our help and I have agreed to help. Vin and Susie are gearing up. What we need is a little bit of your magic; we need to locate Monique Butare."

Sanjay took a moment to consider the ramifications if he agreed to help. Sanjay had a bad feeling, but Tucker never asked for anything. He trusted Tucker with his life. From the moment he walked onto Tucker's boat with a sea bag and a scopolamine patch stuck behind his ear, Sanjay's life began to change, and it had also been full of adventure. It was Tucker's only promise – adventure - and Tucker had kept his promise. They had shared so much together—exotic locations, laughs, friends, parties, boredom, sunsets and storms. Without Tucker badgering him to go, Sanjay knew he would have spent the next ten years of his life hanging out in a Silicon Valley cafeteria, counting his money, and figuring out a way to have sex. It was not until half way around the world, when Sanjay finally understood how much Tucker had done for him. Tucker Finn was the best friend he ever had. His friend now needed his help. Sanjay knew he would give Tucker his kidney, if he asked.

"Alright, Tucker, what do you need?"

"Sanjay, I need you to hack the phone that made the call to Rene. We need to know the location of that phone. You told me once that you could install a GPS onto any phone in the world."

"Okay, let's see what we can do. We need to get freaky now—with a PH - phone hacking, also known as 'phreaking'. Who has the number of the bad guys?"

Rene handed Sanjay his phone.

Sanjay dialed the last caller's number to a system and entered a PIN. He then was prompted to enter the area code and phone number of the people holding Monique and the number he wanted to be identified as calling from, which was again Monique's kidnappers. Within seconds Sanjay is listening to a voice message. Sanjay put it on speaker phone.

"See how easy it is."

Everybody's jaw dropped.

"I was able to get into the voice mail by tricking the mobile operator's equipment into registering the call as coming from the handset—basically pretending to be Monique's kidnappers. I have written a script using open-source telecom software and used a voice-over-IP provider that allows me to set caller ID. Any 15-year-old that knows how to write a simple script can find a VoIP provider that spoofs caller ID and set this up; now their phone is mine."

Sanjay banged away on the phone for a couple of minutes. Sanjay waited for a download to complete.

"Tucker, would you hand me a diet coke?"

Tucker quickly got to his feet and grabbed the drink out of the cooler and handed it to Sanjay. Sanjay took a big gulp then stared at the small screen.

"There, done; just downloaded a GPS App on to their phone. The dopes don't even know it. Let's see, Monique is at 225 Rippon Street SE, Washington, DC."

Rene blurted out, "That's Monique's house! They haven't moved her yet."

Tucker said, "That's a good thing. It means they are not concerned about counter measures."

Sanjay tossed the phone at Tucker and finished his drink.

Tucker caught the phone and said, "Rene and Dan, let's go brief Vin and Susie; it should not take them long to get organized. Monique's in DC, less than an hour away. I think my team can get there and have her out in about three hours. Rene, when the kidnappers text you or call, tell them you will do anything they say—but tell them because of the physical location of the Codex it will take a few hours to deliver the ransom back to their drop point, which I assume, will be in DC somewhere."

Rene looked at her watch.

"Monique's kidnappers will be calling back any minute."

With that bit of news, everybody in the cockpit momentarily went silent, all lost in their own thoughts; each considered their own private concerns.

Rene's phone rang. She followed Tucker's instructions. The Codex was to be dropped off in three hours at the Mandarin Oriental Hotel lobby in Washington, DC.

Chapter 43:

June 13, 11:30 am - Annapolis, Md.
Down the Bay at Fifty Knots

Vin and Susie were ready go in twenty minutes, and took off to DC.

As soon as a plan was in place to free Monique, there was nothing more for Dan to do, and he was anxious to get to the Basilica, and start looking for the Madonna Files.

With Dan heading to DC, Monique already there, and Vin and Susie on their way, Tucker wondered if he should be in DC as well.

"Dan, I think it would be best if we have a base of operation in Washington, DC; I would feel more comfortable with that. I am confident we will free Monique; the kidnappers won't know what hits them. But we should get her in a safe environment as soon as she is free. Also, with the boat in DC, you will have a safe place to get to, once you find the files. I have a boat that can get me to DC in two hours. Also, with the boat, we can stay connected. We'll have access to my server on Pilar. We may need those resources to help us hunt down the folks who are behind these kidnappings."

"All right, Tucker, but I need to get to the Basilica right away, I got to go now; it's about an hour from here. Why don't you take Rene with you and keep me posted on Monique. Rene, you have my cell number, right?"

Rene nodded.

Sanjay chimed in. "I have it as well, Father Dan—I downloaded all of Rene's contacts when I did my little trick." Sanjay glanced at his phone and pressed a key. "And you now have mine."

Sanjay looked down again and pressed another key. "And Tucker's."

Before Dan hopped off the boat, Rene walked over to Dan with her arm stretched out.

"Dan, you are forgetting one thing."

"What's that?"

"The Codex—if Monique is not out in three hours. It's over, Dan. They get what they want. I am giving them the Codex."

There was nothing more he could learn from the Codex—if the path ended at the chapel at the basilica, it was over—he would never find the file – not without more bloodshed. Dan handed the Codex to Rene and took off to the club house parking lot.

Rene turned around and grabbed a hold of Pilar's helm and shook it slightly, making a little noise to get Tucker's attention. She looked at Tucker with a wry smile.

Tucker said, "What?"

"You got another boat?"

Tucker returned Rene's grin with a shrug of the shoulders and his own impish smile.

"I like boats."

Tucker's "other" boat was the stunning Atlantic 54, drawn up by the Italian design firm, Azimut/Benetti. The boat had 1,600 horsepower and cruised at forty-five knots. With a swooping roof line and a long jutting bow, the fifty-four foot yacht, with a navy blue hull, named "Molly," was all power and beauty. Molly Finn was the name of Tucker's daughter who died in her mother's womb.

After gathering some items off of Dan's boat, including Luke, they made their way to Molly's dock, and Tucker fired up the engines as soon as they stepped on board. Sanjay handled the bow lines and Rene took the stern. Tucker turned around and watched Rene handle the lines.

"Rene, you're pretty handy with those lines. Took two ocean passages before Sanjay understood starboard meant the right side of the boat—not his right hand. I'm still not sure he can tie a bowline."

"I enjoy it, Tucker. I like spending time on boats, for sure—mostly sailboats—gets me out of myself."

"Right, understand that."

Tucker looked forward, then expertly maneuvered the boat out of the slip and powered up as soon as they passed the no wake zone.

Rene stood by the stern near the rear seating area, unsure of what to do next, or where to sit. Tucker looked back again and noticed Rene unsettled and looking around.

"Hey, Rene, come on up here; I think you will enjoy the view."

The driver's bench had room for three across. Sanjay was sitting up by Tucker and the middle seat was open.

Rene moved up to Sanjay and Tucker. Sanjay scooted over next to Tucker and Rene sat down on the end seat.

Rene looked towards the Chesapeake Bay Bridge, and said,

"Sorry to seem like such a duck out of water back there. I feel like I am on a spaceship. I don't know what to do. I am afraid to touch anything on this boat. By now, I am usually pulling on something, or I have my hand on a wheel."

Tucker goosed the throttle and opened her up, then scanned the horizon—the bay was quiet, calm, and almost empty.

"Here you go, Rene." Tucker stood up "Come and take the wheel. Sanjay, change seats, will you? Switch places with Rene."

Rene listened to the enormous engines. The speed and power and the displacement of huge amounts of water were intimidating.

"I don't know if that is such a good idea. I am very happy sitting right here."

"No, no, no, Rene. Please take the wheel. There is really nothing to it. It's like driving your dad's Buick. Also trust me, once you are comfortable at the helm you will be at ease with everything else on the boat."

Rene, Sanjay, and Tucker changed seats. Tucker took Rene's arms and helped her around him and got her situated behind the wheel.

Rene stood at the wheel with her backside up against the pilot seat. Tucker stood right beside her.

Rene spoke as she scanned the horizon.

"I can't believe we are already passing Tolly Point."

Rene made a little adjustment to port—slightly more east—and pointed the boat towards Thomas Point. Tucker noticed the slight change in direction.

"You know the Bay."

Rene looked over at Tucker.

"I like it out here."

Tucker looked at Rene and smiled. As Rene turned to check the horizon again looking for the next mark, Tucker kept looking at Rene; he didn't want to look away. He found he couldn't take his eyes off of her. He looked at her profile, her neck and cheeks. He noticed the slight muss of hair resting on her glasses. He thought about last night.

Rene looked back at Tucker and smiled warmly.

Her gentle smile and the tender look in her eyes made something jump inside of him. A powerful, unforgettable sensation rushed through him. Rene looked west towards the oncoming light house and adjusted her stance. More comfortable with the wheel, she stood up and moved slightly closer to Tucker. They were now standing side by side, nearly touching. The engines roared.

After passing Thomas Point, Rene turned the boat south. With the boat on course, they both settled in and peacefully watched the bow eat up the bay.

Molly hummed along at forty-five knots heading due south to Point Lookout—the north point of the mouth of the Potomac River. From there, they would hang a right and power to DC. Rene was getting comfortable with the sound and fury of sixteen hundred horsepower at full throttle.

Sanjay stood up and asked, "Anybody thirsty?"

The engines were loud and Sanjay asked again. Rene and Tucker were lost in their own thoughts.

"Okay, forget it." Sanjay went off to fetch some water for himself.

Chapter 44:

One hour later, after talking with Ben Dirkson, Pat Allen stormed into the President's office with four of his top aides in tow—an Admiral, two three stars, and a one star. Pat Allen had his plan in place.

"Mr. President, we have been going over options on the Arctic Mariner incident. I am recommending to you, Mr. President, if that ship's intentions are to dock in Abbas then we should allow that ship to dock at that port in Iran. Sir, that's a Russian flagged vessel and any illegal interference with the Arctic Mariner will be viewed as an act of international piracy by the Russian Government."

Pat's briefing on the Arctic Mariner incident was totally unexpected. The recommendation took the President by complete surprise.

"What are you saying, Pat? We just let that ship sail right into Iran with a payload of nuclear missiles? What, are you out of your mind?"

"That's exactly what I'm saying, sir. And no, sir, I am not out of my mind. We must get Israel and the Mosaad off the Arctic Mariner as soon as possible. We need to get the United States Navy to stand down, as well. We need that ship docked on Iranian soil. If Iran wants those nuclear missiles, then I say we let them have them. As soon as that ship docks in Iran our military forces will take swift and appropriate action to respond to that specific threat."

The President was dumbfounded. He surveyed the men with a slow, deliberate once over—then turned around and looked out towards the rose garden and the Washington Monument. What the hell are these guys thinking? Pat wants those missiles in Iran? They must have their reasons. He thought about the grueling election, his stump speech, his promise to the American people to get tough—it's what propelled him into the Oval Office. The President of the United States was swept into office to, once and for all, end Iran's saber rattling and nuclear threat. His republican rivals during the debates breathlessly promised to bomb Iran immediately. Hell, he remembered saying on TV, if he had the chance he would take out Iran as soon as the night's debate was finished. The President understood that the election came down to whom the American people trusted most to promptly wage a hot war against Iran.

The American people were not just ready for action—they were demanding it. The President had a mandate. The incumbent, his opponent, lost precisely because he was waiting for WMD's to appear like mushrooms in Iran before using military force. Well, bad luck for the incumbent because now the President had his in a gift-wrapped cargo ship.

As the President continued to look outside the Oval Office, towards the south lawn, he still thought Pat Allen was out of his flipping mind. But just as the words, "What are we supposed to do, let them unload the missiles right there at the dock as we stand by and watch," were set to tumble out of his mouth, a smirking grin came across the President's face. He looked at Pat Allen and playfully waved his pointing finger up and down like a father pretending to be mad at his son's rambunctious cleverness.

"Why you Wiley E. Coyote, you want to blow that ship up right there at the dock and unleash holy hell on those fanatics, including taking out their nuclear research facilities all across the country."

The NSC staff said nothing, understanding the President was thinking through the process.

The President directed his next question at the heavily decorated three star general.

"You really think this is prudent, Sam? Do you think this is the right course of action—letting that ship dock in Iran with nuclear bombs?"

"Yes we do, sir. I really do, and if I may speak frankly, Mr. President."

"Yes of course, by all means."

"Sir, from the first day you sat in this office, our meetings have been dominated by Iran—what to do with that existential threat. You know all this. We have looked at every option to find a peaceful diplomatic solution. We have asked ourselves, hundreds of times, how we can pressure Iran, militarily, economically and diplomatically, to get Iran to act responsibly—and we all know, now, that appeasement will not move Iran to end their efforts to get nuclear weapons. Economic sanctions will not, in any way, slow down Iran's drive to obtain nuclear capability."

"General, that I can agree with."

"Sir, if we stay the course with Iran—if we continue with sanctions and diplomacy, it is no longer if, but when, they become a nuclear power; at that point, our job gets that much tougher. With that ship docked in Iran, we will have what we did not have in Iraq. We will have the evidence the American people will demand to support an aggressive, perhaps prolonged, strike against Iran. We will have caught Iran red-handed, illegally smuggling into their country, weapons of mass destruction—WMD's. Mr. President, the United States military is fully prepared to engage the enemy in this type of operation. Strategic planning is highly evolved to meet precisely this contingency. We have prepared for this. We can move on this immediately."

The President paused and looked at his military advisors and at Pat Allen, again sizing them up.

"Here is what I am going to do. I am going to leave it up to you on how the United States should handle the Arctic Mariner. This is now a military operation and I am authorizing you to take action as you see fit. I trust you to make the right decision to protect this country and our allies. Now, Pat, we have one major problem. I have spoken with the Prime Minister of Israel, and I told him that we will not interfere with Israel's wish to get that boat to Haifa, so we are going to need to sort that out."

"Mr. President, I understand, Israel has notified us of their intentions to tow the Arctic Mariner to Haifa, but we strongly recommend against that course of action. With that ship in Israel, we don't know how Russia will respond—a lot of uncertainties, unforeseen consequences could emerge—and it could get dangerous."

"So what am I to tell the Prime Minister of Israel?"

"Sir, you know I am close to the Prime Minister of Israel. He's a very good friend. We go back a long way. He trusts me like a brother. He is very, very excited about the National Security team of this Administration. If I may, I would like to speak to him about our objectives, and I am confident that he will support the goals of the United States of America. Israel and the United States will stand together on this."

"Okay fine. Now, where is Russia on this? The State Department has reached out to Russia for information, but it has been very quiet.

"It's not entirely clear what the Russian response will be. We have reached out to them, as well, but we have not heard back. I don't think they have any idea what is on that ship. We believe they are in shock over the rumors that a Russian freighter may have smuggled missiles on board. It is pretty clear the Russian military is in lock down until they have a handle on what certainly must be viewed as a colossal crisis within. Sir, the Arctic Mariner is a rogue operation—probably Russian mafia. How they got the missiles, your guess is as good as mine. The Russian Government is going to be paralyzed by this in the short term. But it is urgent, as I said, that Israel and the United States back off the Arctic Mariner and let that ship get to Iran, to ensure that we do not appear to be interfering in Russia's international trade. I will be letting the Prime Minister of Israel know this, as soon as possible".

"Pat, I am not convinced Israel is going to feel comfortable taking the risk of letting that ship land in Iran with those missiles."

"Sir, I think it's important that we leave that ship alone, keep the Russian's out of it until the ship is in port. I'm very confident Israel will see it our way."

"Okay, Pat. You got your deal; you talk to the Prime Minister of Israel, and let's get that boat to Iran."

Chapter 45:

June 13, 12:00 pm - Chesapeake Bay
Molly Down Bay

As Molly was making her way down the Chesapeake Bay just south of the Patuxent River on her way to Washington, DC, Tucker Finn's phone rang. Tucker glanced at the incoming name. It was Pilar's, Captain - Tom Conway.

"What can I do for you, Capt'n Tom?"

"Tucker, we got to get Pilar down to Norfolk. Jabin's says there is a shipyard down there that's better equipped, with more capacity to do the work we need to get done. They have an opening right now. We have to pull her out of the water. You okay on Molly for a few days?"

"Yeah, we're good. Go ahead, do what you have to do."

Sanjay came up with three water bottles. He had been below in the cabin for about twenty minutes. Rene and Tucker were happy to take the chilled bottles.

"Thanks Sanjay."

Sanjay scanned the horizon to get his bearings. It was now second nature to him. Finally, he was getting a little salt in his blood.

"Hey, Tucker, I spent some time browsing the phone activity of the guy who has Monique and I stumbled upon something, and it doesn't sound good. I hacked into voice mail, and your friend's name came up. Professor Bob Baronowski, MIT."

Tucker put his water bottle down slowly.

All the good that was on the boat vanished—gone—overboard. At the sound of Bob's name, Rene's insides went numb and she collapsed in her seat.

Tucker grabbed the wheel.

"Sanjay, get Dan on the phone."

As the phone started to ring, Sanjay handed the phone to Tucker.

"Dan, call your brother. Tell him to get his family and leave town, immediately. He may be next; Sanjay connected the kidnappers to Bob."

Chapter 46:

June 13, 1:30 pm - Washington, DC
Idi Gets Religion

"Monique, I killed your mother. I may kill you today. I have a black heart, Monique. Forget about those times when I was a boy. Idi's head went back down. He glanced at her then quickly looked away.

Monique wondered if she saw tears in Idi's eyes.

"If you are sorry, Idi, why do you still do this?" She waved her taped wrists in the air.

"Ever since I came to America, it is all I know how to do. It is almost like I am in prison, but a prison I know I can run from...but I never do. I have nothing else here in America."

"How did you get out of Rwanda?"

"White men found me. They took me out of Rwanda, two white men. I don't know their names. I know nobody's name. It is the way it has always been since I arrived in America. After the genocide, I went to Goma—refugee camp. I was approached by the white men. They knew I had killed many. I was a tough guy. I had reputation. They were looking for real bad guys. They took me to a tent, and they showed me American dollars. One man wanted to talk to me alone. He was a big man, as big as me. He asked me to talk about my killing. He wanted me to describe everything, every detail, how many strikes with the machete? Did I go for the head at first, or did I hit the body first then cut the head? What did the dying plead for? Did they cry out for God? Did they call for Jesus? We talked for a long time. I told him everything and he showed me a lot of money. He was a crazy white man, that's for sure. He wanted my shirt. He asked me if the blood of the men I killed was on the shirt. I said it was. I gave him the shirt. He gave me more money."

Monique could not believe what she was hearing.

"After that meeting, the other men took me to a helicopter, then a truck with different men. They had money, too. Finally they put me on a plane to America. One man stayed with me and took me to an apartment in New York, in Harlem. I spoke a little English. They gave me very careful instructions. If I did not follow them strictly, they said they would kill me. They told me I should have no friends. They gave me prostitutes. After the man left, I never saw him again. He only calls now. In New York, right away, I dressed nice, I have money, clothes, and after one month I get a call. They want me to kill a man. They want me to kill a friend of a famous rapper or something. I go to nightclub and killed him, just shot him at the bar, and then I disappear. Nobody knows me. Many nights I want to just kill myself, Monique. There is nothing for me in this world. But I wake up each morning and I go first to my door to see if the money has come. The money always comes. Now they want me to hold you. My job is to hold you until they tell me to kill you or let you go. It is what I do, I suppose. I know no other life. It's a small world, I guess, that I am here with you today."

Monique let his words settle into the air, and with her taped hands, she tapped her knuckles on the coffee table to get Idi's attention. She also wanted to connect with Idi's eyes.

She stared at Idi until he looked her square in the eye; then she startled him with her words.

"I forgive you."

Idi looked at Monique with a very puzzled look.

"Monique, what are you saying?"

"Idi, I forgive you. I forgive you for what you did to my family. I don't excuse you, but I forgive you."

"Monique, that is impossible."

"Idi, I leaned something very important a long time ago that it was the only way, the only way I could live with myself."

"What is the only way, I don't understand?"

"For so long, all I wanted to do was strike back. I wanted to only hurt the one's that killed my family, but one night—in prayer—I don't know how to explain it. It was a feeling, but it was real. I felt a presence in my room and when I got to the words in the 'Our Father,' '...forgive those who trespass against us,' the presence became so powerful I was nearly overcome with an unusual sensation of peace and understanding. I felt free, and as I continued with the prayer, it seemed like He—Our Lord—was quietly saying the words along with me. I felt as if Jesus Christ was in the room with me and we were praying together. The moment passed very quickly but from that point I knew, in my heart, what forgiveness really means. Jesus Christ wants us to forgive. He wants us to 'forgive those who trespass against us.' Without that, there can never be any peace. In many ways, the act of forgiveness is at the heart of our Savior's ministry. I knew, right then, we cannot take a vengeful heart with us to heaven. This is something I know. It is why I forgive. This is what I learned that night. Now will you do something for me, Idi Kambana?"

Idi, was dumbfounded. Monique Butare wanted to forgive him?

Idi stared at Monique with the same puzzled look on his face. He could barely register her words.

"Idi, will you do something for me?"

"Yeah, yeah, sure, what is it?"

"Will you pray with me?"

"Pray?"

"Yes, I want you to pray with me, right now."

Monique slipped out of the chair and dropped to her knees.

"I want us both to pray to our Lord Jesus Christ. I want us to pray—from the heart, Idi. Pray for him to forgive our sins. Can you do that, Idi—can you say, 'Jesus please, please forgive me for my sins.'"

Idi wasn't sure what to do and gave Monique a confused look.

"There is no God that will have me."

"Here, Idi, get down like this, like me on your knees. Now, Idi, say it from your heart, say 'Jesus please forgive my sins.' Please ask him to forgive your sins with all your heart."

Idi got down on his knees and clasped his hands in prayer.

Idi began to move his lips. Idi bowed his head and continued to pray. After about a minute, he looked up to a fixed point on the ceiling, and Monique noticed his eyes were full of tears—his eyes were like a dam ready to burst. Tears started coming down Idi's cheeks. His face seemed to contort as if in pain—tears and agony overcame Idi Kambana, and the look on his face almost broke Monique's heart.

Idi's phone rang; it startled them both and it broke the silence. Idi let it ring three times. Idi slowly composed himself. It was the call he had been told to wait for. As he put the phone to his ear, Vin Conway crashed through the living room window—Tucker's security team was storming the house. Susie kicked the front door open. Vin and Susie had a gun on both of Idi's temples before he could take the phone away from his ear.

"Don't kill him!" Monique shouted.

Vin Conway, with the gun still on Idi's temple, took a mobile phone out of his pocket and pressed 'end.' Before heading to DC, in Annapolis, Sanjay had installed Idi's phone number into Vin Conway's cell phone.

Chapter 47:

June 13, 2:00 pm - I-95 Near Baltimore
Alexi Heading South

Nicholas Alexi handed the toll booth operator $2.50. Francis Scott Key tunnel was the last toll that he would have to pay before reaching Washington, DC. Alexi wrote the dollar figure in a notepad he had placed on the center console of his 2006 Dodge Caravan. $2.50 at the Baltimore tunnels, $5 on the JFK Highway, $3 on the Delaware Turnpike, $8.50 on the New Jersey Turnpike, and $13.50 at George Washington Bridge. He stopped reading the notepad; the grim demands from the toll booth operators disturbed him. He looked at his watch—about another hour before he was in DC. Alexi looked at the radio, six hours of traffic and weather, buzzed in his ear. He had had enough. He turned the CD player on.

"Mama Mia there you go again, my, my." The song brought a small smile to Alexi's face, and he started to sing. But Alexi did not really sing the lyrics, but rather he spoke the English line with a thick Russian accent in a hushed monotone voice. It was the only line in the song he knew. He waited in silence for the chorus to return, "Mama Mia there you go again my, my," and again the small smile returned, as did his murmuring. Near the end of the song, he placed his finger on the replay button, and at the last note, he pressed down to start the song all over again. Nicholas Alexi, ex-KGB hitman, weapons dealer, and militant atheist, was a huge Abba fan. The song made him happy and the communist atheist was also in a good mood, because he was very much looking forward to his next assignment.

As Alexi got off the Baltimore-Washington Parkway and onto New York Avenue, he noticed the traffic was thicker than he expected—even for rush hour. He checked the clock on the dash. He had a five o'clock appointment to keep at Catholic University, and he was running a little late.

Chapter 48:

June 13, 2:00 pm - Washington, DC
Monique's House

Vin and Susie could not believe what they were hearing. The kidnapper wanted to help find the people behind the kidnapping; and Monique Butare, the victim, thought it was a good idea.

"Tucker, I have a situation here. After we told Monique that Father Daniel was the reason she had been kidnapped and that her friend Rene had been attacked as well, she kind of went into shock. Initially she thought her capture was some kind of bizarre Rwandan revenge job, but now she thinks the kidnapper is honestly willing to help find who is behind all the abductions—if it will help Father Daniel and Rene. She is adamant; in fact, she won't press charges. She says that before we turn this guy over to the police, we should seek his help."

Tucker considered Vin's briefing.

"What do you think Vin—is he dangerous?"

"He is a big dude, Tucker, so I don't know, but she seems to trust him, and I am getting a pretty good vibe—so is Susie—and honestly, to get an opportunity like this—an inside guy who wants to cooperate is rare; should be helpful."

"I agree; let's bring him to the boat before we turn him over to the cops, and find out what he knows. We will be pulling into the dock at the Gangplank marina in a few minutes—you know the spot.

"Roger that, Tucker, see you there."

Chapter 49:

As Molly eased into her slip at the Gangplank marina in Southwest, Washington, DC, Vin, Susie, Monique and Idi were making their way down the dock.

The quiet marina sat next to the bustling fish market known by all DC residents simply as "Maine Avenue."

Monique set aside pleasantries, permissions to come aboard, and introductions, and jumped onto Tucker's boat and into Rene's arms as soon as she saw her. Monique and Rene hugged tightly and went below to talk. Vin insisted Idi be restrained with an ankle brace attached to the dinette table pedestal. No objections from Idi. Sanjay asked for Idi's phone.

Tucker sat down at the dinette set across from Idi. With everybody settled, Tucker, Susie, and Vin began to interview Idi; Sanjay banged away hacking Idi's phone. But Sanjay was quickly stymied—other than Idi's contact point, there were no leads beyond that—sophisticated encryption software was in place. Sanjay traced the guys pulling Idi's strings to Russia, then the trail went cold. Whoever was on the other end of the line when he called Idi was more than ready for the Sanjay Singhs of the world. The guys in Russia were probably world class hackers.

Tucker asked the first question.

"Who do you work for, Idi Kambana?"

"Please forgive me if I sound difficult, but I don't know."

"When you are paid, the check that you get—is anything on that that could help identify who you work for?"

"They pay me in cash. I told all this to Monique. I came to America from Rwanda, but only on the first days did I meet anyone. He was the man who I did some work for in Goma. I do not know who I work for here in America."

"When you were in Rwanda, how did the men, who brought you to America, find you?"

"I worked delivering food to the refugees. I made sure nobody messed with the trucks. The boss of the delivery company, a white man, he made the arrangements to get me out of Goma."

"Idi, do you remember who that man was? Do you remember his name?"

"I don't know."

"Think, Idi. Can you remember anything about him?"

"I know that he was an American. He was very clever. I do remember hearing his name a few times, but he always changed it when he met new people. So I don't know. He had many names, now that I think about it. I asked one time why his name was always different. He looked at me like he wanted to kill me. He just said it is safer that way."

Sanjay put Idi's phone down; he had been half paying attention to the conversation, but now Sanjay had his own questions to ask.

"Dude, you said you worked delivering food to the refugees. Do you remember the name of that company?"

"Yes, yes, I do." Idi smiled "The name of the company always made the white man laugh- The company was called 'Lessor Reputations' and it had big letters at the end—I, N, C. The trucks all had the name, 'Lessor Reputations, Inc.' painted on them."

"When did you work for the Americans?"

"The year of the genocide—never forget that year - 1994."

Sanjay snapped his fingers and pulled out his laptop that he kept near him at all times. "Goma, right? You worked in Goma in 1994? I take it there were other contractors in the camp, probably U.N. The French were very involved in assisting the refugees. Rwanda was, at one time, a French colony."

"That's right; the French were very involved in the refugee camps."

Sanjay went to work and Googled, Lessor Reputations, Inc.—nothing—then he Googled, "Rwanda genocide French contractors."

The name, Médecins Sans Frontières, came up to the top of the page.

"Tucker, I am going down below, this may take a little time, but I'm thinking 'Lessor Reputations, Inc.' was a subcontractor to Médecins Sans Frontières, there may be some data at Médecins Sans Frontières that can give us some information on Idi's employer. I need to get into their servers; maybe I can get some names."

Chapter 50:

The Prime Minister of Israel was beside himself.

"Our men are not getting off the Arctic Mariner, that's all there is to it, Pat. The Israeli navy is taking that ship to Haifa."

"Mr. Prime Minister, you are going to have to trust the United States on this. It would benefit us all greatly if we get that ship docked in Iran. The United States of America gives you her word that we will strike immediately. The missiles will never leave that ship. WMD's on Iranian soil, imported illegally, will pose a direct and immediate threat to the United States of America. The world will be outraged, and the crisis will give us the political cover to attack, and destroy, Iran's military and nuclear capabilities once and for all. We are going to blow them back to Kingdom Come."

"Pat, I get it, but you can attack Iran's defense without letting those missiles into Iran. We have the boat and the evidence; you have all you need to launch an attack. The American people will support you one hundred percent. I don't need to tell you that."

"Sir, we are concerned that Russia will intervene. It is a Russian ship, and we are very concerned the seizure of the Arctic Mariner will be viewed as an international act of piracy. The press is already calling your boarding of the Arctic Mariner an act of piracy, and we have word that a Russian aircraft carrier has changed direction and is steaming towards the Mariner at attack speed."

"Pat, we have diplomatic contacts in Russia; we think we can work this out."

Pat Allen was surprised and upset that the Israeli Prime Minister was pushing back, resisting his efforts to confront Iran on the terms he set out. Pat had his plan in place and was in no mood to negotiate with Israel on compromises. The President did not hire him to write bold speeches. The President of the United States hired Pat Allen to take action—to implement the President's vision for a safe and secure America, employing the extraordinary capabilities of the greatest armed forces in the history of the world.

"Sir, I am going to give you ten minutes to think it over. You take your men off that boat or we are going to send our men in to do it for you. This is our mission now. That boat is going to Iran, Mr. Prime Minister. This is what the President wants, Sir."

"Pat, my men are not getting off that boat. I am not going along with your cowboy stunt, and I am going to call the President, myself, to let him know what I think of your idea."

"Sir, as head of National Security Council of the United States of America, I have advised the President that Israeli action will be construed as an act of piracy by the world, and Russia, which could lead to unforeseen consequences, perhaps events that we cannot control. Call the President, Mr. Prime Minister, it is your right, but he is going to take the recommendation of the NSC and the leaders of the United States Armed forces. We value the State of Israel as our most loyal and trustworthy ally in the Middle East, but we do not need its help to defend our country. Those missiles are a threat to the United States of America as much as they are a threat to you. This is our show now. You get your men to stand down."

The Israeli Prime Minister decided to call Pat's bluff. The Prime Minister didn't believe, in the end, the United Sates Navy would intervene in the Israeli operation and force Israeli officers off the ship at gun point.

"Pat, I am sorry. As the leader of Israel, I simply cannot take the risk and let that boat dock in Iran, not with nuclear arms on board. We have the boat secured and we are going to continue our efforts to get the Arctic Mariner to Haifa."

"If you don't have your men stand down, Mr. Prime Minister, I am going to order the US Navy to take control of the Arctic Mariner and I am going to let the Russians know that Israel has made an unauthorized boarding. We are going to enforce the United Nations Convention on the

Law of the Sea. Israel is violating the rights of nations in their use of the world's oceans. Mr. Prime Minister, I will give the order in fifteen minutes."

Chapter 51:

June 13, 1:00 pm - Washington, DC
The Basilica

The Basilica was almost empty: a smattering of tourists, a few homeless men and women joined forces in the pews with a handful of faithful who were busy working their Rosary beads and quietly moving their lips in prayer.

Carrying a light weight briefcase, Dan headed directly to the chaplet of 'Our Lady of Guadalupe.' After rounding an enormous Romanesque column standing eighty feet tall, he turned left and fifty feet ahead was the chapel dedicated to 'Our Lady of Guadalupe'. As he moved closer to the painting, he saw the beautiful frescos that covered the walls. At the end of the chapel was the portrait of 'Our Lady of Guadalupe'.

Dan was nearly inside the chaplet when he heard his name.

"Father Baronowski, is that you?"

At a football stadium in Foxboro, Massachusetts, Father Dan Baronowski was just another anonymous fan rooting for his team, but at the Basilica of the National Shrine of the Immaculate Conception, he was an NFL starting quarterback. Nearly every priest in the world had read Dan's text book on discerning Marian apparitions. It was required reading for all clerics who worked at the Basilica. In his small world, he was a rock star.

Dan reached up and ran his fingers along his white collar then admonished himself for being so dumb and careless. Often, wearing the collar helped him cut through red tape. He found clerks and bureaucrats were much more helpful when he wore his collar. He might have felt silly putting on a disguise before heading to DC, but now he felt like a fool. Dan slowly turned around towards the voice.

The young priest quickly walked towards Dan.

"Father Daniel Baronowski, what a great surprise to see you here at the Basilica. You should have called, we would be happy to give you a private tour."

The young priest extended his hand.

"I'm Father Frank Labas."

Dan nervously reached out and took the friendly priest's hand.

"Nice to see you, Father Labas."

"Father Baronowski, I work in the director's office. I am the administrative assistant to Monsignor Fuentes and I can tell you, right now, Monsignor Fuentes would be thrilled to meet you. He would have my head if he knew there was a visitor from the Vatican and I didn't make an effort to bring him by for a quick introduction. Do you have some time, today? The Monsignor is free in about an hour."

"Possibly. Right now I'm doing a little site seeing, little research, and I was headed to the bookstore in a little bit. I have lunch plans, but let me see what I can do. Can I call you in about fifteen minutes?"

Dan slowly turned away from the priest and looked at the painting of 'Our Lady of Guadalupe' in the chaplet. It was large. If he didn't see what he was looking for on the front, he would have to look behind the painting. In that case the painting would have to come down; he would need help, and of course, he would have to inform the Basilica's staff.

Dan turned back around and faced Father Labas, who was pulling a business card out of his wallet.

"Here you go. Please call me, Monsignor Fuentes would love to meet with you."

Father Labas, who was facing the chaplet, handed his card to Dan, then took a long look at the portrait.

"She is beautiful isn't she, Father Baronowski?"

"Yes, indeed, she is very beautiful."

It now dawned on the priest that perhaps he had been a bit intrusive. Perhaps Father Baronowski only came to the Basilica to quietly pray.

"Sorry for the interruption, Father. I will leave you with your prayers. Please let me know if there is anything I can do for you."

Father Frank Labas started walking away.

Dan looked back at the large painting hanging on the wall then started walking backwards towards Father Labas.

"Hey, Frank, just a minute. Maybe there is something you can do for me."

Dan took a business card out from his wallet.

Frank turned around and took Dan's business card.

"Sure thing."

"I'm actually here on official business for the Congregation for the Doctrine of Faith—the CDF. I'm on assignment for the Vatican. I would have called, but the investigation is extremely sensitive; I have been instructed to keep my research quiet. But, here is the deal; I may need help with that painting of 'Our Lady of Guadalupe', right there. I need to examine it carefully, and I may need to take it down and have a closer look. Perhaps you could give me a hand?"

Father Labas looked at the business card. Frank Labas smiled. CDF, Catholic spooks—sure beat ordering light bulbs.

"You bet, Dan. I think we can handle the portrait ourselves, but let me call some security, maybe they can be of help. I will need them to close this chapel anyway, while we take the painting down."

Dan gave it some thought. He was paranoid, but he still believed he was a needle in a haystack. Who would know that Dan Baronowski was rooting around at the National Shrine looking for the "Third Secret of Fatima"—it would be so random if his enemies walked in. Frank's help would also quicken the pace. He wanted to get in and get out as fast as possible. He felt exposed and vulnerable inside the cavernous Basilica.

"Sure thing, Frank."

Dan walked over to the portrait and examined the painting closely. The security team of two, thankfully, arrived quickly and after they set up the crowd control stanchions, Frank and Dan took down the painting.

Dan saw nothing out of the ordinary on the front, then turned the painting around. There was a date and it looked like a person's signature. He saw something that stood apart from the obligatory identification data. In the lower left hand corner there were three words written in hand script: "The Last Tiara." Nothing more—that's all it said. Dan's stomach sank.

"That's it,—The Last Tiara." Was it another clue to the riddle? Would he have to start over? He thought of the riddle, and thought of the "last one buried." Was there a connection?

Hey, Dan, look at that. This painting has not been taken off the wall in a few years, but when I took it down last to clean it, I don't remember seeing that little scribble. You see, Dan, right there? That wasn't there before. It says "The Last Tiara." Is that what you are looking for?"

Dan wasn't sure what to say.

"Perhaps, Frank. Let me take a picture of it with my phone—I'll check with the Vatican. They don't tell me everything. Sometimes it's on a need-to-know basis with Rome."

"I'll bet."

"You say those words were not on the painting last time you took it down. Does it mean anything to you—the words?"

"Sure, absolutely. It's here."

"What? What do you mean it's here?"

"It's the Papal Tiara—the last Papal Tiara, in fact. It's a very popular exhibit, here. It's in the crypt down stairs. Pope Paul VI, at his coronation, refused to wear the crown—he left it on the steps at St. Peter's, after declaring that it was a symbol of pride. The Pope thought that the Papal Tiara was not in conformity with the humble ideals of Vatican II. The Pope's refusal to wear the crown upset a lot of traditionalists in the Church, by the way. After a succession of Popes refused to wear the Tiara, the Vatican put the crown up for sale, and we acted quickly. With our help, Catholics in the United States raised the money to buy it, then donated it back to the Basilica. The Papal Tiara is on permanent display downstairs in Memorial Hall down in the crypt along with the stole that Pope John XXIII wore at the opening of the Second Vatican Council. You know, it's the last crown a Pope ever wore. Ever since the passage of the Vatican II council, every Pope since Paul VI has refused to be crowned with the Tiara."

Father Labas's phone rang.

"Monsignor Fuentes, yes, of course, I'll tend to that right away sir. Monsignor, I was just going to call you, I have with me a distinguished guest with us here today, Father Daniel Baronowki, the great friend of Our Lady. He's come in from Rome; he is a Consular at the CDF."

Dan went cold.

Monsignor Fuentes paused on the other end of the line.

"Father Baronowski, you say, from Rome? Consular at the CDF?"

Monsignor Fuentes had heard the name, and had heard nothing good about Father Baronowski. He knew Baronowski was working on the investigation of Medjugorje; he had also heard rumors of hidden documents that were in his possession. His close associates in Rome had warned him that Father Baronowski was far too attached to Medjugorje—he was not to be trusted.   As Director of the Basilica, Monsignor Fuentes despised unapproved apparitions of the Virgin Mary, and he ruthlessly attacked any of his employees if they talked favorably of Medjugorje, or any other unapproved apparition of the Blessed Mother. Talk of unapproved apparitions only diluted the beauty and special character of the exhibits that were on display at his Basilica.

Monsignor Fuentes was highly suspicious of Father Baronowski's sudden and unannounced visit into his Basilica— the grandest cathedral in the world dedicated to the Mother of Jesus Christ, and he was determined to learn more about his visit.

"Father Labas, please invite Father Baronowski up to my office. It would be ungracious if our community here at the National Shrine did not warmly welcome our prominent guest from Rome. I will see him directly, and we will have a special guest with us: Bishop Cilic, he is here on a visit from Poland."

Father Labas hung up the phone.

"Great news, Dan. Monsignor Fuentes can see you right away. How about it? Do you have time to see him now?"

Father Baronowski was now completely uncomfortable. What to do now? He knew where the file was; he was certain the files were in the Papal Tiara exhibit. He was so close. Dan first thought about telling Frank Labas everything; he liked him, he felt he could trust him. But it would put Frank's life in danger; he was through with that. He would have to take his chances with the Monsignor. What was the likelihood he would run into somebody who was looking for him?

"Sure, I would be happy to meet the Monsignor, but I am on a very tight schedule. Rome wants me to inspect that exhibit and report to them as soon as possible."

"No problem, Dan, the Monsignor has a packed schedule himself today. I'll let security know that we want access to the Papal Tiara exhibit. We'll have a quick chat and head right back down to the crypt. Everything should be ready for your inspection, as soon as we finish our visit."

"Thanks."

Dan's phone rang inside his jacket. Dan crossed his fingers, hoping for good news.

Rene wanted to tell Dan herself.

"Dan, Monique is safe. Tucker's team got her out.

Dan's legs went wobbly—he was overcome with relief.

"Oh, Rene, that's unbelievable news. Thank God…Thank Tucker, Vin, and Susie. Oh my God, I am so thankful."

"Dan, have you found the files?"

"No, not yet."

Dan looked at Frank.

"Rene, I am heading to a meeting right now, but the Basilica is spectacular. I'll call you when I'm done."

Chapter 52:

Dan, Father Labas, Monsignor Fuentes, and Bishop Cilic—an old friend of Pope John Paul II—sat down at a small dining table in the Monsignor's office. Lunch was on its way.

"So, Father Labas tells me you are with the Congregation for the Doctrine of Faith."

"Yes, Monsignor, I have shifted roles recently, the work is similar but I am indeed now with the CDF. I had been with the Congregation for the Causes of Saints; I was very involved with Pope John Paul II's canonization, but now I have a slightly different role."

"Please, Father Baronowski; excuse me, but may I see some credentials. It is highly irregular for clergy to come from the Vatican, unannounced, to my Basilica. I'm sorry for this, but it is my duty."

"Sure, no problem, I understand."

Dan handed Monsignor his business card and his Vatican ID.

Monsignor Fuentes examined the materials carefully.

"So how is Cardinal Esposito?"

"He is doing well, sir, seventy-eight years old, and he can still run circles around all of us intellectually, and you should see him stroll through the gardens—nobody can keep up with him on a walk."

"Yes indeed he is a remarkable man—excellent to hear about his health. So, Father Daniel, what brings you to our wonderful Basilica on this fine June day?"

Dan then did something that did not come easy, but it was too dangerous, he was too close to getting what he needed— he lied, sort of. He told the Monsignor that he was doing some work on the Vatican investigation of Medjugorje. In a way, it wasn't a complete lie. Medjugorje,

Fatima, the secrets—they all were woven together. Pope John Paul II had alluded to the idea that Medjugorje is the fulfillment of Fatima.

"Medjugorje?"

Monsignor Fuentes glanced at Father Labas, sighed, and paused. Dan knew what was coming next. He was almost thankful. The word Medjugorje stirred strong emotions. The Monsignor may not be cooperative, but he would no longer be suspicious of his intentions to show up at the Basilica without calling ahead.

Dan thought of Randall Sullivan, author and journalist, who spent a lot of time in the Vatican writing an exhaustive book on how the Church investigates Marian apparitions including Medjugorje. Sullivan's prescient words from the book "Miracle Detective" came to mind:

"There is no single word I discovered that so instantly could produce a rapturous smile, a derisive snort, or an uncomfortable silence in the Vatican as "Medjugorje." What fascinated me was that those that extolled Medjugorje as a place of sacred virtue of unparalleled power all had made pilgrimages to experience the village first hand while those who scoffed knew only what they had read or heard. The priests inclined to dismiss reports of miracles at Medjugorje (first as an insult to their intelligence and second as an embarrassment to the church) all seemed curiously muted."

Curiously muted. Dan loved that description, and he would slip the phrase in when certain priests, ignorant of the facts of Medjugorje, would challenge his investigation.

"Father Daniel, this thing you call Medjugorje," the Monsignor spat the word out with contempt, "is an unapproved apparition of the Blessed Mother, and we have no place for such silly signs and wonders at the Basilica. I am sorry you have come to our shrine; we will have nothing here for you. Perhaps you should have called ahead and saved yourself the inconvenience. The Basilica only honors apparitions of the Blessed Mother that have been approved by the Catholic Church."

"Yes, I understand, but as the Holy See continues its investigation into Medjugorje, I have been asked to look into Medjugorje to see if a unity exists with other Church approved apparitions."

The Monsignor ignored Father Barownowski's words. It seemed as if the Monsignor had been waiting to unload his piece of mind. Like a cobra, Father. Fuentes was ready to bite.

"Father Baronowski, what troubles me about Medjugorje is that there has been a grave act of disobedience against the local Bishop of Mostar. The Bishop has sole authority over such matters, yet his desires are being ignored. This is what you should concern yourself with. For centuries, the Church has assigned jurisdiction for discerning matters of the supernatural to the local bishop and the local bishop alone. This policy has severed the Church well. The local bishop wants Medjugorje condemned, and because of this the Church should abide by his ruling. I should think this is where the Vatican stands on the matter."

"Sir, it would be difficult to condemn Medjugorje now—the Vatican has not finished its work. I am sure you are aware of this. There is a danger to the Church if we act irrationally."

"We already face dangers. The dangers are obvious to many of my colleagues. We can no longer wait. Medjugorje is out of our control. We need to condemn Medjugorje now, before the movement grows further. Today, too many believe, too many of our young seminarians say they come to the vocation only because of Medjugorje. The Bishop of Austria has said he would have to close his seminary, if not for Medjugorje."

Father Dan had heard it all before—a hundred times—but he decided to engage the Director of the Basilica.

"With all due respect, Monsignor, please understand your point of view. You complain because the Seminaries are full? Also understand confessional lines are long, in many places around the world, because of Medjugorje. Medjugorje is known as the 'Confessional for the World.' Our own Archbishop of Split, has said, 'The Queen of Peace of Medjugorje has done more in six years of apparitions than we bishops, in forty years of pastoral work.' It is known the world over that people convert at Medjugorje, Monsignor Fuentes—this is an indisputable fact that Rome has taken notice of. Jesus Christ himself said 'By the fruits you shall know them.'"

Monsignor rolled his eyes and his tone became sharper.

"Father Baronowski, in my opinion the fruits of Medjugorje come from something else—not from the Blessed Mother—I have heard the devil has his hand in Medjugorje, that it is diabolical. This is what I have been told by experts, and you can take my input back to the Holy Father. It is Satanic—I am sure of it. What you say here today only deepens my conviction. You say we should only look to the good fruits of Medjugorje, but it is the children the priests follow, the so-called visionaries. This is not acceptable—enough of these children. These six, you say we simply turn the Catholic Church over to them—do as they say? They, who are uneducated, married, and not consecrated into the Church, you say they are to lead our Church into the next millennium? How can you not see the danger in all of this? You say approve the hoax because of the good fruits. You say because our seminaries are filled with fools we must not condemn the fraud."

Dan's blood started to boil. After the Monsignor called young priests fools, he lost his cool.

"Monsignor Fuentes, I will not have you speak of our young men called to God, ordained by the Catholic Church, as fools. Monsignor Fuentes, the history of our Church has taught us not to dismiss children because they lack privilege or education and I can assure you, consecration into our Church is not a prerequisite to speak on behalf of God or the Blessed Mother. Look at history. Joan of Arc—a young peasant who led the French army to victory—was killed by a Catholic Bishop because she refused to deny her visions from heaven. She was later made a Catholic Saint. Was it not peasant children of Fatima who even today deepen the faith of so many in our Church? At Lourdes was it not a child who the Blessed Mother spoke to and is it not this child who still calls millions each year to renew their faith and to seek salvation through Jesus Christ. Be careful when you criticize the visionaries for their simplicity and lack of sophistication. It is the height of arrogance to presume the proper intentions of God."

Both men were now nearly shouting at each other.

"The Bishop who controls Medjugorje has spoken, Father

Baronowski! Listen to him and not to the children! He seeks condemnation of the apparitions. That is what we have lost sight of."

"Monsignor, the Vatican—and only the Vatican—will decide what is to be done with Medjugorje. I have been tasked with investigating these events by my authorities, to whom I am bound in obedience. The Church seeks to find the truth, we need to discern. The Vatican must be careful in this work."

The Monsignor snapped bitterly.

"The Truth? The truth is Medjugorje is a Devil's snare! Medjugorje is the Diablos—The Divider. Look at our Church—the schism has begun."

The conversation paused, an uncomfortable quiet dominated the room—then an unexpected movement was sensed. The elderly Bishop, who had sat quietly throughout, began to stir in his chair and all eyes turned towards him. The friend of Pope John Paul II was ready to talk.

Bishop Cilic was revered, respected, and possessed a deep spiritual energy that moved even the most secular, worldly priests. He had spent time in East European concentration camps for the crime of being a priest. The Bishop had been a victim and a witness to the evil of atheist totalitarian regimes. The Bishop was a man of few words and was universally respected.

The Bishop cleared his throat.

"Monsignor Fuentes, some years ago I was asked by a young priest—a journalist—if I believed in the truth of the apparitions at Medjugorje, or does it come from the devil? I told the young man I had been taught by the Jesuits that there are three ways to discern spirits—spirits can be human, they can be divine, or they can be diabolic. I had discussed Medjugorje at length with the young priest and we agreed that Medjugorje was difficult to explain from a man-made point of view—evidence of fraud or hoax to explain Medjugorje was nonexistent. So then we considered if Medjugorje could be of a diabolical nature. I asked him what happens during confession. He understood, of course, the priest who is taking confession is delivering the sinner directly away from the devil. Now, we know that today, Medjugorje is considered the 'confessional of the world.' Monsignor Fuentes, let me say to you, what I said to the young priest—of course,

Satan is adept of many things, but he is not capable of one thing, and that is for Satan to have people to go to confession in order to be delivered precisely from him. So you see, Monsignor Fuentes, the only cause remains in God. And so please understand two points about Medjugorje—one, the good fruits are undisputable; and two, the determination of Medjugorje has been placed in the competent hands of the Vatican—and so any condemnation of Medjugorje is disobedient to the Pope, who is our final authority—and so please see to it that you are prudent in your affairs regarding Medjugorje."

Bishop Cilic finished his lecture, then, abruptly, he stood up to leave. Monsignor Fuentes' tone and bias had upset the Bishop. As the Bishop was leaving, lunch was brought into the room. Dan stood to shake the Bishop's hand. Dan then turned to Monsignor Fuentes, who was still sitting behind his desk.

"Monsignor, I have a meeting with Cardinal Warwinka later this evening. It is critical that I have access to the Papal Tiara exhibit. There are possible items of interest for the Vatican within that exhibit that I must return to Rome. I would like to have a look at that display, sir—as soon as possible."

Without looking at Father Baronowski, the Monsignor spoke to Father Labas.

"Father Labas, see to it that Father Baronowski has what he needs. Good day, Father Baronowski."

"Thank you, Monsignor Fuentes, for your help in this vital matter."

Dan reached into the basket of sandwiches and pulled out a tuna fish wrap and held it up towards the Monsignor. Dan had not eaten all day.

"Help yourself, Father Baronowski."

Chapter 53:

June 13, 12:10 pm - Washington, DC
The White House and Russia

The Russian aircraft carrier, Admiral Kuznetsov, made its way up the Persian Gulf as the United States destroyer, the USS Mason, neared the Arctic Mariner. The Russian cargo ship was drifting eighty miles outside of Iranian waters. The INS Hanit, a Sa'ar 5-class corvette, an Israeli Navy destroyer, ten hours earlier, had taken command of the Russian freighter and was now making preparations to take the ship to the Israeli port at Haifa. Iran authorities, in statements to Al Jazeera, declared that any unauthorized ship in its sovereign waters would be immediately destroyed by its Qhader missiles, Iran's most potent long range land to sea missiles.

As the Russian aircraft carrier closed in on the Arctic Mariner, the President of the United States called Vladimir Putin to explain to the Russian President that nuclear weapons had been discovered on the freighter and the United States viewed the illegal action as an act of war by the Iranian Government against the United States of America and its allies.

The Russian President listened patiently, but without much interest—the Russian Government was determined to seize control of the crisis on their terms—not the US's, not Israel's—a Russian ship had been pirated.

"Mr. President, the Government of Russia has grave reservations and doubts concerning the United States' official explanations into the Arctic Mariner incident. The Arctic Mariner is a Russian vessel and we intend to see that ship into Abbas—its port of call. The freighter has the right to dock in Iran. We will then conduct a legal and proper investigation into the matter. Mr. President, our preliminary investigation leads us to believe the Arctic Mariner is legally transporting Finnish timber to Iran, and we intend to enforce international laws regarding the free flow of commerce on international waters. It is imperative that Israel end its act of piracy."

"Sir, we can confirm the Arctic Mariner is holding nuclear warheads. We have also advised the Israeli Government to end its seizure of the Arctic Mariner and to relinquish the ship's authority back to its rightful operators. But please be advised, this conflict is now between the United States of America and the State of Iran."

"I understand your position, Mr. President, but it is our right to make that determination about the illicit cargo on board and we intend to enforce that right. Let us not be in such a hurry to make war."

Listening to Putin's words, the President of the United States now thought his Security Council had miscalculated. He had been advised that Russia would not intervene. His advisors believed the Russians would allow the United States and Israel to sort out the Arctic Mariner incident—the Russian military, he was told, would be in lock down mode investigating the crime behind the scenes. But, the President of the United States, decided he was ready to move forward with his attack on Iran, even if Russia intervened. The fact that Russia was pressing the matter actually worked in the United States favor. Russia escorting the Arctic Mariner into Iran was not going to change the President's plans.

"Then, you will leave us with no choice. If the Arctic Mariner makes landfall, I will order our military to strike, immediately, Iran's nuclear installations and to destroy its Navy and Air Force in response to the illegal importation of nuclear weapons."

"Mr. President, let us conduct the investigation into this entire incident. We do not believe there are nuclear weapons on board, but if they are found, the international community will decide a proper course of action, including punishments and sanctions. If this is indeed a criminal act, the perpetrators of the crime—including those involved in Iran—will be punished."

"Mr. Putin, I will urge Israel to return the Arctic Mariner back over to its crew and captain, but you have now been informed of our response to Iran. Our response will be swift and decisive."

"Very well"

The President's call to Putin took the decision away from the National Security Council and the Prime Minister of Israel. The Arctic Mariner was going to Iran—and the ship would complete its journey to Iran escorted by Russia. Both navies—U.S. and Israel's—were now to stand down.

Chapter 54:

President Jack Murphy quickly got the Prime Minister of Israel on the phone.

"Mr. Prime Minister, I have spoken with Vladimir Putin. He will be calling soon, if he has not already. I am recommending to you that Israel return the control of the Arctic Mariner back over to its Russian captain; this is to comply with international laws. I have also informed the President of Russia that the United States views the illegal shipment of nuclear weapons to Iran as an act of war by the State of Iran against the United States and our allies. I told Mr. Putin that the United States will respond aggressively."

"Are you suggesting we let that boat dock in Iran?"

"That's correct, Mr. Prime Minister. Mr. Putin has promised me that they will conduct their own investigation, and if there is contraband aboard, then they will allow the international community to decide what to do. They are assuring us of full transparency, but you and I know what is on that boat, Mr. Prime Minister, and so we are not going to wait for Russia to conduct their investigation. In addition, Mr. Prime Minister, our intelligence suggests that Russia will, in fact, be relieved if we destroy that ship. It would preclude a lengthy and potentially embarrassing investigation for the Russians with the international community watching over their shoulders. Their military would be exposed to unwanted attention. Now, Mr. Prime Minister, here is how I have decided to move forward. I will ask the United States Congress to seek a vote declaring war on Iran, immediately. I give you my word on this; I am through negotiating with Iran. I was elected President to rid the world of a nuclear armed Iran. Mr. Prime Minister, the United States of America will see to it that Iran, as a destabilizing force in the region, will come to a quick and permanent end."

"Mr. President, you are going to go to Congress before you hit Iran—before you take that boat out? There will be delays, the United States press and partisan politics will see to that."

"I disagree with you. The outrageous act of smuggling nuclear missiles into Iran will bring this nation together, and declaring war will allow us to respond with our full force—it will galvanize our citizens. Declaring war will give us the ability to wage the kind of war that will guarantee us that our long term security objectives are met."

"Mr. President, the extreme right-wing of my coalition and their ultra-orthodox supporters will be extremely uncomfortable waiting for the United States Congress to declare war, knowing nuclear missiles are in Iran. There will be debates in Congress, which I am certain will lead to delays. We cannot risk those missiles leaving that ship, no matter how quickly or aggressively you act."

Jack Murphy had made up his mind. He could see the Washington Post headlines. He had played out the scenario in his mind of declaring war on Iran months ago—dozens of times. Jack Murphy was ready for this moment.

"Mr. Prime Minister, get your men off the ship. I do not want Russia and you squabbling over this. I will be the first President since World War II to officially declare war, and I want to do this with those Russian missiles in Iran."

"Very well, I will give the order, Mr. President, but I am very concerned about how some will react to this risky maneuver, especially our Foreign Minister; and he is very close to the Commander of Israel's Navy."

Chapter 55:

June 13, 12:45 pm (EST) - Tel Aviv, Israel
Contingency Plans

Israel's Prime Minister sat down to discuss the Arctic Mariner crisis with the Commander of Israel's navy, and the Foreign Minister. The Foreign Minister was furious with the decision to be submissive to the United States.

"Mr. Prime Minister, we simply cannot wait for the United States Congress to declare war against Iran. This is our operation; we are in control at this point. It would be a crucial mistake to allow this dangerous situation to be placed into outside hands—those missiles are a threat to the very existence of Israel. One delay, one mistake, one miscalculation, and we could have those missiles pointing at us—launched against us!"

"I understand your point, but, the United States of America seeks a solution that includes allowing Russia to save face. The U.S. President believes Russia is humiliated that nuclear weapons were smuggled out of their country, but right now Russia is preparing to accuse us of piracy. We don't need that complication right now. Russia's involvement in this incident will compromise our security objectives of ending Iran's nuclear capabilities. The missiles on the Arctic Mariner are a long way from being a threat. If there are delays, I am prepared to take out the missiles—before the act of war is voted on in the United States. But right now, I am ordering you to turn the Arctic Mariner back over to the Russian civilians operating that ship."

The Chief of the Israel's navy complied with the Prime Minister's direct order, but he was not walking away from the threat. He had his own secret plan. After the Israeli Admiral told the commanding Israeli officer on board the Arctic Mariner his plan, the Israeli navy and the Mossad commandoes left the boat promptly.

One hour later, the Admiral called the Prime Minister of Israel.

"Mr. Prime Minister, my men are nearly off the Arctic Mariner. I have complied with your order, sir, though I strongly disagree with it. Now, I would like to give you my recommendation."

"Yes, by all means."

"Sir, I understand the President of the United States intends to ask the United States Congress to declare war against Iran, but I think we can help the Americans, our great friend."

"Okay, Admiral, and how do you suppose we do that?"

"I think the Israeli people would demand we either seize the Arctic Mariner or sink the ship ourselves. Israel is a strong nation and we can defend ourselves. We do not need America's help. I am prepared to launch two cruise missiles to sink the Arctic Mariner. Russia will be angry, at first, but I think they will not act. The people of Russia understand our tough proactive defense policies, perhaps, better than the United States."

"I understand what you are saying, but no, Admiral, we will work with the United States on this. We will let them lead this operation."

"Sir, as Commander of Israel's navy, I cannot stand by and have a ship—a criminal operation—pull into Iran with a cargo full of nuclear missiles. The Israeli people will not stand for this kind of risk taking. It is an outrage to our people, to the people who fought and died for our country. One of the founding principles of this nation is that Israel defends itself first and foremost."

"Admiral, I understand your point, but that will be all for now."

The Commander went back to his office, called his friend, the Foreign Minister, and told him that he was going to sink the Arctic Mariner—and he was going to give the order in an hour.

The Foreign Minister was thrilled with the Admiral's decision to act.

"Admiral, you will be a national hero, I can promise you that."

"And you, my good friend, when that boat hits the sea floor, you will be the next President of Israel."

Chapter 56:

Dan, Father Labas, and two security guards walked towards the Papal Tiara exhibit. In the crypt of The National Shine, on permanent display in the Memorial Hall, is the last Papal Tiara, along with the stole worn at the opening of the Second Vatican Council by Pope John XXIII. The exhibit sits in the middle of the cavernous lower level of the National Shrine, and is ensconced inside a large glass cabinet. The Papal crown is shaped like a bee-hive, has a small cross at its highest point, and is also equipped with three royal diadems ornamented with precious stones and pearls.

Father Labas unlocked the glass encasing, and opened the cabinet door. One of the security guards carefully removed the tiara and handed it to Dan.

Dan held the crown away from his body and studied it. Dan didn't think much of it. It was heavy, cumbersome and downright homely. He turned the tiara upside down and examined the insides—leather, cloth, and velvet were sown along the rim of the crown. Dan put his hand inside and felt around, and right away he knew he had the file.

Dan looked at Father Labas.

"I need to take off the cushion. What I need is underneath the stitching."

"Fine. Go ahead. We can tend to the repairs. The tiara is rich in history, but it is hardly a priceless work of art."

Without much trouble, Dan took off the cushion and reached inside. There it was—The Madonna Files. Dan glanced at the contents quickly. They were mostly letters and notes written by Pope John Paul II.

As Dan was handing the tiara back to the security guard, so he could more carefully review the file, and to verify that the Fatima letter was actually there, Monsignor Fuentes was walking towards him at a quick pace. Monsignor Fuentes noticed the file in Dan's hands.

"Hold it right there, Father Baronowski. I want to thank you for your efforts on behalf of the Vatican, but those documents—at this time—still belong to the National Shrine. I would like you to please hand everything over."

"Monsignor, as Consular for the Congregation for the Doctrine of Faith, I have jurisdiction over this matter. I have explained everything to you and to Father Labas."

"Well, Father Baronowski, I have had a change of mind, and since I am the Director of this cathedral, I am the one who has the final say on all property at the Basilica. If you would like to take possession of the files, in your hands, we must follow the rules governing the transfer process. We will need paper work completed, and, of course, verification of authority. It is important we handle this matter with great care. I am sure you understand., Confidentially will be maintained. You have my word."

"Monsignor, I have authority in the matter, Rome has sent me here to return these documents back to the Head of the Congregation for the Document of Faith and no one is to interfere in my efforts."

Dan knew his entire mission was covert. He did not have any official Vatican paperwork he could show the Monsignor that he, indeed, had been authorized by Rome to take possession of the file—the file is not even known to exist. All he had was his Vatican ID.

"Father Baronowski, you are simply not going to walk out of my church with documents that clearly belong to me—to the National Shrine—without proper approvals and due process."

Dan started putting the file into his brief case.

Monsignor Fuentes turned towards one of the security guards.

"Mr. Johnson, I would like you to secure Father Baronowski. He has, in his possession, stolen property that belongs to the Catholic Church."

Dan was now sure somebody had gotten to Fuentes.

"Monsignor, one moment please, let's be reasonable here. We can expedite this matter with a phone call. Let me call Cardinal Ruini, head of the CDF." Dan took his phone out.

"It's the middle of the night, Father Baronowski, and we are not going to settle this matter on the phone, standing here in this hall like a bunch of school children—no matter who you get on the phone. I will hand that material back to you as soon as we have properly followed procedures for transfer of artifacts that belong to the National Shire. Now, hand them over at once."

As the Monsignor was talking, a phone call came in. Dan glanced at the phone number—it was his mother. It was a strange time of day for his mother to call. Dan's mind went numb.

"No, no more bad news, please no." Dan said to himself. It was as if the Monsignor and the guards did not exist.

"Hello, Mom?"

Seeing Dan answer the phone, the Monsignor's face tightened and his lips pursed, a maneuver the prelate had mastered over the years.

"Father Baronowski—how dare you take a call while I am addressing you; I demand you hand over the files at once."

"Daniel. Daniel, Bob is dead, he's been murdered—in his office—nobody knows anything. You must come home right away. Dear Jesus!!!"

Daniel's mother then sobbed uncontrollably.

"Mom, I'm coming. I'll be there, right away."

Dan never felt so alone—and so angry. The need to strike out overcame him. He felt the urge to knock the teeth out of the condescending Monsignor. He now saw him as part of the enemy, but what good would it do? He needed to get back to the boat. The gloves were going to come off—he was ready to blow the roof off the Vatican to find out who was behind this evil.

Dan turned his phone screen to the Monsignor. He wanted the Monsignor to know who called.

"Mom."

Dan then simply took off running.

"Seize him, he must be stopped; shoot him if you must!"

Deafening sounds of gunshot cracked throughout the Basilica. The chase poured outside into the parking lot. The security guards had never used their guns in live action, and came to complete stops before firing. Dan pulled away on foot, jumped into his car and peeled away from the National Shrine.

"Call the Police Father Labas, I want Daniel Baronowski arrested for theft immediately."

Father Labas slowly put the tiara back inside the glass cabinet.

"Labas! I told you to call the police, call 911, and I mean this instant."

Father Labas quickly shut the cabinet door and took out his phone and got someone on the line.

"Sir, they want to know where the suspect is"

"Give me the phone."

"Yes, this an emergency...No, I am not in any immediate danger...Yes, the suspect is gone, he has taken stolen property and fled...No, I do not believe he is on the premises any longer...What do you mean, you will send a crew over to get the details and file a stolen property report. We need to apprehend this man immediately...No, I don't know how many reports of stolen property are called in each day in the District of Columbia...What do you mean call this number, this IS an emergency...Hello...hello?

Monsignor Fuentes stared at the dead phone for a second, then rudely tossed the phone in the air towards Father Labas, not caring if he caught it or not.

"You better hope you did not know anything about this, Father Frank Labas."

One of the guards returned, nearly out of breath.

"We got his plates—it's a white Crown Vic, late model."

"Well don't just stand there—you're security, for crying out loud. Go get your man; get the police on this, right away."

Dan chirped the tires as he took a hard left on to North Capitol Street off of Michigan Avenue.

His brother was dead. What next. He reached into his pocket, held his rosary, and said a prayer. Dan came up to a stop light; traffic was thick and there was no way to get around. With his eyes tearing, he checked the rearview mirror—no keystone cops—he then looked ahead, into the distance. The United States Capitol loomed majestically on the horizon. The sun was flattering; the Capitol looked like a postcard. Dan's eyes settled on the colossal twenty foot tall statue that crowns the Capitol's spectacular dome. Most casual observers think the statue is of a Native American Indian because of the distinctive plumage adorning the bronze figure's top. Dan thought of the great irony. The statue was not an American Indian at all—far from it. But rather, it was that of a white woman, handling a long sword, and wearing a headdress of eagle feathers. How perfect, Dan thought—a white woman with the headdress of a defeated Native American sits atop of the United States Capitol. He thought of the Virgin Mary and Juan Diego, the peasant Mexican Indian, who humbly did what he was told by the Mother of Jesus Christ.

Beep! Beep! Beeeeeeeep! Behind Dan's car, a driver, sat on his horn demanding him to pay attention. Dan looked up and saw the light was green.

As he stepped on the accelerator, he reached for his phone.

"Hey, Tucker, where's your boat?"

Chapter 57:

Rene and Monique scurried down to "Molly's" master bedroom suite and plopped on the king-sized bed and stared up at the ceiling. For a moment, they both laid there in silence, not knowing where to start. For Monique, there were a lot of unanswered questions—the boat, where was Dan; who, what, where, when, why, and who the heck was Tucker Finn? Rene and Monique had a lot to talk about.

Sanjay stepped back up into the main salon.

"Hey, Tucker, I may have something here."

Vin and Susie were keeping watch on Idi. Idi sat at the dinette table.

Sanjay struck gold quickly. Sanjay went to Médecins Sans Frontières server, and there he found images of old contracts—contracts with subcontractors that Médecins Sans Frontières had hired in Rwanda during the time of the genocide. Sanjay quickly found Lessor Reputations, Inc. Turns out, in order to get paid in real currency—dollars or francs— a MediaCom officer was required to sign the contract. The signature had been faxed—it was George Tela. Sanjay then went to work inside MediaCom's records. He quickly searched the database, hoping to connect somebody at MediaCom to Goma. Two people came up in the data base. George Tela and Carl Beckett, CEO of MediaCom, had gone to Goma in 1994. The CEO? —now that was surprising. Sanjay searched annual reports and Googled images looking for photographs of Carl Beckett. Sanjay saved a handful of pictures of Beckett from the 1990's, and some others taken recently, to his iPad. He did not find any photos of George Tela.

Sanjay and Tucker left the main salon, walked aft to the dinette and put the iPad, with Carl Beckett's portrait taking up most of the screen, on the table so Idi Kambana could see it.

"That's him. Yes, I remember him—big man, big head—no doubt it is him."

Sanjay quickly walked back to the main salon and returned with his laptop.

"MediaCom—Carl Beckett, CEO—let's see if his secretary knows where CEO Beckett is."

Sanjay gave the old maestro's cliché of stretching his fingers, but before he started typing he glanced at the flat television screen on the bulkhead adjacent to the main salon facing the dinette table. CNN breaking news—something got his attention.

Using the remote, Sanjay turned up the volume.

Breaking news: *CNN has learned that at least one errant Israeli cruise missile has hit the Russian aircraft carrier Admiral Kuznetsov. Heavy damage has been reported with significant casualties. The President of the United States will make an announcement within the next two hours. What we know now is that the Russian Aircraft carrier was escorting a Russian freighter—the freighter named the Arctic Mariner— had been reported missing in the Strait of Hormuz. It has been reported that an Israeli commando force seized the ship, suspecting that the vessel was transporting weapons of mass destruction to Iran. Israel has apologized for the tragic incident. CNN was also reporting that Iran had fired missiles at U.S. Naval boats that were in the vicinity of the tragedy. No reports of damage have been announced."*

Sanjay pulled his phone out of his pocket—it was buzzing madly. His phone was programmed to notify him when volatility targets were reached. He looked at his CNBC app—the stock market had triggered its circuit breakers. The Dow had halted trading after falling 1,000 points in a matter of minutes.

Luke started barking. It was Father Dan trotting down the docks heading to Tucker's boat, holding a briefcase. Tucker and Sanjay stood up and moved towards Molly's stern to meet Dan.

"Tucker, Bob's dead. He's been murdered."

Dan stepped into the aft salon and saw Idi, and staggered nearly losing his balance.

His first thought was he had been set up by Tucker—the whole thing—he'd been stung, duped. And now they had Monique and Rene, and his brother was dead. How could Idi be on Tucker's boat? There could not be any other possible explanation. Dan looked again at Idi, then at Tucker.

"Tucker, where are Rene and Monique?" Dan asked again, this time shouting, "Where are they!?"

"Dan, they are safe. They are down below talking, resting. My God! They got Bob? I am so sorry."

Sanjay found what he was looking for.

"He's here in DC. Carl Beckett is staying at the Mandarin Hotel.

Tucker and Dan both turned towards Sanjay, and both said at the same time, "Who?"

"Carl Beckett, he is the guy. I am willing to bet he hired Idi—he's the guy Idi works for. He is staying at the Mandarin Hotel—the place where the Codex was to be dropped off. I think he is behind the kidnapping of Monique. Carl Beckett is behind this whole thing I am sure of it." Sanjay picked up his iPad "This guy, right here, is your man Father Dan. I am so sorry about your brother, but, Carl Beckett, I'm betting, had him murdered."

Dan said, "What? How can you be so sure?"

"He had a meeting yesterday, in Milan, with a guy named Father Roberto Indellicotta."

"How do you know all this?"

"I have his phone; I have it all right here—every call he has made in the last week. He talked to Indellicotta for seven minutes yesterday. Indellicotta's number is 555-676-5551. Tucker, you tell me why Beckett is talking to priests in Italy and then the next day his employees are abducting people tied to Vatican intrigue and the Codex. And this Beckett dude is staying at the hotel where the secret relic was to be dropped off. Carl Beckett is behind all this—guaranteed."

Tucker had not put the pieces together completely, or perhaps he was looking for more certainty, more answers. But the news of the murder of a friend took precedent.

"Dan, what the hell is going on? Your brother, why?"

Dan turned away from Tucker. He was not ready to answer. It would take two thousand years of history and the entire Vatican library to answer the question, "why." There had always been a human element in the Catholic Church—pride, vanity, lust for power, sex, and ambition, in the midst of the Holy Spirit. The human component—sin—had been a corrupting force in Christianity since the beginning of the ministry of Jesus Christ, starting with the betrayal of Judas for a bag of coins.

Dan's thought through Sanjay's speculation starting with Indellicotta—he knew him. Back in Rome he heard he had been acting strange. Indelicotta was known as a "Fatimist," and most definitely aligned with ultra-traditionalists who were viewed as enemies of the sitting Pope.

Dan had planned to give the Fatima letter to Cardinal Warwinka. Could Cardinal Warwinka be next? Maybe they had the secret list of names.

Rene and Monique appeared from down below.

Dan moved quickly to Rene and took her in her arms.

"Bob's dead."

Sanjay kept fiddling with his laptop and cell phone.

"He is not in his hotel room. This is weird; he's on the campus of Catholic University."

Dan turned back towards Sanjay before helping Rene onto a seat. Monique raced over to Rene and sat with her.

"Cardinal Warwinka—Cardinal Warwinka is speaking there in about an hour. I've got to warn him; nobody, who is connected to me, is safe."

Tucker walked up next to Dan.

"Dan, maybe now is the time for the police. Let's see if we can have this guy Beckett arrested for the kidnapping of Monique."

"I don't know, Tucker. I don't know if there is time. If this guy Beckett is behind all this, then he is at Catholic University for a reason. I need to warn Cardinal Warwinka. I need to get him to cancel the speech. My brother's dead, Monique was taken, and they almost got Rene. No more risks. If I can get to him now; I am going to stop him myself."

Dan quickly dialed two numbers hoping to get word to Warwinka to cancel the speech—he called Warwinka's cell phone, then Catholic University's administration office—voice mails. He put his phone way. He then made his way towards Sanjay and picked up his iPad and stared at the photo of Carl Beckett. Dan pulled out his car key; he was going to go straight to Catholic University and hunt down Beckett himself.

Idi, unexpectedly, spoke up. His deep voice, at that moment, resonated with unexpected sincerity, and all eyes turned to him. Idi, with his feet still handcuffed to the table pedestal, looked at the priest who he had almost killed in Rwanda. Now the priest's brother was dead—killed by people he worked for. A momentary shot of bloodlust returned. He looked at Monique—the word, "forgiveness." It meant everything to him, but now he thought forgiveness would have to wait; it would have to come after justice. Carl Beckett did not deserve forgiveness—he deserved punishment.

"Father Daniel, I should go with you. You will need an extra set of eyes to find him. I know what he looks like. Also, you must understand, Father Daniel, if we find him I can be very persuasive—I think he will tell you everything you need to know to get at the root of all this evil. I can get him to talk to you without lawyers."

Dan looked at Idi and thought of the American nun and the horror of Rwanda, but he had also heard Monique talk about forgiveness—that it was the only way to repair and to retrieve one's humanity. He thought of his brother. Dan thought of justice.

"You would recognize him, Idi?"

"Yes, Father Daniel—I have seen the pictures—I'll know him."

"Tucker, are you okay with it?"

"Set him free, Vin. Dan needs somebody to watch his back."

Dan checked his watch. Time was of the essence, but he had to look at the files first, he had to make sure the "Third Secret of Fatima" was in the file. It was the only way to keep Rene and Monique safe, if the trail did not end with some guy named Carl Beckett.

"Tucker, before I go, I want to review these files. I did not have a chance to verify everything. If it is what I think it is, I want to make sure

Cardinal Warwinka gets the files. It will only take a minute. I just want a little privacy."

As Dan made his way down below, Sanjay, who had been keeping one eye on the TV, turned up the volume.

"Tucker, are you watching this? Israel accidentally hit a Russian Aircraft carrier with one, maybe two cruise missiles."

Dan stopped and turned around.

"Did you say a Russian aircraft carrier?"

"Yeah, Israel just accidentally hit a Russian aircraft carrier in the Strait of Hormuz, one hundred miles from Iran. What about it?"

"Forget it; I'll be right back."

Sanjay checked his CNBC app again; markets overseas were plunging. Sanjay checked his proprietary trading programs. Sanjay's models were highly complex math equations that analyzed stock market data instantly around the world.

"Hey, Finn, there is some real crazy stuff going on. U.S. markets just halted trading and my trading algorithms are freaking out. Vix indexes, volatility measures, are just blowing through the roof. This situation in Iran looks like it is getting out of hand. Tucker listened carefully to Sanjay then moved closer to the television screen. Tucker Finn was now starting to pay close attention—his probability and statistics brain was starting to engage. A Russian aircraft carrier was sinking off the coast of Iran.

Tucker was surprised at what he was now thinking about. Was it the priest, Fatima, end times talk, prophecies? Was it because he found himself around people he cared for—was it Rene? He stopped thinking and watched the scrolling news dumbly at the bottom of the screen for a moment.

"Russian aircraft carrier has been accidentally hit by Israeli cruise missiles..."

The professor now started doing some probability analysis—he could not believe what he was thinking. The crisis, unbelievably, had the potential to turn in to WWIII, and they were sitting at a boat dock one mile from the United States Capitol—the bulls-eye.

Tucker took out his phone and called the captain of Pilar.

"Tom, get Pilar out to sea—the Atlantic Ocean—and get her there as fast you can; push hard with everything she has."

Chapter 58:

Alone in the forward cabin, Dan opened up the brief case and took out the file. He was now so close—so close to reading the third secret, words from the Mother of Jesus Christ, words that only a few people on earth had ever seen. As much as the apparitions at Fatima are venerated, they are also steeped in great controversy. The secret letter starts with the most controversial incomplete sentence in Church history. *"In Portugal, the dogma of the faith will be preserved, etc…"* Books, international conferences, even secret catholic sects have madly attempted to decipher the truth of the words that followed " etc," and now Father Daniel would know. His heart began to pound. Dan first took a look at a letter on top of the stack of papers making up the "Madonna Files": It was a letter from Pope John Paul II, titled "Be not afraid!" Dan thought about Pope John Paul II's iconic cry, "Be not afraid." Dan, long ago, decided he wanted those words carved into his tombstone. It was in his will.

Dan then read the Pope's letter:

Christ said to the apostles and to the women after the Resurrection—"Be not afraid!" According to the Gospels, these words were not addressed to Mary. Strong in her faith, she had no fear. Mary's participation in the victory of Christ became clear to me above all from the experience of my people. Cardinal August Hlond, had spoken these prophetic words as he was dying: "The victory, if it comes, will come through Mary." During my pastoral ministry in Poland, I saw for myself how those words were coming true.

After my election as Pope, as I became more involved in the problems of the universal Church, I came to have a similar conviction: On this universal level, if victory comes it will be brought by Mary. Christ will conquer through her, because He wants the Church's victories now and in the future to be linked to her.

I held this conviction even though I did not yet know very much about Fátima. And thus we come to May 13, 1981, when I was wounded by gunshots fired in St. Peter's Square. At first, I did not pay attention to the fact that the assassination attempt had occurred on the exact anniversary of the day Mary appeared to the three children at Fátima in Portugal and spoke to them the words that now, at the end of this century, seem to be close to their fulfillment.

.

Dan re-read what Pope John Paul II had said: "*Jesus wants the Church's victories now and in the future to be linked to her.*"

He had encountered those words of the great Pope before, and he was fascinated to see them alongside the "Third Secret of Fatima". He sifted through the papers; he was ready to read the secret letter— to verify that he had, in his possession, the Fatima letter. The file was small, and he quickly found what he was looking for—it was easy to find; it was handwritten and was the only document in the file written in Portuguese. Over the years Dan had forced himself to learn Portuguese precisely because Fatima was so important in his world. He put the other papers back into the briefcase and started to read.

"*In Portugal, the dogma of the faith will be preserved. Dear Children, I am the Mediatrix between you and God*"

Dan stopped reading. He was jarred by the sound of the unfamiliar words. He had read the sentence so many times before and the short sentence always ended with the infamous "etc." But not this time—the "Etcetera" was missing. He knew he had the third secret—the hidden text—text that included words given to Sister Lucia directly from the Blessed Virgin Mary of Fatima. He went back to the letter:

"*In Portugal, the dogma of the faith will be preserved. Dear Children, I am the Mediatrix between you and God. Be not afraid, my Immaculate Heart will be your refuge and your safe path to God. I am the Mediatrix of all graces and my heart will triumph. **Christ will conquer through me, because He wants*** *the Church's victories now and in the future to be linked to me. I am the Advocate for mankind and I told you, if men do not repent and better themselves, the Father will inflict a terrible punishment on all humanity, and Russia will be the instrument of my chastisement.*

Dan stopped. There, again, were the Pope's words of the future linked to the Virgin Mary. Pope John Paul II had read the Fatima secret. It made perfect sense now. But the Virgin Mary calling herself the Mediatrix. "I am the Mediatrix of all graces." It was a shocking surprise, but Dan understood right away—it seemed obvious now. In fact there was no other way. The Mediatrix—it was a reference to the so-called "Fifth Dogma."

"In Portugal, the dogma of the faith will be preserved," Millions of Catholics and thousands of bishops and priests, for years, have petitioned the Pope to recognize the Virgin Mary as Mediatrix of all graces and have asked that her role as the universal advocate for mankind be established as the fifth and final Marian Dogma. By establishing the fifth and final dogma, the Church would have an immense tool—an infallible tool to guide the faithful to Jesus Christ, specifically through the heart of the Virgin Mary leading to the truthful and sacred purification of souls. It was how her heart would triumph. It would be how the dogma of the faith would be preserved. Portugal, of course, referred to Fatima. Dan understood, now—the dogma of the faith including the fifth dogma would be preserved through the Virgin Mary's heart, and only through her triumphant heart. Dan looked at his watch; he had to get going, but he could not let go, also, of the reference to "Russia" in the secret letter. Dan thought—Fatima-Russia, of course, but the Vatican's official release on May 13, 2000, never mentioned Russia. Dan put the letter down and considered what he had just read. Experts for years have insisted Russia had to be a part of the third secret. Experts and theologians who studied Fatima had always been puzzled by Russia's unique status in the messages and secrets. Why was Russia, that tragic nation with such a rich tradition of venerating the Blessed Mother, specifically mentioned? Famous author and Vatican insider, Fr. Malachi Martin, who claimed to have read the "Third Secret" in the 1960's, hinted that Russia was the key to the 'Third Secret of Fatima'. He wrote:

Sister Lucia's single-page letter of the "Third Secret" covers three topics—
1. A Physical chastisement of nations
2. A spiritual chastisement
3. The central function of Russia in the two which in fact, the physical and spiritual chastisements are to be gridded on a fateful timetable in which Russia is the ratchet.

Malachi Martin said that, *"Russia, according to the text of the 'Third Secret', was the regulator of the Fatima timetable. Russia's role in the 'Vision of Fatima' is very important because, if we're to believe the Vision of Fatima, salvation for the world, the cure for the world ills, will start in Russia, and that was why the Virgin Mary, in the Fatima vision of 1917, was supposed to have spoken actively about Russia."*

Russia, according to Malachi Martin, first of all, has to be cured of her errors. And then, Russia will help the entire world to get better and to cure itself of its sins. Martin wrote:

"It's a very bizarre message in that sense because one would have said that salvation was going to come from the West as we always think because we are Westerners, but no, according to the message of Fatima, salvation will come from the East, and particularly, from the State of Russia itself, which is extraordinary."

Dan was obedient to the Church, but he had always suspected that the 'Third Secret of Fatima' had, indeed, been politicized. For many reasons, Dan had always believed Russia was the dominant element to Fatima as well—it made perfect sense. Pope John Paul II had obliquely referenced Russia as part of the third secret and had gone along with the politicization. The Pope once said, when asked about the Fatima secret:

"Because of the seriousness of its contents, in order not to encourage the world wide power of Communism to carry out certain coups, my Predecessors in the Chair of Peter have diplomatically preferred to withhold its publication."

Dan knew Pope John Paul was speaking of Russia. A chill ran through him, as his thoughts went back to an ominous message from Medjugorje. In the fall of 1981, a time when Russia was still very much the communist atheist empire, the Blessed Mother told the children of Medjugorje: "Russia will come to glorify God the most; the West has made civilization progress, but act as if they are their own creators."

He shook his head. Then, without reading anymore, he slipped the letter back into the briefcase. It was not for him to read, not without the permission of his Superior. He was asked by his Superior to return the files back to Rome—he had not been authorized to read the 'Third Secret'. He must turn it over to Cardinal Warwinka. He trusted the Cardinal; they were great friends. He closed the briefcase, and locked it. He needed to get to Cardinal Warwinka as soon as possible.

As Dan was making his way back to the main salon, Sanjay's voice bellowed throughout the cabin.

"What the F…This is unbelievable!"

Sanjay stood up and pointed at the television. Dan was still making his way up, and Tucker was at the navigation table looking at charts and weather.

"Father Daniel, Tucker, you won't believe what just happened. Tucker, you have to see this!"

Chapter 59:

June 13, 2:40 pm - Washington, DC
The White House

"Sir, Vladimir Putin is on the phone."

"Mr. President, I am calling you to inform you that I have ordered the Russian Navy and Air Force to destroy the Israeli Navy in Haifa, at once. We have aircraft, in the air, on the way now. I urge you to not interfere with this appropriate punishment. Good day, sir."

The President dropped to his seat.

Pat Allen charged into the Oval office.

"Mr. President, we have detected highly unusual activity. We are getting recon intel that has a fleet of Russian bombers, Tupolev Tu-95's heading across the Caspian Sea. Their route takes the aircraft straight to Israel."

"Pat, get me the rest of your team into my office, right now."

The President's national security team walked into the Oval Office, one by one. Pat Allen spoke first.

"We have to stop those Russian bombers, Mr. President. We have the USS Eisenhower in range. We can have fighter jets in the air in minutes. We can take those planes down quickly."

"And start World War III? Look, the fact is Israel just destroyed a Russian aircraft carrier with two cruise missiles. God only knows how many Russian sailors are dead."

The President surveyed his national security team with disgust; men with enormous egos preoccupied with their place in history— with these men it was all about taking hills, collecting medals. These prideful men with a chest full of decorations are now responsible for possibly starting WWIII. He should have seen it coming.

"You pathetic, prideful, ego-maniac eagle scouts. You men are nothing but a bunch of peacocks! Why should I listen to anyone of you?"

The President went nose to nose with an Army General and flicked one of the colored awards on the General's chest. The trophy case on one side of the officer's chest was so large that the imbalance unintentionally projected a sense he was listing—like a flagship caught on rocks.

"So, Sam, they give you this one for packing your family in a station wagon and driving across our country—was that your mission, General?"

Pat Allen interrupted the President.

"Sir, right now we need…"

The President turned towards Pat Allen.

"Pat, did I ask you for your opinion?"

"Sir, we really…"

"Pat, did you hear what I said?"

"Yes sir, but…"

"I asked you a question, Pat. I guess I'll have to ask again. Now, did I ask you for your opinion?"

"No, sir."

"Okay good, I don't want your opinion. And when I want your opinion, I will ask you for it. Is that understood?"

"Yes sir."

"Okay, good, now I want you all to listen to me."

The President looked first at Pat Allen, then up and down the line. He looked at the line of men who had made their careers beating the hell out of illiterate goat farmers and over-matched third world dictators. The President wondered if he had the right men, with the right stuff, to respond to a foe that had nuclear missiles.

"You bunch of stinking no good cowboy yahoos…You hot-shots may have just started World War III…on my watch—are you aware of that? A few hours ago, the United States Navy had an opportunity to take control of the Arctic Mariner situation, from the start, and we talked them out of it. We should have taken that ship, but, no; you all wanted to pull your two-bit stunt. Are you aware, that your reckless egos, have just put the life of every man, woman, and child in this country in grave danger? I am as guilty as the rest of you, but by God—you are the professionals." The

President stood up and looked back out towards the rose Garden. "Somebody get me Reverend Powell on the phone."

Reverend Jerry Powell had been the President's spiritual advisor for years.

When the call came in, Reverend Jerry Powell was already be fit to be tied, and itching for a fight, after news reports that the Russian aircraft carrier had been hit in Iranian waters. He was like a wild animal.

"I told you Mr. President, the Russians couldn't be trusted. I have been warning you, sir, my congregation, and the country about this for years."

"Jerry, hold it right there. Israel just hit a Russian aircraft carrier—unprovoked. Blew the ship up with two cruise missiles."

"Doesn't matter. They deserved it, they had it coming to them. Now you wait and see what they do next. This is not going to be pretty, Mr. President. It's all in the bible—we have talked about this day. I have been warning about this for years. I've written books on this."

For twenty years, Jerry Powell had been hell-bent on marshaling in Armageddon. He'd made a fortune telling Evangelical Christians that the end-times were close, and that Russia was the satanic country that would start World War III. Reverend Powell had gone on national TV on many occasions and declared that Vladimir Putin was the anti-Christ, and that the Russian Orthodox leadership was nothing but god-hating KGB agents in disguise. The Reverend proclaimed that it was just a matter of time before Russia and the Middle East would join together and attack Israel.

Reverend Powell had many opinions, on many subjects, but talk of Russia would have the edges of his lips white within minutes. The pastor, with all the gusto he could manage, proclaimed that the principal force of Evil in the world is, and will always be, Russia. And Russia, as the the sworn enemy of America, is divinely revealed in the Bible.

"Jerry, Russia has planes heading to Israel and I want to pray with you, right now. I need to feel God is with us as we prepare to defend the United States of America and the great State of Israel."

"Mr. President, I will be happy to pray, but please understand the developments in the Middle East are preordained by God, none of this is your fault—you are a good man, you are a blessed man. Sir, we have talked about this before in our Bible meetings. Sir, this confrontation is willed by God, who wants to use this conflict to erase his people's enemies before a New Age begins. Mr. President, it is important to accept this, and there can be little doubt that the forces at work have been fated by God. Sir, an attack against Iran is the fulfillment of a Biblical prophecy in which you have been chosen to serve as the instrument of the Lord."

"I don't know, Jerry, I really don't know. But let's pray right now. Let's pray for the American people, the people of Israel, and let's pray that God Almighty will guide us and lead me to make the right decisions to protect this country."

As soon as the prayer ended, Pat Allen again spoke up; this time forcefully.

"Sir, we need to move forward on our plan to destroy Iran's military capabilities. They have fired on our ship in the Strait of Hormuz. And we need to stop those Russian bombers heading to Israel."

Chapter 60:

June 13, 3:00 pm - Washington, DC
The War Begins

Russian nuclear submarine, the Aleksandr Nevsky, outfitted with its own Orthodox chapel and named after a Russian Christian Saint, was ordered to fire. The Sub's payload consisted of sixteen ballistic missiles, each carrying multiple re-entry vehicle warheads capable of shattering ten separate targets. In addition to the sixteen warheads, the sub carried six cruise missiles. All six of the cruise missiles were now, in flight, across the Indian Ocean streaking towards Haifa, Israel's largest port, at six hundred miles an hour. The missiles would hit Haifa in less than an hour. The war had begun.

Just before noon, after passing over Temple Mount in Jerusalem, the missiles hit their targets. Haifa was Israel's largest port town and also home to the Navy's Third flotilla. US Air Force AWACS planes had picked up the projectiles in flight and issued warnings, but nine hundred people were dead along the waterfront before there was time to seek safety. The Russian missile strike, in an instant, transformed Haifa into Israel's own version of Pearl Harbor. Russia's attack had sunk, or heavily damaged, eight of the twelve Sa'ar 4.5-class Navy Corvettes docked in the harbor. Gas terminals exploded, ballistic missiles detonated from the stricken naval ships—Haifa was on fire. Iran then sent everything they had, that could reach Israel, to Tel Aviv, mostly missiles packed with nerve gas.

In Washington, DC, at 2pm, CNN installed a breaking news scroll across the bottom of its telecast, concerning the rumored Russian missile attack against Israel. Reports of the attack were everywhere—Al Jazeera was already calling it the start of World War III, but the news was too shocking to truly accept, so before 24/7 news coverage was launched announcing that WWIII had just started, CNN producers urgently scrambled, seeking confirmation from the White House. In newsrooms across the nation, an odd sensation overcame almost everybody who worked in the industry. Perhaps for the first time in television history, people were scared. Three nuclear powers were moving uncontrollably towards war. Journalists were accustomed to covering "wars" from swanky international hotels—wars that were essentially staged battles. This was different - a collective nervousness infiltrated newsrooms. The Afghan and Iraq wars had been great for careers. Covering Middle Eastern wars, newsrooms and reporters worried mostly about ratings, job assignments, and airtime—but, with Russia bombing Israel and a new unpredictable, hawkish White House administration—veteran war correspondents found themselves worrying about their children.

By 4 pm., gas stations on the east coast started to raise prices. Slowly at first and as lines began to form, the filling stations panicked, and prices skyrocketed to eight dollars a gallon. Worried motorists rushed home from work or to the nearest gas station or to the grocery store. Radios and smart phones flooded the airwaves with the latest reports of the cruise missile attack against Israel by Russia. Citizens across the United States collectively worried about what would come next. How would the United States respond? Would the U.S. launch a counter attack against Russia? Cell phone networks began to fail due to heavy use. Every citizen of the United States was searching for their loved ones at exactly the same time. The President scheduled a speech at 6pm. Gas prices continued to rise. Global financial markets plunged. Germany, France, England, all fell fifteen percent. Gold surged past its all time high. The dollar and euro plummeted against the Chinese currency. Except for the major petroleum producers, stock prices on the New York Stock Exchange collapsed in heavy volume.

A terror alert in New York City was launched and they were preparing to declare martial law. The Governor of Virginia ordered the National Guard to fully mobilize.

Chapter 61:

June 13, 4:00 pm - Washington, D.C
Idi and Carl Beckett's Reunion

The Russian attack on Israel was the tipping point for Tucker Finn; he was going to get the hell out of Dodge—out of Washington, DC—and fast. But he agreed to give Dan some time to find Carl Beckett and complete his business with Cardinal Warwinka.

Dan and Idi got into the Crown Victoria and made their way to Maine Avenue. Dan noticed that traffic was starting to get thick. Drivers were anxious and in a hurry; horn blasts were heard in all directions. Catholic University was not far from the marina—ten, fifteen minutes, depending on traffic. Dan was going to go right by the U.S. Capitol, then up North Capitol, before taking a right on to Michigan Ave.

As traffic began to slow his progress, Dan began to sense something in the air, like animals before a tsunami or earthquake. The atmosphere in Washington, D.C. had changed. Dan could feel a strange energy all around him. It felt like the barometric pressure was plunging. Dan wondered if the collective mindset of millions of people—a measurable wave—could actually change the atmosphere, physically. The thought made Dan think of the Blessed Mother and how She asked the world to pray together—pray as one—and that prayer could literally change physical laws—she had said so much, at Medjugorje, and added that prayer could even stop wars. He understood it now. He could tangibly feel the impact in the air of millions of people simultaneously thinking that nuclear war in the United States was close—that it was truly possible and that millions of people could, in fact, die—soon.

Idi spoke up. "Something bad will happen at the campus. There will be evil in that room."

Idi's words surprised Dan.

"Why do you say that?"

"Father Daniel, this man Beckett seeks out evil. He lives for it. He likes to be near it. He told me as much in Goma. Years ago in the tent in Goma, he was obsessed with me, my clothes, my eyes; he kept looking into my eyes. I asked why he does this. He said he was looking for Satan. He believed he could see him behind my eyes. He knew I had murdered many people, and he was certain Satan was close to me, inside me. He was obsessed with things like that. I can tell you one thing, Father Daniel, he is not there for the lecture."

"Idi, I've got to get Cardinal Warwinka—nobody is safe right now. I want to get him out of harm's way; get him to the boat. Right now I think that is the only safe place. I don't know who I can trust anymore. Anybody close to me is in danger."

"You find the Cardinal, let me find Beckett. He is a tough guy, but I might have some luck getting him to talk. Maybe Beckett is the key to getting to the bottom of this evil, maybe he is the serpent's head. I will find out what he knows; I have a lot of experience in that line of work."

Dan suddenly thought of his brother and a deep sadness overcame him, but it passed quickly. He then felt a rage—the kind of rage he felt standing in Rene's hallway closet, but before justice was dispensed, he wanted to talk to Beckett. He needed to find out who was involved; get to the root and destroy it, like Idi said.

"How are you going to get him to cooperate, Idi? How are you going to get him to admit his involvement?"

"Father Daniel, Carl Beckett will do as he is told; He will understand. He will believe my threats without hesitation."

"Alright, Idi, let's talk to him. I want to get to the bottom of this, right now, before we turn him over to the police; I am not even sure we have enough on him to have him arrested. My brother is dead, Monique was kidnapped, but right now we can't tie it to this man named Beckett—not yet. You are the kidnapper, and you don't even know who you work for. Just because you met him once means nothing. His attorneys will have him free, at least until some case can be made against him. If I don't talk to him now, I may never get the chance, again. He could walk free, and I would spend the rest of my life afraid of my own shadow."

Dan tuned into the university parking lot and, like any college campus, parking was hard to find. Dan pulled into the handicap parking, reached over, and took his pistol out of the glove compartment, put it in a holster inside his jacket and headed to the Edward J. Pryzbyla building, Catholic University's student union and conference hall.

Cardinal Warwinka's lecture was scheduled to start in twenty minutes, in "Great Room A." The event was free and open to the public—about three hundred people were expected. The college President would be in attendance, as well as dozens of priests and a smattering of bishops from the Washington, DC metropolitan area.

Dan and Idi walked into the lecture hall. The conference room was large, and unadorned—standard middle brow hotel conference room fair. A simple lectern adorned with potted plants was the extent of the circumstance. Room dividers had been pushed open, doubling the size of the room. Students and faculty mingled in the hallways, munching on snacks, cokes, and coffee. It was still early when Dan and Idi walked in. The room was a third full. Dan felt a twinge of guilt; he should first go find Cardinal Warwinka. He should warn him, but he was overcome by a wide range of emotions: anger, sadness, grief, and now he had an overwhelming need to find the source of evil, Bob's killer. He had to find Beckett first; the Church would have to wait. It was now personal—there was a monster behind the attacks and this was Dan's first chance to see what the monster looked like. Beckett was all he wanted. He took out his phone to look at the photo of Carl Beckett that Sanjay had sent him.

Idi saw him first. He was standing across the room examining the seating arrangements. Beckett was as big as he remembered, fit and strong for a man his age. Idi nudged Father Daniel. Dan saw him. The smile on Beckett's face, his smug air of superiority made Dan sick to his stomach.

Dan said to Idi.

"I would like to get him somewhere where I can talk to him. How do you want to get him out of here?"

"I'll just ask him nicely."

Carl Beckett made his way to the front of the room. He wanted a front row seat to the execution of a man who, he believed, could one day complete the destruction of the Catholic Church. As far as Beckett was concerned, he was on a mission to kill one of Satan's secret agents.

Seats were still available along the first row. As soon as Beckett sat down, Idi made his way towards him.

Idi weighed three hundred and ten pounds, and took up a lot of room. He could tell Carl Beckett was very annoyed that the huge overweight black man would sit down right next to him with other seats available.

Beckett did not recognize Idi. To Carl Beckett, Idi Kambana would have been the last man on earth he would have guessed would be sitting next to him in a conference room on the campus of Catholic University, getting ready to hear a talk from an eminent Catholic prelate. What Beckett did know, is he didn't like the fat man sitting next to him at all.

"Excuse me, sir, but I am actually saving that seat for a friend of mine."

Idi didn't look at Beckett.

"I like this seat. Maybe you should move."

Beckett was totally surprised to hear the sharp rude response coming from the piggish oaf, particularly on a Catholic campus. Beckett's size and intimidating demeanor and powerful position had, for the most part, allowed him to go through life unchallenged. Beckett could not remember the last time somebody spoke to him in that manner. Beckett always got his way, no questions asked.

"Look, sir, there is a seat right there. So just scoot over one and we will both be happy."

Idi leaned over and whispered in Beckett's ear.

"I like this seat, Mr. Carl Beckett, and if you ask me one more time to move I will remind you how I made a living in Rwanda."

With his mouth open, Beckett took a quick look at the man sitting next to him, then he remembered—Goma. The refugee camp—the grand epic horror. He also remembered why he hired the man sitting next to him. He was the best man in camp at killing people. A sudden chill coursed through his body, from head to toe—a feeling he had never had in his life.

Idi sensed that Beckett was uncomfortable. Beckett was stirring. Good. He remembered, but he wondered if Beckett was ready to bolt out of the room. Idi kept up the conversation in a whisper.

"Beckett, you need to do what I say. Understand first, I'm here right now on a mission of redemption. I owe somebody something...no, make that everything, including my life. So if I snap your neck, right here in front of all these people, it would not be of any concern of mine—they can do what they want with me after I have killed you. It would be my penance. Now, I would like you to do as I say. DO you understand me?"

Carl Beckett considered his options. The fact that Idi Kambana was in the room with him, he knew something big was up. Nobody on earth knew where he was; he had not told a soul—not even Father Indellicotta. How was he traced? He stayed in his chair. He wondered if he was being double crossed, but who could it be—had Idi gone rogue? Beckett needed answers.

"What do you want from me?"

"I want you to meet someone. I want you to meet Father Daniel Baronowski."

Beckett's face spun towards Idi; he was astonished to hear Baronowski's name. This was not part of the plan. Was Idi upping the stakes? Was he hustling him for more money? Christ, where the hell is Baronowski; was he in the room?

"Baronowski? What is this, some kind of sick joke?"

"No, Beckett this is no joke."

"Then what the hell is this all about? Where's Baronowski? Does he have the Codex del Rio Grande?"

"Beckett, I ask the question and you do what you are told."

Beckett's teeth clenched, nobody speaks to him that way.

"Now listen to me, you fat ass; you work for me. Now, does the priest have the Codex?"

Idi made some deep, but subtle noises, chortles, throat clearing. Then a menacing gesture; Idi rolled his shoulders, like a wrestler, then jerked his neck and head from side to side.

He was ready to strike, but he wanted Baronowski to have his chat with Beckett. One thing for sure, the negotiations were over.

With his vice grip-like hands, Idi took his thumb and finger and grabbed a chuck of Beckett's soft side of his torso, pinched hard, then leaned towards Beckett and whispered in his ear.

"Move to the exits, right now, or I will kill you."

Beckett got up and did what he was told.

Dan, still standing by the entrance, saw Idi coming his way, with Beckett. Dan gestured to Idi to follow him outside. Walking outside, Dan looked for a place that was quiet and away from the student foot traffic. Dan headed to the parking lot and stopped between two tall SUV's. Idi patted Beckett down, then scanned the parking lot and entrance to the student center. He didn't know what he was looking for—just anything suspicious—Idi was sure Carl Beckett had evil intentions. Idi knew Beckett was not on campus to take in a religious lecture. Beckett was looking for action.

Beckett fumed, but was unsure of his next move. Beckett was convinced he was being double-crossed by Idi, but rather than engaging in measured conversation—like a psychotic bully with no governor—he lashed out at Idi again.

"Do you have any idea who you are messing with—you better know what you are doing or you are a dead man."

Idi was in no mood to talk. Idi landed a vicious punch into Beckett's stomach, buckling him over and knocking the wind out of him.

"Beckett, just answer Father Daniel's questions."

Dan did not want to talk to Beckett just yet, instead he wanted Beckett's phone. He wanted to call Father Indellicotta from Beckett's phone. Dan wanted Indellicotta to hear his voice. Dan was sure Father Indellicotta was the evil, inside the Vatican, behind the search for the 'Third Secret of Fatima'. He was also certain that Indellicotta was behind the killing and kidnapping.

"Give me your phone."

Beckett was at a complete loss now. Idi was working for Baronowski? But how? It seemed impossible.

"Idi, if this is about money...Is this priest paying you off? Is the Church paying you off? Did he get to you? If it's about money, I'll double what anybody is paying you."

Idi hit Beckett again, in the same spot. This time Beckett went to the ground and vomited. Idi reached into Beckett's pocket, took out the phone, and handed it to Dan. Again Idi scanned the campus grounds.

With Beckett's phone in his hand, Dan spoke to the man who had his brother killed.

"Now, Mr. Carl Beckett, I have a good source that tells me you talked to Father Indellicotta, yesterday, in Milan. Are you behind the chase to find the letter?"

Beckett did not answer, and not because he was still recovering from Idi's blow.

"Look, Beckett, it's over. You and Indellicotta are the ones who want the Codex."

Picking himself back up, Beckett decided to give up the tough guy act. Idi was looking for his chance. Idi would kill him so much as look at him. Beckett had not heard yet, but it was very likely the priest's brother was dead and the priest knew about it by now. He figured the priest and Idi were looking for a reason to do some real damage. Beckett did have one asset. Over the years he had spent untold sums of money designing an elaborate system, a maze, a massive Chinese wall that kept his secret world of CIA covert adventures and private security operations at least six degrees of separation apart from him. The system, he was told, was impenetrable. Legally, he still felt he was on strong footing. It would be difficult to prove his involvement in criminal attempts to acquire the Codex. They would never tie Idi back to him. Hell, he would not have taken a front row seat at Warwinka's lecture if he had any doubts. So what about Idi? Alright, Idi claims he knows him from Goma. High profile executives are constantly being blackmailed by crooks looking for a payday. Nothing could be traced back to him. And having lunch with Roberto Indellicotta in Milan? Sure, they had been friends since college. But still the unanswered question: How did the priest get to him? He must have been hacked, or somebody talked. Somebody had gotten in. Beckett was not going to make it easy for the priest.

"I don't know what you're talking about."

Dan ignored Beckett's response and scrolled though Beckett's calls and saw the Rome area code. It was Father Indellicotta's number. As Dan was dialing the phone, Idi looked around the parking lot. This time he saw something—he saw a slight flicker, a light, a twinkle. It was a shiny chrome whistle.

Chapter 62:

June 13, Midnight - Milan, Italy
Father Roberto Indelicotta and Sofia

In bed, but unable to sleep, Father Indellicotta felt the pains return—sharp punches from inside, as if somebody was trying to fight their way out of his rib cage. Roberto got up and walked, hunched over, to the hotel room's balcony. Sofia slept comfortably. The return of the pain made him extraordinarily depressed; he thought it had gone away—permanently gone away. He looked at his watch—he had done everything the beast had asked. Cardinal Warwinka would be dead, shortly. He was learning to obey the Demon. Standing on the balcony of the Four Seasons Hotel, Roberto put his hands on the railing, and as he looked down, he noticed his fingernails had grown and the tips were elongated and sharp, almost like talons. Looking at his fingers, nausea came over him. Roberto knew the possession was intensifying, the Demon was coming and going like a raging fever. He turned around and looked back into the room; Sofia was breathing gently, at peace and asleep, and this simple human act suddenly filled him with rage. He walked back into the room, trying to calm down. He sat on the edge of the bed. He softly stroked Sofia's hair, as she slept, then, gently, he put his hands around her neck, being careful not to scratch her with his nails. As he began to squeeze, he felt the warmth of her neck. He squeezed a little tighter and, just before he was going to snap her neck, he managed to gain control of his humanity. He let go. Sofia, still happily asleep, turned over on her side. He got up from the bed and shook his head, horrified about what he had almost done. He looked at his nails; his defeat was nearly complete. Prayer, he thought—it was now called for. It is what he was trained to do—start the exorcism—he was the best in the world. But with the first silent words of prayer, the blows to his ribs intensified—the blows were so fierce he collapsed to the floor. The fight was on.

Lying on the floor, his phone started to vibrate on the bedside table and with the sound of the phone, the punching stopped, almost as if the demon was curious; the Demon wanted him to answer the phone. He stood up and looked at the screen—it was Beckett.

Roberto answered the phone.

"Beckett, is he dead?"

Father Roberto Indelicotta heard no reply, then bellowed into the phone, "Carl, damn you!, Are you there? Did you take care of Warwinka?"

Dan heard the question, but he wanted Father Indellicotta to deal with the silence, hear his own words.

"Carl, why don't you answer me?"

"Father Indellicotta, I know who you are—I know what you've done."

Roberto looked down at Sofia, then quickly moved to the balcony.

"Who is this? Carl, what is this, some kind of sick joke. Is Warwinka dead or not?"

"No, but my brother is dead. And Cardinal Warwinka is safe."

Roberto looked at the phone screen again. It was Carl Beckett's number.

"Who is this; who are you. Where is Carl Beckett? I demand to speak to him at once."

"Father Indellicotta, this is Daniel Baronowski, Father Baronowski of the CDF. I am here with Carl Beckett on the Catholic University campus. I want to put Beckett on the phone with you and he is going to tell you that Cardinal Warwinka is alive, he is safe, and I will be coming for you to ask you some questions."

Roberto quickly hung up the phone.

With the words, "Warwinka is safe," Indellicotta fell to his knees and looked skyward. The pain returned. The pounding from inside his chest was almost more than he could bear. After a moment, Roberto managed to stand up. He put his hands back on the balcony rail, and looked up at the moon and stars. Roberto violently vomited over the balcony. As he coughed and spit, he noticed a slow growl coming from inside him; he knew it was not from him and he knew he could not control it. Warwinka was alive, and the beast was wounded and rabid. The growl became louder, then a sound that could not possibly have come from a human being, erupted from his lungs, throat, and mouth. The noise and physicality seemed to tear open his esophagus.

"Noooooooo!!!"

After the howl, and still in agony, Roberto noticed his fingernails. His nails were horrific; they were now the claws of the beast, and they were wrapped around the mobile device.

With the scream, Sofia woke up and sat up in the bed and saw Roberto pacing, drooling and breathing heavily on the balcony.

"What's wrong Roberto, are you ok? Roberto, honey, are you ok?"

Roberto looked at the phone one more time; his clawed hands still wrapped around the device. Roberto looked at Sofia, then threw the phone, as hard as he possibly could, at Sofia.

"You are a whore; you are a filthy stinking whore!"

The phone missed Sofia by inches, and shattered against the wall. A cold chill ran through Sofia's entire body. She noticed his eyes were almost glowing; was he sick? She was at a loss of what to do; the priest had always been so gentle, so she tried one more time to help him with soothing words.

"Roberto, what's wrong. You look awful. You need a doctor; I'll take you there, right now."

Roberto knew what was happening, and he knew what was coming next. He looked at Sofia, and with his last shred of humanity and faith, he shouted out, "Holy Mary, Mother of God, save this woman and my soul from the eternal fires of hell."

The demon raged and howled and commanded Roberto to kill the woman that he loved. Almost supernaturally, Roberto started to move towards Sofia.

Sofia was too afraid to move, but she knew something was horrifically wrong—all she could do now was scream for help.

Roberto grabbed the balcony doors, fighting with all his strength to stay outside on the balcony as the beast tried to pull him into the room. Roberto saw the terror and tears in Sofia's eyes. He knew he was about to take her and leap with her out of the room, down to the street below—he was being commanded—but with one last gasp, and all that he had left inside of him, Roberto cried out, "Jesus, deliver me from evil—deliver me from evil, Lord and Savior—carry my soul, carry my soul to you in heaven!"

With his last breath and ounce of strength, he turned around and leaped to his death from the balcony.

Chapter 63:

June 13, 4:30 pm - Washington, DC
Alexi and Idi

The whistle - it belonged to Nicholas Alexi, and he was heading to the student union at a rapid, but disciplined pace.

Air raid sirens sounded off and people came pouring out of the student union, all looking at their phones, reading the breaking news or calling friends and families.

"Father Daniel, the assassin is here. Forget Beckett, we will deal with him later—another day. Go, find your friend."

Idi, very overweight but surprisingly nimble, took off after Alexi.

While Dan found himself alone with Beckett, a rising tide of pandemonium was beginning to grip the college campus. Like flood debris, students, faculty, employees of all sorts poured out into the sunlight. Howling sirens and blasting car horns filled the air. Frantic students and faculty poured into the parking lot, heading for their cars, anxious to be with family and friends. Dan took out his gun—he didn't want to take a chance on Beckett getting tough with him. Beckett spoke first—despite a gun pointed at him, and understanding the futility of asking an obedient priest to break a vow, Beckett had to ask about the Fatima letter.

"Father Baronowski, why do you keep the secret of Fatima from the world, from the faithful? If the world would know the secret we would know the Pope lied. We would know the errors of the faith. We could begin to rebuild the Church. Don't you see it—a crisis of faith is leading to the destruction of the Catholic Church. With the secret, we could begin to restore our faith to its former glory. Millions of souls are at stake, Father."

"You can keep your glory, Beckett, Jesus Christ did not seek glory—he sought humility and peace. You are a cold-blooded killer, how dare you talk to me about faith."

Suddenly, the grief-stricken cries of Dan's mother came back to him. Thinking of his dead brother, Dan was nearly overcome with sorrow. Holding back tears, Dan pointed the gun at Beckett.

"You killed my brother, you evil bastard. What do you think, Beckett—eye for an eye? Is that how you see the future?"

Dan put the gun up close to Beckett's head.

"Get on your knees."

Looking down at Beckett, Dan felt the cool steel of the gun in his hand. As Beckett looked up at him, Dan had his hand on the trigger. He thought about his brother—his big, happy, loving, innocent brother. He thought of Rene and Monique, and what had almost happened to them. Beckett was a monster. He put the gun on top of Beckett's head.

"You killed my brother."

He put pressure on the trigger.

A tear came down Dan's cheek; he looked to the sky. Looking up at the sky, he felt the gun trigger; he felt the muscle on his finger, as he squeezed the trigger more firmly.

"You killed him in cold blood—He did NOTHING!"

Carl Beckett lowered his head.

The small fatalistic gesture of defeat and resignation probably saved Beckett's life. Had Beckett made a willful move, Dan would have shot him—he knew it. Dan moved the gun away, then his cell phone rang. Dan answered the phone with his free hand. The gun still pointed at Beckett.

It was Tucker Finn.

"Dan, this place is about to blow; we are on ground zero. There is talk of nuclear war. I'm getting my boat out of here and heading to sea. I need you to return, now."

As Dan listened to Tucker, his thoughts returned to the Fatima letter and Cardinal Warwinka. The world around him came back into focus, police sirens, students pouring into the parking lot, cars all starting at the same time. Dan looked back down at Beckett.

"You have not seen the last of me."

Tucker didn't understand what Dan was saying.

"Father Dan, I did not copy you."

Dan spoke directly into the phone this time.

"I am on my way Tucker, hold tight."

Dan put the gun back in his holster, then took off for the student union to find the Cardinal. The air raid sirens blared loudly, as he swam against the tide of humanity streaming out of the student union.

Chapter 64:

June 13, 4:45 pm - Washington, DC
The President' Speech

Tucker, Sanjay, Monique, and Rene sat in the salon talking anxiously, and watching TV, when the President of the United States interrupted Wolf Blitzer on CNN.

"My fellow Americans, you have, by now, seen the news reports; you have heard that Russia has attacked the State of Israel in retaliation for the accidental missile strike against a Russian aircraft carrier. The attack against Israel, at the port of Haifa, has resulted in thousands of casualties, including the deaths of hundreds of innocent civilians. Iran has also launched an attack against our naval forces and have attempted to fire at Israel. Israel is preparing for war against Iran—and Israel has not ruled out the use of nuclear missiles. The United States of America has, as of 5pm this evening, notified the Russian Government that any additional hostile actions against Israel will be viewed as an act of war against the United States of America. Russian leader Vladimir Putin, has informed me, that hostile action, or a nuclear strike, against Iran will lead to war. But, I stand before you, this evening, to tell you, that we will stand by our ally in their great time of need. My fellow Americans, the United States of America is faced with a grave crisis; the peace and security of the world is now threatened by the hostile acts of the State of Russia. In addition, the United States of America has discovered that an illegal shipment of Russian nuclear missiles has made their way into Iran. Because of this hostile action, I will ask the United States congress, this evening, to join forces with our friends in Israel and declare war against the State of Iran. The United States of America, for over two centuries, has been a force of good for the world, and today this great country will stand tall against this threat. Our freedoms and our way of life are at risk and now as I stand here before you this evening, I urge all Americans to prepare for war, including reviewing and understanding evacuation routes and procedures. USA-dot-gov will provide information on courses of action. Thank you, and God Bless

America."

As soon as the President's speech ended, CNN had cameras at the Russell Building on Capitol Hill. Politicians and Congressional staffers were charging out of their offices; the streets, roads, and highways were overflowing—traffic was quickly coming to a standstill. Tucker had been in DC on the day the Twin Towers and the Pentagon were hit by Osama Bin Laden—9/11. On that day, DC came to a halt. Cars were abandoned, or ran out of gas—hundreds of people simply left their cars on bridges and roads and walked home. The President's speech was frightening, and Washington plunged into panic.

Tucker was the first to speak.

"Sanjay, get the dock lines; I'm going to top the tanks off. We are leaving."

Chapter 65:

Idi saw Alexi ahead, and he gained speed as he neared the Russian. Alexi was on the steps to the entrance of the student union, weaving his way through the hordes of students. A moment before he reached for the door, Alexi's fine tuned ability to sense danger kicked in and he turned around—Idi was coming at him at full speed. Alexi was too late to react. Idi's body-tackled Alexi, sending them both to the ground. All three hundred pounds landed squarely on Alexi. Idi overpowered Alexi, but the trained assassin quickly reached for his knife and plunged it into Idi's back. Idi barely flinched. Idi's hands were now around Alexi's neck. People storming out of the student center ignored the fight. As the two deadly foes wrestled, Alexi managed to get the knife back into Idi. This time Idi was hurt, but the pain sent Idi into a blind rage. With nearly superhuman strength, Idi picked up Alexi, and with a pro-wrestler's maneuver, he had Alexi locked in a full-nelson. Idi then lifted him in the air. He turned the Russian upside down then drove the assassin's head into the edge of the concrete steps, crushing his skull and snapping his neck, killing him instantly. Idi collapsed to the ground, bleeding heavily.

Idi, with great effort, reached into the dead man's pocket, looking for his wallet.

Idi, now sitting up, pulled out the wallet and rummaged through it. A photo with the name Professor Robert Baronowski written on the back was the first item he pulled out.

Dan neared the entrance to the student union and saw Idi sitting on the ground next to a man who lay motionless.

"Idi!"

Dan could see that Idi was bleeding.

Idi slowly got to his feet. He wanted the priest to think he was not hurt.

They both looked down at the man lying on the ground. Idi bent down towards the dead man and pulled out a gun.

"He came for your friend." Idi handed Dan the photograph, "and I think he killed your brother. I knew him in Rwanda. He was a gun dealer—a Russian assassin."

Dan stared at the photo and shook his head.

Idi reached down again and ripped the whistle off of Alexi's neck and showed it to Father Daniel.

"This whistle. Father Daniel, you may not remember it, but it probably saved Monique's life—it got me out of the church that day. I am sorry about your brother."

Dan and Idi looked at each other in silence for a moment. Dan could see Idi was bleeding heavily.

Idi spoke first, "Father Daniel—go to your friend. Leave me. I will be fine. I am sorry for everything, everything. I just want to go away now—disappear. Good luck to you, and tell Monique that I love her and tell her that every day I will pray for her family."

With that, Idi put the whistle in his pocket, turned, and walked away.

Dan watched Idi slowly make his way down the stairs, and soon he was lost in the crowd.

With Idi out of sight, he ran into the student union and headed for the conference room. Weaving through the crowd, he made his way to the conference room and found Cardinal Warwinka standing by the podium, talking with a group of priests. Monsignor Fuentes was among the group. They were discussing the extraordinary international news and sorting out plans of action.

Dan thought this was not a time for Catholic hierarchal protocol. He stepped into the middle of the group.

"Excuse me, gentlemen, but I must have a private word with Cardinal Warwinka, on a matter of great importance to Rome."

Monsignor could not believe his eyes.

"You!"

Dan ignored the Monsignor and immediately spoke to Cardinal Warwinka, not giving the Basilica's Director a moment to speak.

"Your Eminence, I must have a private word with you. It is a matter of great importance." Dan turned toward Fuentes, but continued to talk to Cardinal Warwinka, "I am acting under orders from the Vatican."

Somewhat startled, but given the fast-moving political events around the world—nothing now would be a complete surprise to the Cardinal.

"Daniel, yes, yes what is it?"

Monsignor Fuentes tried to interrupt, but Dan cut him off sharply. "This is an urgent matter, your Eminence."

Cardinal Warwinka never liked the pompous Director of the Basilica, and he sensed great urgency in Father Daniel's voice.

"Monsignor Fuentes, it can wait."

The Cardinal then gave Dan his full attention, turning his back on the Monsignor.

Dan moved Cardinal Warwinka away from the group and spoke quietly.

"Your Eminence, Rome, with instructions from the Pope, has asked me to put in your possession an important document. Your life may also be in danger. I would like you to come with me. I have a place where I can keep you safe.

"My life is in danger?"

"Your Eminence, my brother was killed yesterday, and I have reliable information that you are also a target."

Cardinal Warwinka looked at Dan with alarm. Cardinal Warwinka moved further away from the group. The Cardinal knew Daniel well. They had spent time together as friends, also professionally; they had worked closely over the years, monitoring events coming out of Medjugorje.

"You're brother? This is terrible, terrible news. Please, Daniel, what is this all about?"

"Your Eminence, there is a plot in the Vatican. It is about the 'Third Secret of Fatima'. There is a group, inside the Vatican, that very much wants the Fatima letter. I have it. It's the document I spoke of. I do not have all the answers, and there is much to explain. It is best we go. I do not feel safe here."

"The Third Secret', you have it with you?"

"I have it, I will explain everything, but, Your Eminence, we should go."

"Very well, we shall go at once."

The Cardinal stepped back to the group and excused himself.

Monsignor Fuentes was still fuming, but like everybody on campus, priorities had shifted dramatically in an instant. Fuentes huddled with the other men and discussed plans of action. Mass in the Basilica's crypt was agreed upon.

Dan's phone rang. It was Tucker again. Rene was now at Tucker's side.

"Dan, meet me at the fuel docks. The fuel dock is just south of Molly's slip—a hundred feet to the left as you are looking at her. And listen, Dan, you have your work cut out for you making your way back. It is getting crazier by the minute. Russia and the United States are heading to war. Airports are jammed, Reagan is shut down; mandatory evacuation orders have been given. There is no way to get out of DC—absolute gridlock."

Traffic was at a standstill as soon as Dan turned onto Michigan Avenue. Dan didn't have far to go, but he had to get to the boat fast. The sidewalks were empty of pedestrians, and down by the Mall the sidewalks were wide and generous. But nearing Maine Avenue, a few blocks from the marina, traffic came to a complete standstill. People now were shouting and honking their horns. Dan managed to find a spot to pull over that would not impede traffic. Dan and the Cardinal, who was in good physical shape, walked at a fast pace the rest of the way to Tucker's boat.

With the engines idling, Tucker looked at the fuel gauge one more time. He knew how much fuel he had—the tanks had just been topped off, but given their new extended cruising itinerary—at full throttle—there was nothing more critical. Pilar would be passing through the Chesapeake Bay Bridge Tunnel about the time they shoved off. By then, Pilar would have a one hundred and fifty mile head start. Wide open at fifty knots he should catch Pilar about sixty miles off shore. Tucker looked at his weather reading—light air for now—should be a good ride.

Tucker looked down the dock and saw two clerics. They looked like oversized flightless birds—a cardinal and some kind of blackbird —heading quickly towards the boat. Tucker blasted his horn and goosed the throttles. Molly roared like the king of beasts. It was time to go.

Chapter 66:

June 13, 6:45 pm - The Potomac River
Molly Chases Pilar

Cardinal Warwinka sat down with Dan in the main salon. Molly was heading down the Potomac River, to the mouth of the Chesapeake Bay, on the way to the Atlantic Ocean, at fifty knots.

As Dan reached into his brief case, Cardinal Warwinka popped open an ice cold Diet Coke, and helped himself to some peanuts that had been placed on the table. After introductions had been made, Cardinal Warwinka and Dan were left alone to talk. On the television set, news of the impending war droned on in the background.

Dan opened his brief case, took the Fatima letter out and handed it to the Cardinal.

"Peter, this is for you; it is the 'Third Secret of Fatima'. I have been instructed to give it to you; you are permitted to do as you please with the letter. You can read it if you want."

Cardinal Warwinka looked up at the television screen; it seemed likely that Russia and the United States were headed to war. It was astonishing to think Russia and the United States were going to war while he held the Fatima letter in his hand.

The Cardinal looked at the letter for a moment, then put it on his lap; he had not decided to read it, yet.

"We need the prayers of the Holy Father, Daniel, but sadly, he is too weak. He is now too far gone—I'm told he is in a comatose state."

"Yes, Peter it is very sad, we do need his prayers, but we will get to Rome, and there, the Holy Spirit will guide us. Perhaps, Peter, you will be the one that leads us in the future. If the Holy Father passes, and a Conclave is called, they will wait for you, before they close the doors of the Sistine Chapel."

Cardinal Warwinka tapped the letter on his lap.

"The world is being punished right now, Daniel, perhaps not punished, because man has free will; it is more that man has brought this upon themselves. Too much war, no prayer for peace, only prayer to kill or defeat our enemies; it is how I see it. But what is not clear is something else. What is not clear, to me, at this time of war, is, whose "side" is God on, or does God even take a "side"? Most Americans think God is always on their "side"; but who knows?"

"Peter, in my work for the Vatican, as a "Miracle Detective" investigating apparitions of the Virgin Mary, I have learned many things about the Mother of Christ."

Dan pointed to the television set and said, "I don't know whose "side" God is on, but I can't help but think that She is watching over the world, in tears. In times of great upheaval, The Virgin Mary reveals herself to the world, and when the Virgin Mary comes, She brings special messages for the world. Her messages implore us to return to God— to seek salvation through her Son, Jesus Christ, but so few listen."

"Yes, Daniel, precisely, She is always with us, pointing the way back to her Son. And what is important is that the Bible clearly states that. The Bible also tells us that a woman will lead Christians in the victory of 'Good over Evil.' It is written, in the book of Genesis and the Book of Revelation, that in the final battle, the "side" of "Good" will be led by a woman; that much I know, but that is an unfamiliar concept for many Christians. But for me, at this time—a time of nuclear threat—an apocalyptic event to be sure, I am compelled to seek out this woman. From the beginning, the Sacred Scriptures have taught Christians that it would be a woman who defeats Satan. At the beginning, in Genesis 3:15, it is written: 'I will put enmity between you and the woman, and between your offspring and hers; he will strike at your head, while you strike at his heel.' Then in the Book of Revelation, chapter 12: 'A great sign appeared in the sky, a woman clothed in the sun, with the moon under her feet, and on her head a crown of twelve stars.' We are taught, in the Catholic Church, that the "woman clothed in the sun... and on her head a crown of twelve stars", is the Mother of Jesus Christ and because if this, Daniel, I find it most interesting that the Virgin Mary, at Medjugorje, appears to the 'visionaries' 'with a crown of twelve stars.' This fact is of critical importance."

Cardinal Warwinka looked down at the letter again and wondered if Medjugorje and Fatima were, indeed, connected. In 1991, the Medjugorje 'visionaries' said that the events at Medjugorje were to be understood as the 'continuation and fulfillment of Fatima'. After a moment of silent contemplation, Cardinal continued to speak.

"Daniel, not only does the Virgin Mary at Medjugorje come with a 'crown of twelve stars', She also gave the world a prophetic message. I believe this prophecy, from Medjugorje, explains many things. At Medjugorje, in 1981, the Virgin Mary said, 'Russia will come to glorify God the most; the West has made civilization progress, but without God, and they act as if they are their own creators'. These shockingly, prophetic words are worth considering at this time."

Dan nodded his head. Having just read a part of the 'Third Secret of Fatima', he understood Russia would play a decisive role in the future of Christianity.

Dan said, "Peter, with this pending war, I can't help but think the fulfillment of the prophecies at both Fatima and Medjugorje are upon us. 'Our Lady of Medjugorje' has given us beautiful messages of peace for over thirty years and She has beseeched the world to reconcile with God. If only the world had listened and we had prayed to the Blessed Mother, prayed for Her protection, I believe this war could have been avoided. "

"Yes, Daniel. I wonder if I have failed in my duties. I ask myself, could I have done more? But then I think, it was just too much to overcome. The ship could not change direction."

"The ship?" Daniel asked.

"What I mean is the West is a slow turning ship. The ship could not change directions – it was weighed down with love for itself and self-righteousness. The ship also disregarded rules by abandoning the commandments. It all was too entrenched. The ship could not change directions. This war, Daniel—Russia and the West, Israel, Iran, the United States— it is vital that we do not look at our faith through the eyes of nations. God does not choose nations; God does not choose sides—God chooses hearts. We all have such myopic principles when it comes to

Christian faith. We have convinced ourselves that God has chosen the West and the United States, but we must understand that this point of view is established mostly because the West has power and wealth, and dominates modern culture –it dominates the narrative in all things. We never consider Russia when it comes to faith. The faithful in Russia venerate the Blessed Mother unlike any country on earth."

Dan listened carefully and thought about Russia's Christian faith and its love for the Virgin Mary. He glanced at the Fatima letter on Warwinka's lap. Was the Book of Revelation now being fulfilled? Was the apocalypse unfolding before his eyes? Was Russia really some kind of instrument of a chastisement against humanity? Dan looked up at the television as he continued to listen to the Cardinal.

"But because American and European 'exceptionalism' seeps into everything, even Christianity, we are predisposed to believe God is on America's "side". How can we be so certain that God has chosen the West? I have always asked myself: if Western ideals of Christianity are unassailable, why then did the Virgin Mary, at Fatima, speak so often about Russia? The other important aspect, we must contemplate are John Paul II's words about the Virgin Mary. He said: 'The victory, if it comes, will come through Mary.' What this means is that the triumph of the Virgin Mary's heart is intended to reunite all Christianity. What this means is, that in order to participate in the triumph of Christianity, Protestants, Orthodox, Evangelicals must seek salvation by accepting that the ONLY true path to Jesus Christ now runs ONLY through the heart of His Mother. The Virgin Mary must be in the meditative prayers of all Christians. Without Mary as the Mediatrix, Christians will suffer. Look now at the trouble. Look at the trouble with their pastors—the Pat Robetsons of the world. Christ sacrificed for us, Daniel; the Protestant faith, today, lacks that element – suffering and sacrifice. It is all prosperity promises; it is all about praying for the good life on earth. The way I see it, Daniel, Protestant preachers, with their haircuts and their American-centric, 'patriotic' politically-focused, evangelization, has just about crucified Christ all over again. I don't see a shred of Christ in those men on TV. Daniel, we need a woman to sweep away the corruption that is so prevalent in the

Protestant faith – a faith that is led by charismatic businessmen. Christianity will wither away unless people find their way back to Christ through Mary – his Mother."

Cardinal Warwinka looked up at the television. CNN was broadcasting live from Moscow. Behind the CNN reporter was Saint Basil's Cathedral, the Russian Orthodox Church on the grounds of the Red Square, inside the Kremlin. Warwinka listened to the man talk about nuclear war. He was impressed with the man's cool demeanor. Warwinka helped himself to more nuts, then took his diet Coke and leaned back comfortably in his seat.

"Daniel, it is important also for Christians, in the West, to understand Russia's long and complicated relationship with the Blessed Mother. At Fatima, the Virgin Mary asked the Holy Father to consecrate Russia to the Immaculate Heart of Mary, and with the consecration, a period of peace would follow. On March 25, 1984, the consecration took place and, incredibly, the Soviet Union, almost immediately, began to crumble. Within a few short years, in 1991, the year the Virgin Mary said that Medjugorje is the fulfillment of Fatima, on Christmas Day, Russia lowered the Soviet Union Flag—the hammer and sickle came down from the Kremlin rooftops on Christmas day, Daniel. And now we see that Russia has slowly begun to mend her ways in such surprising ways that we can consider Russia as one of the most Marian and Christian countries in the world."

Cardinal Warwinka thought about the triumph of Our Lady's heart and glanced back at the TV—fear was taking over the country. Cardinal Warwinka then took the letter off his lap and began to read it to himself.

*"In Portugal, the dogma of the faith will be preserved. I am the Mediatrix between you and God. Be not afraid, my Immaculate Heart will be your refuge and your safe path to God. I am the Mediatrix of all graces and my heart will triumph. **Christ will conquer through me, because He wants the Church's victories now and in the future to be linked to me.** I am the Advocate for mankind and I told you, if men do not repent and better themselves, the Father*

will inflict a terrible punishment on all humanity and Russia will be the instrument of the chastisement. It will be a punishment greater than the deluge, such as one will never have seen before. Fire will fall from the sky and will wipe out a great part of humanity, the good as well as the bad, sparing neither priests nor faithful. The survivors will find themselves so desolate that they will envy the dead. The only arms which will remain for you will be the Rosary and the Sign left by my Son. Each day, recite the prayers of the Rosary. The work of the devil will infiltrate even into the Church in such a way that one will see cardinals opposing cardinals, bishops against bishops. The priests who venerate me will be scorned and opposed by other priests, churches and altars will be sacked; the Church will be full of those who accept compromises and the demon will press many priests and consecrated souls to leave the service of the Lord. The demon will be especially implacable against souls consecrated to God. The thought of the loss of so many souls is the cause of my sadness. If sins increase in number and gravity, there will be no longer pardon for them. The devil has succeeded in bringing in evil to the Church under the guise of good and the blind are beginning to lead others.

Cardinal Warwinka placed the letter back on his lap, took a sip of Coke, and went back to the television. After a few moments, the Cardinal handed the letter to Dan and leaned back in his chair and then pointed to the TV.

"Daniel, I think the outcome of this war is very uncertain. The religious faith of Russia could surprise many Christians here in the United States." The Cardinal then added, "Did you know that Padre Pio, the great Italian stigmatic mystic, once said that the Russian people would be converted and their conversion would happen very fast."

"Yes, Peter, I read that somewhere."

"Yes, good, but what is really fascinating, Daniel, is that Padre Pio cryptically added that Russia would teach the United States a lesson in conversion—"teach a lesson", Daniel."

The Cardinal continued to watch the television—live feeds were pouring in from across America, and its citizens were panicking throughout the land— grocery stores were gutted, a gun fight broke out over a generator at a Home Depot, gas station lines stretched for blocks. CNN then cut to a scene taking place outside the front steps of St. Mathews Catholic Church in Washington, DC. On the streets, surrounding the church, traffic was at a standstill. People were abandoning their cars and rushing into the Church. The cathedral was overflowing. The stairs of the church were packed with hundreds of people, on their knees in prayer.

"It is sad, Daniel—now they turn for salvation and redemption. But, as I said earlier, I am partly to blame. I should have spoken up. I should have been more forceful. The Christian faith has been corrupted for far too long. Faith has become too attached to politics. It is a diabolical disorientation and far removed from the message of Jesus Christ. Evangelical and Protestant preachers, even some of my Catholic brothers, interpret the teachings of Jesus Christ with human, worldly, political, hearts. They stopped believing in miracles. They have ignored the Virgin Mary's tears for generations. What is sad, is that for two thousand years, we have overlooked Jesus Christ's decisive words about his mother's role in Christian faith. The last words of Christ, on the cross at Calvary, were 'Behold your Mother.' He said this to his favorite Apostle, John, and what he meant by this was, 'Behold the Mother of the Church.' Why so many Christian leaders belittle and dismiss these final words of our Savior, has always been a great mystery to me."

More shouting on the TV by the network anchors. Cardinal Warwinka looked back up at the screen—Tehran had just been hit with a nuclear bomb; and reports were coming in that missiles were nearing Seattle, Washington.

Chapter 67:

June 14, 8:30 pm - Somewhere in the Atlantic Ocean
Tucker and Rene

Sitting comfortably in the boat's roomy cockpit, a gentle breeze ran though Rene's hair. Water quietly lapped under Pilar's stern. Rene looked west then up at the sky wondering if she would see anything. She turned her gaze to the ocean's edge. It was 8:30 in the evening and the sun, wearing a halo of purple, orange and red, rested on the horizon.

Earlier in the afternoon, Molly, Tucker's power boat, had rendezvoused with Pilar, sixty miles off the coast of Norfolk, Virginia in the Atlantic Ocean. After Tucker and his crew boarded Pilar, Captain Tom took the motor boat to Bermuda. Tucker wanted to keep his options open on the ocean. Tucker felt safe on his sailboat. Captain Tom and his wife were happy to take their chances in Bermuda.

Tucker sat down across from Rene. He opened a bottle of Chardonnay and poured Rene a glass, then put the bottle into a wine bucket filled with ice. Tucker opened a beer.

There were no more words about the war. There was nothing to say that would make a difference. The war happened. All that mattered was the wind. It was light and from the east. The boat drifted; there was nowhere yet to go.

Anything but the war. Rene wanted to know about Tucker, his boat, the places he'd seen; she wanted to talk about storms, sail trim, and sea monsters.

Rene just wanted to talk.

"Tucker, you know the dumbest question I get from really smart people about ocean racing?"

"No, what's that?"

"What do you do at night…do you, stop, anchor?"

Tucker Finn chuckled.

"Yeah, I've heard that one before, too."

Tucker then looked away from Rene and started fidgeting. He looked uneasy. He rubbed his cheeks with both hands, then his chin.

Tucker wanted to get to know Rene, but he felt unsure where to go, he had no preconceived tactical approach.

"Rene, there is something you need to know about me."

Tucker took a long drink from his beer.

"Ok, Tucker, sure, what's that?"

"It' s kind of a confession."

"Not my department, Tucker. You have your own private priest on board—not to mention a Cardinal; no lines, and they have a lot of time on their hands, right now."

Tucker smiled, but then his forehead wrinkled and eyes narrowed as he looked at Rene.

"Rene, I just have to tell you how I feel: sitting down with you, just the two of us, like this, makes me really nervous. I don't know why. It shouldn't, but it does."

Tucker's question surprised her. After Tucker's decisive move to leave DC before the evacuation was mandated, Rene thought Tucker went through life without any doubts or second guesses.

His confession surprised her.

"Huh? What do you mean, why do you say that?"

"Well it's just how I feel, I feel it right now. Honestly, I'm just not really comfortable talking to people—not just with you—but most people. Not like this, anyway."

Tucker moved his pointing finger back and forth between the two of them.

"You know, one on one, "conversation." All the time I have spent on this boat has turned me, basically, into a mute—all my time alone. Look Rene, all I have done for the past year is read, and look at jellyfish, plankton, man o'war, and birds. I'm checked out. I don't engage. I don't have exchanges, not with humans, not...like this."

"I think you do fine, Tucker."

"I'm not sure about that."

"You and Sanjay never seem to be at a loss for words."

"Forget that. He's like a kid brother. Sanjay is great. He is a lot of fun, but offshore it can be real different. Sometimes, it gets a little lonely out there—and quiet, I have to admit. I am not really complaining; I would call it a good lonely, if there is such a thing. It's peaceful. But you know, there are long periods of time at sea when I don't talk to anybody. I mean, for days."

"What about the crew, your captain. They all seem friendly."

"Oh yeah, they are great. My captain, god bless him—he is in love with his wife; they HAVE a life. I really don't deserve those two, they are amazing, but mostly he only talks to me about navigation, weather and maintenance. He likes it that way, and it is as it should be. Sanjay, offshore, texts his girlfriends, trades stocks all day, and is basically on another planet. My crew is professional and friendly, but hanging out with the owner is not their idea of a good time. And they don't always do the long passages—they fly in and meet us at our destination. So out on the water, don't get me wrong, Rene, I love it, but on the wide stretches of the ocean, it's quiet, and so I end up talking to myself or to animals, to creatures."

"Creatures, you mean like dolphin?"

"Yeah, like dolphin, but I have seen so many of them it's now like looking at goldfish in a bowl. There is a lot of amazing sea life, but my favorite animal is without a doubt the Albatross—the giant Wandering Albatross—that bird is the king of beasts in my book. I'm lucky to have seen my share. They are unbelievable animals."

"Yes, I've heard they're great. Someday I hope to see one, but what's this Dr. Doo-Little stuff about you talking to them?"

"What I mean by that is, when I run into an Albatross on the southern ocean, when you see them gliding by off the beam of the boat—a thousand miles from nowhere—it gets you thinking about important things, you start talking to yourself, you start asking yourself questions, big questions, about life, its meaning and all that. So you find yourself, at first talking to yourself, but soon you're talking to the bird."

"Those lonely birds are probably starved for company; they sound like they would make good listeners."

Tucker smiled slightly and thought about the giant birds.

"They are, Rene, for sure. I love those animals. They are a big part of me, now. You've read the books and poems and I am here to tell you, it's all true. I understand why they have captured the hearts of so many artists. They really have a mystical power, when you see them free on the ocean."

Rene offered up a line from the well-known poem by the English poet Samuel Taylor Coleridge:

"The Rime of the Ancient Mariner—with my cross-bow…I shot the albatross…water, water everywhere."

"Very good, Rene, but I am happy to say my experience was different than that. It's all been good. I've had Albatrosses glide right beside me for hours without a flutter; it's really fantastic to see."

"Someday I hope to see one Tucker, free on the ocean, but they do seem lonely. Who knows, maybe one day I can keep one company. But what is this about questions? What kind of questions do you ask them?"

"You ask them the same kind of things we ask ourselves when we are alone late at night. You know, big question about life, like I said, like whether or not you measure up. Have you made the world a better place? Did you help enough little old ladies across the street. Is your life shallow or vain, have you made the right choices, or does your life basically suck? What's interesting to me, Rene, is the Albatross is like a mirror or a looking glass into your life. When you look up at them instead of seeing their loneliness, you see what's inside of yourself. Do you know what I mean?"

There was that word again—Mirror. She thought about her closet. She thought about the other night—before everything changed.

"Mirror? What do you mean by that?"

"What I mean is that they are like a mirror, but not like a mirror on a wall, it's more like a mirror into your soul. When the bird is near you—when you look at them—somehow it makes it easier to see into your own heart, into your essence. There are no lies or pretenses on the southern ocean with an Albatross looking down on you. No way. Sometimes, it seems, you see yourself the way God would see you on judgment day—you get to the foundation of your soul; your naked core. It's been great medicine for me, Rene. I've learned a lot about myself. I can watch them for hours, skimming across the tops of waves; it's beautiful to see them out on the water, so free. It helps you understand what freedom really means. It sorts out the important things in life."

He took a sip of his beer, looked into the sunset, and felt the light breeze against his face. The long shadows from the stern stanchions had made their way to the cockpit. He looked over at Rene and their eyes settled on each other for a moment. He could stay there forever, he was beginning to realize…but it was too early, too risky. The last thing he ever really cared about had been taken away from him. He looked away and his eyes moved up to the top of the mast to check the wind direction. The light wind was still from the east.

Rene liked the way Tucker looked at her, but like Tucker, she was nervous and uncertain. But with his eyes, she felt movement in her heart. With his eyes, she seemed to find a gear. She realized, again, she had been stuck hard aground for a long time. But she wanted to navigate carefully. She decided to keep the moment light.

She put her elbows on the table and her hands on her chin, and the playful affect brought a smile to Tucker. It also brought her physically closer to him.

Rene spoke up.

"Well, I like penguins."

Tucker Finn was unable not to smile as she said the words. Her playful snap, "I like penguins," intended to amuse him, and it did.

Holding back a chuckle, he finally responded.

"Penguins?"

"Yes, penguins. I love them and I have a little secret about them that I don't share with just anybody."

"A secret? Are you sure you want to tell me?"

"I'll take my chances. Who are you going to tell anyway? Sanjay was right about that, it's just birds and fish with you, Tucker."

"You learn fast Rene; now about your penguins."

"Okay, you know the story about the Emperor Penguin – the whole romantic business of taking care of their babies, loyalty to the ones they love and all that. If you do, I think you will agree there is no greater male role model in the animal kingdom. As an example of virtue, Tucker, this amazing bird is unequaled."

"I'll buy that; I understand their appeal, but the secret, what's your secret?"

"My secret, Tucker, is when I meet someone for the first time—a guy—in the back of my mind I am thinking of penguins, and I am thinking, 'does the guy measure up—to a penguin, for Pete's sake;' Quite honestly, it's really pretty messed up."

"It's not that messed up at all, I have the same problem with albatrosses."

"You really do have a thing about the albatross don't you."

"Well, Rene, I guess I do. I think about them almost every day. Let me say one more thing about them."

Rene put her wine glass down and opened her palms, inviting Tucker to continue.

"Like I said, when they come to you on the ocean you never forget it. The birds find you in the most desolate places on earth, in the southern ocean, in the lower latitudes of the Atlantic Ocean, halfway between Cape Horn off the southern tip of South America, and the Cape of Good Hope. On those waters, Rene, it's gray, it's cold, it's rough and so why the Wandering Albatross chose that sad and lonely spot on earth to seek his fortune is a mystery. But for me, after spending time with them, I now see something more—I guess it's my little secret— I now believe when they show up, they are looking for more than simple companionship. They also come with something to share. Like all of us they want to share with someone what they find beautiful in the world. I think it is inside of us all - that need."

Rene looked at Tucker and thought of his words, "all of us need someone to share what we find beautiful in the world." His words suddenly seemed to have power; the words reached her.

"Rene, let me try to explain this a little bit. It starts with a dance." Tucker turned his hand into a flying object. "Most of the time, the albatross arrives at sunset and these lonely creatures want to dance with someone when they come. The dance begins when the long narrow wings appear out of the sky. The bird then rolls down towards the boat. As he gets close, he banks into a long slow swoop. This is followed by a slow loop around the boat near the water, his wings flutter just above the sea and at the right moment he peels away, towards the bow and the setting sun. Once he is aligned in front of the boat, his dance comes to its end and he begins to paint. He knows we are watching him. Ahead of the boat, his picture is framed by the earth's edge. The bow of the boat, the water, the clouds, the sky, the colors, the sun, and the silhouette of perfect wings, all combine to paint a picture you never forget. It's so beautiful to see him flying towards the setting sun in that lonely place, you find yourself giving thanks to all that's around. Out on the ocean, Rene, you often realize there is not much separation between your soul and God. It's a thin line out there on the ocean and I am very thankful for it all."

Rene said nothing. She thought about her own quiet nights on the Atlantic.

He looked up again, into the setting sun, and thought about his wonderful flying companions that had kept him company on so many lonely days.

Lowering his voice and leaning forward slightly Tucker put both his hands on the table.

"You know, Rene, when I see them reaching out, there are times when it also makes me sad. Like you said, I do think they are lonely, lonely as can be. In fact, sometimes I think they may be the loneliest creatures on earth. I really do; you can't help but think that. I think that's why they come by and stay for so long."

Tucker looked away and up to the sky. He listened to the gentle lapping of water against the stern. It was dusk and the North Star had arrived. Rene thought about Tucker's birds; he called them a mirror—a lonely mirror. He also said you see inside when the bird is near.

The sun was gone and the shadows would rest until tomorrow. Tucker looked across the table into Rene's eyes, and seeing her dark black hair falling onto her forehead, he sensed again what he had felt on the dock the first time they met. Everything about her seemed to make everything fit the way it was supposed to—with her eyes, she gathered all his shattered pieces and set them right. He felt something good inside of him.

He now realized he was falling in love. He was about to say something, then paused, and after a moment he quietly said, "Rene, are you ever lonely? Do you miss sharing? You know – moments, little things that in the end, are really the big things."

She had not seen it coming; at least not the impact of his words, and it took her by surprise. His words popped something open. It seemed now that the words had been standing right in front of her all the time but she had always looked away - convinced the emptiness that came with being alone was not hers, it belonged somewhere else. She reached over and took his hand—his hand was warm and she liked the feeling it gave her. She ran his words through her mind again. She now understood that it had been that way for a long time. Yes, she missed it. With Tucker, she now understood, she missed it more than anything in the world.

She looked at Tucker with warm, open eyes, the lonely edges gone. She squeezed his hand gently and said, "Do I miss sharing, Tucker?" At that moment, she was never so certain of anything in her life. She pressed his hand more firmly, and looked at Tucker in a way that asked him to be close to her. As their eyes settled together on a quiet place meant for only them, Rene finished her answer.

"Not now, Tucker, no, not right now."

Tucker Finn's free hand joined Rene's. After a moment, Tucker stood up and moved closer to Rene. He took her hands and gently guided her up and out of the cockpit to the back of the boat. They both stood, looking west, out towards the horizon, holding hands. The sun had set. Tucker put his arm around Rene's lower back. She moved her body closer. Tucker turned towards Rene and held her gently by her arms just beneath her shoulders. Rene leaned against Tucker's chest put her arms around him and let her new life pour in.

Epilogue

As the sky in the west burned, Rene and Tucker made their way back to the cockpit to sit down. Out of routine, Tucker scanned the whole horizon. Then from the north, Tucker saw something.

"What's that, Rene? you see that over there, it looks like masts."

Tucker pointed towards little specks dotting the northern horizon. Rene right away had a good idea what Dan was seeing on the ocean's edge. She jumped into the cockpit and grabbed the binoculars that hung by the wheel then hopped back up on the stern.

"It's them."

"Who?"

"The fleet—A2N"

"A2N?"

"Tucker, it's the fleet—Annapolis to Newport —the race. They must have turned around and headed south- headed out to sea. The fleet is probably headed to Bermuda. My brother, he's there, he's on one of those boats."

Rene jumped back into the cockpit, this time she snatched the hand-held radio.

"This is sailing vessel, Pilar, Wharf Rat, do you copy? This is sailing vessel, Pilar, Wharf Rat, do you copy?"

About thirty seconds went by and just as Rene was set to hail Wharf Rat again, a voice came on.

"This is sailing vessel, Wharf Rat. We copy you Pilar—over."

Rene recognized the voice—she caught her breath; it was her brother.

Rene took Tucker's hand and held it firmly.

"Teddy, Teddy, it's me, Espy, you see that big damn mast to your south—that's me!"

About the Author

Stephen K. Ryan owns and operates www.ministryvalues.com. Ministryvalues.com is a faith based online news magazine which averages over 200,000 visitors a year. Stephen also operates Castine Investment Management, a wealthy advisory investment company. Stephen is married to Tania and lives in Alexandria, Va. They have two children, Andrew and Meredith. When he is not banging away on his computer he can often be found somewhere on an ocean racing sailboats.

*For your reading pleasure,
we invite you to visit our web
bookstore*

WHISKEY CREEK PRESS

www.whiskeycreekpress.com